"This story is lightened by witty banter yet realistically deals with tragic, timely issues. A hanky or three might come in handy." —*Library Journal*

"With strong storytelling and a tender plot, this tale is equal parts heartwarming, romantic, and genuine."
—*Romantic Times*

A Time for Home

"An enchanting tale about believing in love, forgiveness, and acceptance." —Reader to Reader Reviews

"An emotional roller coaster. I couldn't put it down! Loved it!" —*New York Times* bestselling author Susan Mallery

PRAISE FOR THE NOVELS OF ALEXIS MORGAN

"A bit of mystery, lots of action, plenty of passion, and a story line that will grab your attention from the get-go."
—Romance Reviews Today

continued . . .

"Suspicions, lust, loyalty, and love create a heavy mix of emotions."
— *Romantic Times*

"Magically adventurous and fervently romantic."
—Single Titles

"Whew! A unique paranormal story line that sizzles with every page."
—Fresh Fiction

"This book sucked me in, and I didn't want to stop reading."
—Queue My Review

"Morgan delivers a great read that sparks with humor, action, and . . . great storytelling."
—Night Owl Reviews (5 stars, top pick)

"Will keep readers entranced."
—Nocturne Romance Reads

"This action-packed paranormal romance has a little bit of everything—especially if you love interesting immortal warriors who are sexy as all get-out—and enough action and suspense to keep you riveted until the last page."
—Black Lagoon Reviews

"The spellbinding combination of passionate desires, fateful consequences, and the supernatural . . . [is] totally captivating throughout every enthralling scene."
—Ecataromance

A Reason
to Love

❧ A Snowberry Creek Novel ❧

Alexis Morgan

Ⓔ
A SIGNET ECLIPSE BOOK

SIGNET ECLIPSE
Published by the Penguin Group
Penguin Group (USA) LLC, 375 Hudson Street,
New York, New York 10014

USA | Canada | UK | Ireland | Australia | New Zealand | India | South Africa | China
penguin.com
A Penguin Random House Company

First published by Signet Eclipse, an imprint of New American Library,
a division of Penguin Group (USA) LLC

First Printing, May 2014

ISBN 978-0-451-41773-2

Printed in the United States of America
10 9 8 7 6 5 4 3 2 1

PUBLISHER'S NOTE
This is a work of fiction. Names, characters, places, and incidents either are the
product of the author's imagination or are used fictitiously, and any resemblance
to actual persons, living or dead, business establishments, events, or locales is
entirely coincidental.

I want to dedicate this book to all of my son's friends: Hey, guys, thanks for growing up so great! We are so proud of the men you've become.

Chapter 1

A last name shouldn't be a burden, but Melanie's sat as a heavy weight on her shoulders as she strolled through the cemetery. The pressure increased dramatically as she passed the neat rows of nearly identical markers, all bearing the familiar inscription: Wolfe.

The library in town had the same name carved in the arch over the front door, and the name appeared on the local high school as well. As the sun edged its way down toward the western horizon, Melanie moved on down the hillside, taking her time to enjoy the fresh air and the last of the warm sunshine.

There was no escaping her family heritage here in Snowberry Creek. Her great-great-grandfather Josiah Wolfe had parked his covered wagon next to a small stream tumbling down through the foothills of the Cascades and planted the family's roots down deep into the rocky soil. He'd been an ambitious man, one determined to make his mark in the world—and the town of Snowberry Creek was his creation.

There, under his firm hand, the family had proudly flourished in both number and wealth for two generations. Even the stock market crash and the Great Depression had been mere setbacks. Since that time, the size of the family had dwindled dramatically until now there were only two Wolfes left in town: Melanie and her mother. At least their family fortune was rock solid.

Or at least that was the fairy tale Melanie had always been told.

She reluctantly started down the slope to where a new granite headstone had been set in place. Her mother had instructed Melanie to ensure that everything had been done properly. Melanie had bitten back the suggestion that if her mother was worried about it, she could always come back to check it out for herself. After all, there were other more pressing things on Melanie's to-do list screaming for her attention right now.

Instead, here she was, playing the dutiful daughter again. It was a role she'd never been well suited for, but right now she had no other choice. Not when something inside her mother had shattered the day her husband's heart stopped beating. Three weeks after the funeral, the reality of their changed circumstances had come crashing down. She'd immediately left town on an extended visit with her sister, Marcia, down in Oregon, abandoning Melanie to deal with the fallout from her father's death alone.

It would take a better person than Melanie not to resent having her whole life uprooted, especially when she'd worked so hard to escape the confines of Snowberry Creek in the first place. But unfortunately, according to Melanie's aunt, Sandra Wolfe had become little more than a shadow of herself and only rarely left the house. Figuring out what to do about that was also on Melanie's list.

She coasted to a stop a short distance from her father's grave. From afar, the gray granite marker blended in seamlessly with all the others. It was only on closer inspection that she could see the polished stone was a little shinier than those on either side of it.

Edmond Wolfe would've approved. Even in life, he'd preferred to maintain a quiet, dignified lifestyle. The only anomaly had been a bright red pickup truck that he'd loved to drive around town. Looking back, Melanie should've known something was wrong when he'd sold it only days before he died. What other signs had she missed that all was not as it should be? She'd grown up believing her parents were financially secure and that her father had inherited her great-great-grandfather's head for business. It had never occurred to her to doubt that.

As it turned out, she'd been wrong on both counts.

The silence in the cemetery was oppressive, but what could she say to a slab of granite? She settled for the obvious. "Well, Dad, looks like they got everything right on your headstone. It suits you."

Considering all it contained was his full name and the years that spanned his life, there wasn't much that could've gone wrong. The Wolfe family didn't go in for inspirational sayings or emotional displays, in public or private. Melanie snapped a picture with her phone to text to her mother later. For now, she set down the small bouquet of lilies she'd brought for her father's grave.

Staring down at the headstone, she whispered, "Dad, I'm doing my best to figure things out, but I've got so many questions I wish I could ask you right now."

Not that he would've liked answering them. He'd never discussed finances with his wife, much less his only daughter. No, like his father before him, her father preferred to shelter women from the hard realities of the business world. Well, that train had left the station. Melanie now knew all too much about the precarious state of the family's finances.

It was time to get moving. She had other, happier places to be this evening. But as she turned to leave, she realized she was no longer alone on the hillside. A man dressed in a camouflage uniform stood by a grave on the far side of the cemetery. He had his back to her as he stared down at one of the markers. From the slump in his shoulders, the name on the headstone had to be causing him great pain.

She knew why because she knew who was buried there: Spence Lang. Last summer, the whole town had turned out for his funeral to pay homage to one of their own. The war was being waged on the other side of the world, but that day it had come home to Snowberry Creek.

Although she'd been living in Spokane at the time, Melanie had taken the day off work and driven down to attend the service. She'd owed Spence that much. The solemn ceremony had been excruciatingly painful in its intensity. As the final strands of "Taps" faded away, the army honor guard had carefully folded the flag that had covered the coffin and presented it to Vince Locke, Spence's uncle.

Melanie bet she hadn't been the only one who had wanted to snatch it right back out of that bastard's hands. Considering the despicable way the man had treated his nephew in life, Vince didn't deserve the honor of claiming that last reminder of Spence's service to their country. It had been a relief to see Callie, Spence's best friend, take it away from him before he left the cemetery.

Even now, months later, the memory of watching Spence's coffin being lowered into the ground still made

Melanie's heart ache. He'd been such a force of nature, always a bit wild but with an easy smile for everyone.

Even the shy daughter of the first family of Snowberry Creek.

God, she'd had such a crush on Spence back in their senior year, not that she'd ever admitted how she felt about him. If anyone had found out, it would only have embarrassed Melanie in front of the whole school. Not to mention her parents would've been horrified to learn their daughter was attracted to the town bad boy.

No doubt the soldier had come to town for the wedding, the same one Melanie was about to attend. Callie was marrying Nick Jenkins, who had served in Afghanistan with Spence. The couple had met when Nick drove across the country to bring Callie the dog their unit had adopted over there. The couple might have bonded first over their shared loss, but there was no doubt about how much they loved each other. In truth, Melanie was a little envious of the connection they shared.

It was time to get moving if she was going to arrive at the church on time. But before she left, the least she could do was introduce herself to the soldier and maybe nudge him along, too, since he hadn't moved since she first spotted him. Visiting Spence's grave was no doubt hard for the guy, and who could blame him? How many of his other friends had been wounded or killed over there?

As she made her way across the cemetery, she decided to do more than simply exchange names. For Spence's sake, she would offer to show him the way to the church. If he was in town by himself, maybe she would even invite him to sit with her. That way he would have met at least one other person in the crowd of locals besides the groom and his best man, Leif, another member of Spence's unit.

If the soldier was aware of Melanie's approach, he gave no sign of it. He remained frozen in that one spot even though Melanie made no effort to be especially quiet as she approached. She stopped a few steps away, pausing right in front of the double headstone that marked the grave of Spence's parents.

"Excuse me? I don't mean to intrude, but I was wondering if you were in town for the Jenkins-Redding wedding. If so, I'm headed there myself and thought you might like to follow me to the church."

The soldier's shoulders snapped back as if he was coming to attention. He didn't turn to face her, but something about his rigid stance and clenched fists bothered her. Melanie backed up a step, keenly aware that she was a woman alone with a strange man on an isolated hillside.

Suddenly, she didn't want him to turn around even if she couldn't pinpoint the reason for her misgivings. When he finally glanced back over his shoulder, her pulse went into overdrive as she tried to make sense of what she was seeing. That jawline. That profile. They were all too familiar even as her head tried to convince her heart that what she was seeing—no, make that *who* she was seeing—just wasn't possible.

"Melanie?"

With that single word, her lungs quit working altogether as her knees buckled and the ground came rushing up. She heard a muttered curse as a pair of strong arms caught her right before she hit the ground. She stared up at the soldier's face, blinking hard as if that would clear her vision. When that didn't change the new reality of her world, she pointed out the obvious.

"Spence?"

Chapter 2

❦ ❧

Son of a bitch, he hadn't meant to send Melanie Wolfe into a tailspin. It had been a risk stopping at the cemetery, but he'd wanted to visit his parents' graves to say hello and leave a bouquet for his mother. She'd always loved flowers, and he'd thought she'd like the colorful mix of red and yellow roses.

It hadn't been until he'd bent down to place the bouquet on the ground that he noticed the headstone next to theirs. He'd freaked out, but then seeing his own name carved into the granite marker had come as one helluva shock. Hearing that everyone thought he was dead was one thing; standing over his own grave was another.

And leave it to his bastard of an uncle not to have bothered having the headstone removed when he found out Spence was alive.

If he hadn't been blindsided, Spence might have handled the whole situation with Melanie better. Right now he was standing in a cemetery holding an armload of woman and not sure what to do about it. Finally, Melanie struggled to get down. He set her back on her feet but stayed close by in case she was still feeling wobbly.

When he released her and started to move away, Melanie reached out to grasp the sleeve of his ACU. "Spence, you're not dead."

Was she trying to convince herself? Or him?

"No, I'm not." Trying to ease the tension, he forced a smile. "Sorry to shock you like that, Mel. But like the man said, the news of my death was greatly exaggerated."

Melanie didn't laugh. Instead, she punched him in the arm. "There's nothing funny about this, Spencer Lang. We buried you. Do you have any idea what that was like for me . . . for everybody who knew you?"

She was right. There was nothing funny about any of it. In fact, he was royally pissed about the whole situation. However, Melanie wasn't the right target for his anger. "I'm sorry. I'm having a bit of a problem dealing with all of this myself."

Her gray eyes filled with sympathy. "I can only imagine."

To Spence's surprise, she gave him a hard hug, her arms clamped around his waist and her head against his chest. Damn, it felt good. When was the last time anyone cared enough to hold him close? He couldn't even remember. Wrapping his arms around her, he took both comfort and pleasure in the embrace. It was just a hug between friends. That didn't mean he was totally unaware of the fact that he was holding an attractive woman, one whose flaming red hair felt soft against his cheek.

Then he realized Melanie was crying.

Well, shit, now what should he do? Unable to think of any words of comfort, he settled for keeping her close as he softly rubbed her back and tried to soothe her pain.

When she finally moved to step back, he reluctantly let her go.

Melanie scrubbed at her cheeks with her hands, wiping away the tears that were still streaming down her face. The sight made him want to haul her right back into his arms. Instead, he pulled out his handkerchief and handed it to her.

"Thanks, Spence. I don't mean to cry, but this . . ." She paused to wave her hand in his direction from head to toe. ". . . is all a bit much." She managed a wobbly smile. "Not that I'm complaining, mind you. You're looking pretty good for a dead man."

He shrugged. "Yeah, I wouldn't have sprung it on you like this, but damned if I could think of an easy way to let people know. I know the army notified my uncle as my next of kin, but I'm guessing he didn't see any need to spread the word."

Actually, it came as no surprise that Uncle Vince hadn't bothered to tell anyone. The coldhearted bastard didn't give a flying fuck about anybody but himself. He'd hated Spence from the day he was adopted into the family. Vince had made it all too clear that his feelings toward him hadn't changed when the army sent someone to notify him that Spence had been found. Spence had planned to call Callie and his friends, but Vince had taken great delight in informing him that his best friend and the woman he'd wanted to build a life with had hooked up.

Spence's initial reaction had been relief that he hadn't been the only one to survive the blast from the IED that day in Afghanistan. His second was a towering rage that fed on the knowledge that Leif and Nick were busy rebuilding their lives on the ruins of Spence's life right in the town where he had grown up. It was *his* home, and his former friends had no place there. So rather than calling ahead to warn anyone of his impending arrival, he'd flown halfway around the world to arrive in Snowberry Creek unannounced and unexpected.

Damn, he couldn't wait to see the expression on Nick's face when he realized Spence had returned from the dead and wanted his life back. The only question was how Nick had managed to steal it in the first place, the sneaky rat bastard.

Melanie had finished drying her tears. She thrust the handkerchief back at Spence and then grabbed his other hand. "Speaking of letting people know, did you know that Callie is getting married? In fact, the wedding is about to start. She's marrying Nick Jenkins, a guy from your old unit. If we hurry, we should just make it."

"Yeah, I'd heard."

If Melanie noticed his lack of enthusiasm, she gave no sign of it as she towed him up over the hill to the small parking lot on the back side of the cemetery. He'd left his motorcycle parked on the other side of the mortuary building, where it was unlikely Melanie would have seen it. Would she have recognized the old Harley if she had? He'd just gotten it out of storage, but it was the same one he'd driven in high school.

Before he walked away, he asked, "Are you okay to drive, Mel? You still look pretty shaken up."

She kicked her smile up a notch. "I'm fine, Spence. Better than fine, in fact. After the past few months, I could use some good news, and finding out you're alive is as good as it gets."

It sounded as if she really meant that even though he and Melanie hadn't known each other all that well back in high school. She and Callie had been tight, but her parents had kept her on a pretty short leash. For sure, they would never have liked her hanging around with him. Back then, he'd had a well-deserved reputation for running wild.

He watched her walk away, telling himself he was just making sure she was all right. Even so, that wasn't the reason he admired the gentle sway of her hips and that thick tumble of wavy red hair that reached nearly half-way down her back. The combination was the kind of thing that grabbed a man's attention.

Now that he'd gotten a better look at her, he realized Melanie had changed a lot since the last time he saw her. That must have been nearly ten years ago, right after high school when she'd left Snowberry Creek to go to some college back east. In those days, she'd been cute enough despite the dark-rimmed glasses that had threatened to overwhelm her delicate beauty. Melanie had been shy, and he'd always suspected she'd worn those glasses as armor to hide behind.

Not anymore, though. Now that she'd regained control of herself, she moved with more confidence. It looked good on her. Maybe later she'd catch him up on her life. That is, if she was still speaking to him after the wedding.

She glanced back in his direction and frowned, a reminder that it was time to get with the program. He hustled his ass around to the other side of the building and traded his cap for his helmet. He'd rather ride without either one, but he also didn't want to draw the attention of the police on his first day back in town.

After tonight, though, all bets were off. He revved the engine and roared off to catch up with Melanie.

*   *   *

Ten minutes later, Spence followed Melanie's car into the church parking lot. She pulled into the last available slot while he drove his motorcycle onto the grass and turned off the engine. When he took off his helmet, he could hear music coming from the church. Evidently, the wedding was already in progress. His temper instantly flared hot and furious.

He'd been running on the edge like that ever since he woke up in a hospital to find out all of his friends thought he was dead. He might not have died after their vehicle had hit an IED, but there'd been plenty of times in the following months that he wished he had. That part of his life had been filled with darkness, pain, fever, and fear. Rather than get sucked too far down into the mire of the memories ripping through him, he dug his fingernails into the palms of his hands, using the small pain to help him focus on the present.

He didn't want to miss a single minute of what was about to happen.

Melanie caught up with him. "It sounds as if they've already started. I'm guessing we'll have to wait to be seated until after the bridal party is up front."

When they slipped inside the narthex of the church, Callie and her father were already halfway down the aisle. Spence leaned closer to Melanie. "You can go on in, Mel. I think I'd better watch from out here."

That much was true. He wasn't sure he could keep his mouth shut if the minister actually asked if anyone had any objections to the marriage. Hell yeah, he did. However, even if he did want to kick Nick's ass up and down that aisle a few times, Callie didn't deserve to have her big day ruined with a brawl.

He watched as Mr. Redding lifted Callie's veil and

kissed his daughter's cheek before stepping back to join his wife in the front pew. Mrs. Redding pressed a tissue to her eyes as she watched her daughter move up to stand beside the groom in front of the minister. With a huge lump in his throat, Spence forced himself to look at the man who used to be his best friend.

Watching Nick hurt too much, so he dragged his gaze to the woman standing next to Callie. Leaning forward a little, as if that small distance would help bring everything into focus, he recognized Bridey Roke. It made sense that she would be Callie's maid of honor.

Shit. Leif was up there, too. He should've expected him to be there, but his presence only served to make their betrayal that much worse. The three of them had gone through hell together. When men put their lives in one another's hands, it formed a bond that was unshakable. At least, that's what Spence had always believed.

But as he watched Nick smile down at Callie, his expression intensely possessive, that bond shattered into jagged shards of pain. He must have made a sound, because Melanie took his hand in hers and gave it a quick squeeze.

"Are you all right, Spence?"

He didn't trust himself to speak, but she seemed satisfied when he squeezed her hand back and nodded. A full-out retreat would probably be the smartest thing to do, but he couldn't tear his eyes away from the drama playing out in front of him. Right now the minister was talking, probably asking a question since first Nick and then Callie nodded and answered.

Then the happy couple turned to face each other. There was a movement that had the entire wedding part staring down toward the floor with huge grins on their faces. What were they waiting for?

He got his answer when Mooch, the dog that he and the rest of the squad had adopted back in Afghanistan, stepped into sight with a small basket dangling from his teeth. Nick reached down to pat the dog on his head and then took something out of the basket, no doubt the wedding rings. After that, Mooch dropped the basket at Nick's feet and sat down to watch what happened next. The entire congregation broke into applause.

Now it was Spence's turn to have his knees turn to jelly like Melanie's had back at the cemetery. While he'd languished as a prisoner of war, feverish and wounded, he'd suffered through unending nightmares that both Nick and Leif had died in the explosion. His captors had been only too glad to taunt him that he'd been the lone survivor.

But even after he'd been rescued, the one question no one had been able to answer for him was what had happened to Mooch. On that last deployment, they'd been on a foot patrol when that silly-looking mutt trotted out of an alley, half-starved and filthy. Spence had tossed him a couple of strips of beef jerky, which was evidently the dog's price for undying loyalty. In return, it was Mooch who'd sounded the alarm right before they would have walked into an ambush.

The fur ball's good deed had been rewarded with a bullet in his shoulder. Against regulations, Spence had carried the wounded animal back to camp while the rest of the squad formed up around them to hide what he was doing. With the help of one of the vet techs, they'd nursed Mooch back to health, and the dog had become an unofficial member of their squad. Unfortunately, Spence's plans to ship him to the States had yet to be finalized when he was captured. He was so afraid Mooch had been left behind to starve.

Spence's eyes stung as he studied his four-legged friend. Mooch's coat was shiny and clean, and his spots stood out in stark contrast to his white fur. Hell, it even looked as if the mutt had put on a couple of pounds. Good for him. At least one nice thing had come out of the war.

While Spence's attention had been focused on the dog, the service continued. It looked as if the pastor was bringing things to a close, and any second now Spence's friends would be headed his way. When Nick and Callie turned to face the wedding guests, the need to get the hell out of there hit Spence hard. Feeling as if all the oxygen had been sucked out of the air in the church, he stumbled back toward the door, dragging Melanie right along with him.

Damn, he'd forgotten he was still holding her hand. When he released it to rush out into the night, she followed him anyway. At least he could breathe again, but damn, he wished Melanie hadn't come with him, not when all he wanted to do was punch something. He settled for cutting loose with a string of curses he'd have to apologize for later.

Rather than retreat, Melanie planted herself right in front of him. "Spence, tell me what I can do to help."

He shook his head, still fighting for control even as the foul words poured from his mouth. For the second time that day, Melanie wrapped her arms around him, holding him close. It didn't help; he was too far gone for a simple touch to be enough to soothe his fury.

He managed to keep his touch gentle as he tugged her arms off him. "Get away from me, Mel. I don't want to hurt you."

Her chin took on a stubborn tilt. "You won't, Spence."

She sounded sure of that. He wasn't. "I wouldn't mean to, but I can't promise anything right now."

Before she could respond, people came pouring out of the church, laughing and having a great time. They all formed up in two lines in the glow of the front lights of the church as they waited for the bride and groom to make their appearance. Spence lost track of Melanie in the crush. Rather than risk being recognized too soon, he faded farther back into the shadows and waited for his former friends to appear.

He hadn't thought through what he wanted to say to them, but he'd make damn sure it was memorable.

Chapter 3

❦ ❦

A handful of minutes later, Leif and Bridey finally made their appearance, followed closely by Callie's parents and another couple, most likely Nick's folks. It wouldn't be long now. Spence's gut did a slow roll as he waited to confront them. His conscience, what was left of it, was screaming at him that he should just leave. He was mad at Leif and even more so at Nick, but before tonight he would've sworn there was no way he'd ever risk hurting Callie.

As it turned out, he was wrong about that. He couldn't seem to find the strength to jump on his Harley and haul ass out of there. Even if he had been able to go, it was too late now. The happy couple had just stepped out of the church.

Then Nick yelled something, but Spence couldn't hear anything above the roar in his own head. Whatever had Sarge hollering also had Leif charging through the crowd and—oh, shit!—heading straight for Spence.

And he wasn't alone.

Mooch cleared the crowd of people, his nose to the ground. Two more steps and he brought his head up to look straight toward the shadows where Spence had taken refuge. He yipped and charged forward. A few feet out, the dog took to the air, clearly trusting Spence to catch him. He held out his arms and stumbled back several steps from the impact of the happy dog hitting his chest.

The furry beast wriggled with everything he had, which made it impossible to hold on to him. Rather than risk dropping him, Spence knelt down to set Mooch back on the ground. He remained at the dog's level, letting the dog lick his face like crazy, the whole time whining and wagging his tail at a million miles an hour.

For the first time since touching down in the States, Spence felt as if he was back with family.

A pair of shiny dress shoes appeared at the edge of his peripheral vision. Leif. It had to be. Spence kept his face buried in Mooch's fur for another few seconds before releasing the dog to stand up.

The familiar sound of Leif's voice washed over him. "Damn it, dog, let the man stand up. Sorry, buddy. Mooch likes soldiers."

Spence lifted his eyes to meet Leif's gaze head-on and waited for the man to make sense of what he was seeing. It didn't take long. Leif's eyes widened in shock and his mouth opened and closed soundlessly like a damn guppy's.

He managed to choke out, "What the fuck? Wheels, is that really you?"

Spence nodded as he stood up and moved back out of reach when Leif would have started toward him. "Yeah, it's me."

Evidently, some of the other guests heard what Leif had said, because a shocked silence spread through the crowd, punctuated by a series of stage whispers as people spread the word. It took everything Spence had to step into the soft glow of the lights of the parking lot and stand his ground in front of all that intense scrutiny. It was too late to retreat. All he could do was let the drama play itself out.

Eventually, the news reached the bride and groom, because he heard Callie cry out as Nick shouted his name. A few seconds later, the pair broke through the line of people facing Spence. He glanced briefly at Nick, noticing he wore a tux instead of dress blues. Guess that confirmed that Sarge had left the military.

"Wheelman, where the fuck have you been?" Spence's friend's voice was little better than a growl choked with emotion.

Spence ignored both the question and the man, choosing instead to focus on the woman who had been his best friend for most of his life. "You look beautiful, Callie."

Her eyes were huge and shiny with tears and her face looked ghostly pale in the dim light. "Spence."

He wanted to grab her, hold her, maybe stake his claim, but that sparkling diamond band on the hand that she held out toward him stopped him in his tracks. She already belonged to someone else. He understood that. She'd thought he was dead, and she'd moved on. He hadn't expected her to pine away for him and wouldn't have wanted her to. It was who she had chosen that had him clenching his hands into fists.

When she tried to close the distance between them, he shook his head and crossed his arms over his chest. She gasped and looked to Nick for help. Spence hated that his actions had hurt her, but he couldn't stand the thought of her touching him. Not now.

When she tried again, he shook his head. "No, Callie, don't."

Nick pushed his way in between them. "Wheels, what the hell happened to you? Where have you been?"

"Like you care, you bastard!"

When Spence tried to shove him away from Callie, Leif joined the party. "Spence, cut it out. It's their wedding."

Yeah, like that truth didn't just pour gas on the fire. "Believe me, I know."

He got right up in Nick's face. "What's the matter, Sarge? Feeling a little guilty for stealing my life when you couldn't find one of your own?"

Nick gave him a hard shove. "What the hell is wrong with you? We thought you were dead! The whole fucking squad dug through the dirt with their bare hands looking for you. All we found were your bloody dog tags!"

He ran his hands through his hair, leaving it standing on end. "Damn it, Spence, I thought I got you killed."

What could Spence say to that? Even if he had the words, right now his throat was nearly closed shut with pain and regrets. He closed his eyes, trying to figure out what to do next. When he opened them again, all he could see were the tears streaming down Callie's pretty face.

He did an end run around Nick to get to her. Already he could feel Leif's hand on his shoulder, trying to pull him back. He shook him off. "Let go of me, damn it. I just want to tell her something."

He stared down at her, memorizing how she looked

at that moment and feeling sick that he'd put that expression on her face. "Sorry, Callie. I shouldn't have come. Forget I was even here. Be happy."

He pressed a kiss to her forehead and went into full retreat. Turning his back on her and on the future he'd hoped to have was the hardest thing he'd ever done, but he did it anyway. He had no memory of how he reached his motorcycle without falling apart completely, but somehow he made it. Shoving his helmet on his head, he straddled his bike and tore out of the parking lot.

Melanie hovered on the outskirts of the parking lot, horrified by what had just happened. Yeah, she hadn't heard that Spence was alive before seeing him at the cemetery, but she'd figured that was only because she'd been out of town on business and only just returned. If she'd had any idea that neither Nick nor Callie had known about his return from the dead, she would have done something to soften the blow. Called Callie or maybe her mother. Anything to have prevented this whole fiasco.

In a sudden outpouring of sympathy laced with a goodly amount of shock, the other wedding guests surrounded Nick and Callie. No one seemed to know what to do exactly, but finally the pastor took charge and started shepherding everyone toward their cars with instructions to head for the hall where the reception was to be held.

He asked for everyone's patience while the bridal couple took a few minutes to recover and regroup.

Good. Maybe with his help, some of the evening's celebration could be salvaged. For Callie's sake, she hoped so, but they'd have to do it without her. Someone needed to keep an eye on Spence. She wasn't sure why she felt such a powerful need to volunteer for the job, but it was obvious no one else was going after him.

Melanie ran for her car. Spence had gotten enough of a head start that he was out of sight by the time she pulled out of the parking lot in hot pursuit. Where would he go? It was doubtful that he was headed for his family home if for no other reason than that it was in the opposite direction.

No, Spence had looked more like a man in need of a stiff drink. She'd start by checking the closest bars in the area to see if she could spot his motorcycle in the parking lot. If that didn't work, she'd go to plan B. She wasn't sure what that would entail; all she knew for sure was that she wouldn't rest easily until she made sure he was all right.

Luck was with her. She'd almost given up when she remembered there was one more bar out past the city limits. Sure enough, there was a Harley that looked like Spence's parked at the end of the graveled lot alongside five or six other motorcycles. She pulled up behind it to get a better look and decided it was his.

Melanie left the engine running, contemplating her options while staring at the blinking neon sign in the window that simply said BEER. Dare she go in? She wasn't in the habit of hanging out in any kind of bar, especially not on her own.

As she tried to make up her mind how to proceed, a pickup truck pulled into the parking lot in a spray of gravel. Two guys got out and headed inside. They both wore jeans, heavy work boots, and hoodies. Okay, they didn't look so tough. More like a couple of construction workers stopping for a cold beer on the way home from the job.

"Come on, Melanie. Either get out of the car or go home. Dithering isn't doing anyone any good."

Neither was talking to herself. After parking the car, she headed for the entrance to the bar. There was nothing saying she had to stay any longer than it took her to find Spence. Once she knew he was all right, she could march right back out of the bar and head home.

"Right. So here goes."

She drew one last deep breath and opened the door. Once inside, she stayed within easy reach of the door and kept her back to the wall while she studied her surroundings. Where the heck was Spence? It was hard to see anything clearly in the dim interior of the bar. The few bright circles of light were centered over the line of pool tables. But unless one of the players was taking a shot, they all stood back in the shadows.

A few people sat at the bar, but no one in a uniform. That left the row of booths across the back wall, but she couldn't see those clearly from where she stood. Pushing off the wall, she took her first shaky step toward the other side of the room.

The bartender came out of the back room carrying a case of beer. Thinking he might know something, she veered in his direction. "Can you help me? I'm looking for someone."

"Maybe." He set the heavy box on the counter and gave her a narrow-eyed look. "Maybe not. Most people come in here wanting to be left alone."

Yeah, she believed that, but she had to try. "I think my friend Spence came in here. He's in an army uniform."

When he didn't immediately respond, she stepped closer to the bar and dropped her voice. "I'm worried about him. He just got back from being deployed and is having a tough time. I just want to make sure he's all right, and then I'll leave if you want me to. I promise I'm not here to cause trouble."

For some reason, he seemed to find that amusing. "Lady, in a place like this, you're the very definition of trouble."

He stared at her for several seconds and then jerked his head in the direction of the booths. "Your soldier is in the back corner booth."

He popped the top on a pair of beers. "He's probably ready for another one of these. The second one is for you."

She reached for her wallet in her purse, but he shook his head. "This round is on me."

Melanie reached for the beers. "Thank you."

He winked at her. Then as she walked away, he called after her, "If you need any help with your friend, come get me."

She nodded and kept going. Sure enough, there was Spence. He had his back to her as he stared down at a bottle identical to the ones the bartender had given her. There were also three more empty ones just like it lined up in a neat row on the table in front of him.

Wow, Spence had been a busy boy in the short time since leaving the church. He didn't say a word as she slid into the opposite side of the booth. Rather than break the silence herself, she set the new beer down in front of him and settled back to sip her own. She would've preferred a soft drink, but maybe this night called for stronger stuff. Judging by the number of beers Spence had already consumed, he thought so, too.

He finally looked up. "Mel, you shouldn't have followed me here. You were never one for pool halls and beer."

"And how would you know that? Before today, we hadn't seen each other, much less spoken, since high school. As far as you know, I come here all the time."

Although he didn't smile, she suspected that he found that idea humorous. "Well, as I recall, we didn't talk much back then, either."

She couldn't argue with that point. "So talk now. What was all of that about at the church?"

His face turned rock hard. "Don't go there, Melanie. In fact, finish your beer and leave. Better yet, I'll finish it for you. We'll both be happier that way."

"Sorry, but you're not in charge here, Spencer Lang." She took a long drink of her beer to prove her point. "Talk or don't talk. It's up to you, but I'm not going anywhere."

The nameless bartender wandered by and plunked down two plastic baskets, each containing a cheeseburger and a huge pile of sweet potato fries. He pulled a couple of forks and knives out of the pocket in the stained apron he wore tied around his waist. "Here."

Spence leaned back in the seat to glare up at their host. But when he didn't say anything, Melanie spoke up. "I'm sorry, but we didn't order those."

The bartender didn't even glance in her direction as he concentrated all of his attention on Spence. "Eat them anyway."

Spence finally joined the conversation. "I'm not hungry."

Their host put his hands on the end of the table and leaned in close. "I didn't ask if you were, but you're eating them. I'm cutting you off until you do. Got that, soldier?"

Finally, Spence nodded and pulled one of the burger

baskets closer to him and ate some fries. Melanie did the same in the hope that would encourage Spence to continue eating.

The bartender nodded in approval. "The nice lady is worried about you, so try not to be too much of an asshole. Let me know when you're ready for another round."

When he finally met Melanie's gaze, his stern expression softened just a bit. "Like I said before, if you need anything, come get me. The name's Liam Grainger."

She smiled, grateful for his support. "Thank you, Liam Grainger, I'll do that. I'm Melanie Wolfe, and he's Spence Lang."

Liam's eyebrows shot up, but she didn't know which name had surprised him. He didn't explain and she didn't ask. When someone across the room hollered his name, Liam gave the burgers one more pointed look and walked away.

Spence ate another fry and then picked up his burger with both hands and took a huge bite. Melanie cut her own hamburger in half before trying it. She'd been expecting it to be barely edible, but it was one of the best burgers she'd had in ages. "This is delicious!"

Spence merely grunted but kept eating, alternating bites with sips of his drink. Obviously he'd believed Liam when he said eating something was the price of getting more to drink. At the rate Spence was downing the beer, she doubted the food would do much to slow down his determined efforts to get drunk.

Maybe if she knew him better it would have been possible to talk him into taking it easy. But somewhere along the way, the boy she'd known had morphed into the angry man sitting across from her. Earlier in the cemetery, there had been a few recognizable flashes of the old Spence. Something in the way his eyes crinkled at the corners when he smiled.

But there was a hardness about him now that hadn't been there before. Yeah, he'd acted out as a teen, especially after he lost both his parents, yet he'd never been known for getting into fights. But back at the wedding, the sense of barely controlled violence simmering just below the surface had been all too clear.

When he finished off the last of his fries, he lurched up out of the booth and started toward the bar. After going only a few steps, he turned back. "You ready for another one?"

One of them needed a clear head. "I'd prefer coffee with cream and sugar."

He was already on his way. She watched as he tossed his empty basket on the bar. Liam looked past Spence toward Melanie. She wasn't sure exactly what he wanted to know, but she nodded anyway. As soon as she did, he popped the top on two more beers and set them on the bar. Spence pulled out his wallet and dropped a credit card on the counter before snagging the two beers and heading back to their booth. Maybe they didn't serve coffee here.

Spence set both beers on his side of the table. "Your bartender friend said he was brewing a fresh pot. He'll bring your coffee when it's done."

Liam wasn't her friend, but she wasn't going to argue the point. "Thanks."

"Why aren't you leaving, Mel? I don't need a babysitter. And besides, won't Callie be hurt if you don't show up at the reception?"

"I doubt that she'll even notice." Although that same thought had crossed her mind more than once. Glancing at her watch, she decided it was too late now anyway. If she did show up at the reception now, she'd have to explain where she'd been and why. It was that last part that she had no easy answer for, so she stayed right where she was.

Besides, right now Callie and her new husband were surrounded by friends and family.

In contrast, Spence was painfully alone. Even if he preferred it that way, she wasn't in the mood for a big party, either. She'd rather sit here in this dingy bar with an angry Spence than hang out with her friends, the odd girl out.

"Believe me, she'll notice, Mel. You're one of her best friends, or at least you used to be." Spence was like a dog with an old bone.

"The same could be said about you." She stopped and looked at their surroundings. "And yet here we are."

Her coffee arrived. Liam set it down in front of her along with a carafe in case she wanted more. He walked away without a word.

Spence winced as if her words had hurt him.

"Sorry, Spence. I know all of this has to be hard for you. Them, too."

"Fuck that and fuck them." His fist came down on the table hard enough to cause her coffee to splash over the rim of her cup.

Okay, so maybe they'd both be better off if she just kept her mouth shut. Spence lapsed into a sullen silence as he made steady inroads into his beer. When he started on the last bottle, Melanie went up to the bar and ordered two more. Liam didn't say a word, but there was a wealth of opinion in the look he gave her.

"After these, I'll try to get him out of here," she said.

Liam looked past her and laughed. "Yeah, good luck with that."

If he said anything else, it was drowned out by a sudden blast of music. She headed back to their booth; it was empty. After setting down the beers, she turned around to look for Spence, only to find him standing right behind her. He took her hand in his and towed her over to the opposite side of the bar where a couple of spotlights were focused on a small open area.

She tried to drag her heels, but she was no match for her determined companion. "Spence, what are you doing?"

"I want to dance."

His grip on her hand was gentle but firm. Even so, she suspected if she really wanted to break free, he'd let her. She couldn't find it in her to even try, which scared her enough to at least make a token protest. "I don't think this is a good idea, Spence."

He gave her one last tug right into his waiting arms. "Too bad. I do."

Before she could even sputter a response, he gave her a quick twirl, and the battle was lost.

Chapter 4

✾✽

Earlier in the church parking lot, Spence would've sworn his conscience was dead, lost that day in the streets of Afghanistan when his whole life went off the rails. But like him, it had somehow survived, battered and bruised perhaps, but definitely alive. He knew that for a fact because right now the damn thing was shoving its way through the pleasant fog of beer to point out that he shouldn't be forcing Melanie to dance with him.

In his own defense, he hadn't asked her to follow him to this hole-in-the-wall bar, not to mention he'd repeatedly told her to leave as soon as she found him. Obviously Melanie was still there because she wanted to be. God knows why, but it was her choice, her problem.

His conscience wasn't buying it. *Yeah, and you're being a complete asshole. She's still there because little Melanie Wolfe has grown up to be some kind of misguided do-gooder out to save the world. Or, in this case, one Spencer Lang.*

Okay, fine. He'd paid for two songs, which were almost over. They'd finish this dance, he'd thank Melanie for her concern, and then he would send her on her way. If necessary, he'd shove her out the fucking door. He gave Melanie another twirl as the final strains of the song faded away.

Unfortunately, someone else must have fed quarters into the antique jukebox, because the opening strains of a slow song about lost loves and roads not taken filled the room. Three notes in and all of Spence's good intentions shattered. He'd already dropped Melanie's hand when the previous song ended. Now all he could do was stare down at her. She studied him for what felt like an eternity even if it was only a few seconds.

He wasn't sure which one of them moved first, but between one second and the next she was back in his arms and slowly swaying to the music. Melanie was a bit shorter than Callie, making her about five-seven, and so more than half a foot shorter than his six-three. The heels she wore made up enough of that difference to put her head right at his shoulder, the soft silk of her hair against his cheek.

He breathed in her scent, an intoxicating mix of warm skin combined with a hint of perfume. He knew he should be shot for the thoughts he was having, because this was Melanie Wolfe, not some random woman he'd picked up in a bar. He shifted so there was a little more room between them, praying the song would end before he did something stupid like kiss her.

She might forgive him for it; he wouldn't.

For the moment, all he could do was enjoy the sweet hell of simple human contact as the music cocooned them with bluesy guitar notes and sad lyrics. The song suited his mood perfectly, but he'd be glad when it was over.

When it ended, Melanie walked away, heading right toward their booth in the back corner. He followed after her, promising himself he'd make her leave now. It was getting late, and he had some serious drinking left to do. He didn't need or want those big, worried eyes of hers watching every time he lifted a bottle to his mouth.

He'd earned the right to get drunk on his first night in town; he'd paid for the privilege with both blood and pain. Nothing and no one was going to stop him. Before Melanie could sit down, Spence blocked her way. "It's getting late. You should go home."

Despite his best efforts to sound like Sarge making it clear to a new recruit that his orders were not to be questioned, Melanie stood her ground. "I told you earlier, Spence, I don't take well to being bossed around. This is a public place, and I can stay here as long as I want to."

Okay, she was starting to piss him off. "But I don't want you here."

She flinched as if his words hurt her, but she stood her ground. "Tough. I'm staying. Deal with it."

"Is there a problem?"

They both jumped. That the bartender could sneak up on them like that showed just how rusty Spence's survival skills had gotten. "No problem. I just asked her to leave."

"And I said no," Melanie said as she used the distraction to sneak past him to reclaim her side of the booth. Once she was seated, she poured herself another cup of coffee, clearly settling in for the duration.

Fine. He'd tried. "I'll have two more beers."

Liam nodded. "If either one of you wants something else to eat, now's the time. My short-order cook leaves at midnight."

"I'd love another order of fries," she said.

Spence mumbled, "Nothing for me."

He couldn't help but notice the bright smile Melanie had given Liam along with her order. If she liked that guy so much, why was she sitting with him instead of parking her backside up at the bar? Rather than ask, he finished off his last beer even though it had gone warm and flat. He didn't care. It would hold him until the fresh ones arrived.

By the time Liam delivered his drinks and Melanie's fries, Spence's nerves were stretched to the breaking point. He jerked his head in Liam's direction to show his appreciation. "Thanks. Put it all on my tab."

"Will do."

After he left, Spence watched Melanie pouring a puddle of ketchup next to the heaping pile of fries. He snagged one for himself and washed it down with a big swig of beer. The combination tasted good to him, so he did it again. Melanie didn't complain about him pilfering her snack, probably glad that he was tempering the effects of the alcohol with food.

"Don't you have someplace better to be?"

She shrugged. "Obviously not."

Okay, that cracked him up or maybe it was the beer laughing. He took another long drink and set the empty bottle to the side. After a few more swallows, the haze was back, softening the edges of everything that had happened. Tomorrow, he'd probably hate himself for how he'd acted at the church, and he figured a world-class hangover would be suitable punishment.

At least Liam kept the beer coming. He'd stop by every so often with two more bottles and to take the empties away. On the last trip, he grinned at Melanie. Spence looked over to see what the man found so entertaining. Her head was nodding, as if she couldn't keep her eyes open another minute. This despite having finished off the entire carafe of coffee by herself.

Liam walked away, his shoulders shaking as if he were laughing. Clearly he found the pair of them amusing for some reason. Right now Spence was too drunk to care.

As a rule, he'd never been much of a drinker, mostly because his bastard of an uncle had been a mean drunk. Spence was adopted, so they hadn't crawled out of the same gene pool. Even so, he had seen up close and personal what a lifetime of hard drinking did to a man. He had more respect for himself than that, or at least he used to. By now he'd lost count of how many beers he'd had.

Too many by anyone's count.

He'd also lost track of time. How long ago had Melanie fallen asleep? She looked pretty damn uncomfortable wedged there in the corner with her back against the wall, her legs up on the bench, and her head angled against the back of the seat. What should he do about that? He blinked several times to clear his mind. It didn't work, but he had to do something.

"Hey, Melanie."

No response. He tried again, louder this time. "Melanie! Wake up. It's time for you to hit the road."

She shifted, but her eyes remained closed. He reached across the table to shake her. "Mel, wake up. You need to go home."

Damn it, he meant it this time. She couldn't risk being seen like this. She was stone-cold sober, but anyone who saw her would think she was passed-out drunk. That was his goal in life right now, not hers. When he shook her again, she batted at him with her hand but still didn't wake up. Had she always been this stubborn? He caught her flailing hand in his and gave it a squeeze. "Wake up before Liam throws your sleeping ass out into the Dumpster."

Melanie wanted to burrow deeper under the covers and ignore the guy telling her to wake up, especially because his voice sounded an awful lot like Spence Lang's. That couldn't be, though. Everyone knew Spence was dead. She hated knowing that, and if she woke up right now, even the dream Spence would disappear. She reached for the blankets and found none.

Reality slowly filtered in. She wasn't in bed; she was in a bar. And the voice she heard wasn't coming from a phantom Spence, but the real thing. Her eyes finally fluttered open. Still thickheaded and confused, she sat up taller and looked around.

Spence settled back into the corner of his side of the booth. His eyes looked as bleary as hers felt. He saluted her with a half-empty beer bottle. "Yeah, you're really here."

Dropping her feet back down on the floor, she smiled back at him. "So are you."

That simple truth improved both her cognition and her mood considerably. Meanwhile, Liam must have been watching, because he appeared with a pot of coffee in his hand. He filled her cup and shoved it in front of her. "It's almost closing time. Drink that before you go."

Melanie wrapped her hands around the mug and stared down at the hot liquid as she soaked up its warmth. After a few seconds, she finally doctored it with cream and sugar and took a sip.

She shuddered. "God, that's strong. It tastes like pure caffeine."

Not that it kept her from chugging it down. The taste improved only slightly after she toned it down with two more packets of sugar and another one of those little plastic tubs of half-and-half. As soon as she finished it off, she picked up her purse. It was way past time to head home.

"Okay, Spence, finish that last one so we can go."

He reached for the beer. "Yeah, I should walk you out to your car. Not safe for a woman. There's a bunch of drunks around."

She didn't point out that he was one of those himself. After he downed the beer, he set it down with a loud clink and carefully lined it up with a neat double row of others just like it.

He cocked his head to the side to admire his work. "There, neat and tidy like a squad of soldiers reporting for duty."

As he studied them, his smile looked a bit loopy. "I'll be back, guys. Just gotta see the lady out."

Melanie didn't bother to correct him. Once she got him outside, she wasn't about to let him head back into the bar. For one thing, he'd had enough to drink. Spence might have good reasons for consuming that much alcohol, but he would suffer tomorrow for it. Besides, the bar was about to close.

When he stood up, though, he reeled from side to side as if the whole world had done a back spin, and he stumbled slightly as if the floor rippled beneath his feet. Flailing his arms for balance, he staggered across the aisle to bump up hard against the empty booth on the other side of the aisle.

Spence narrowed his eyes and glared at everyone in the bar. "Whoa! What the hell just happened?"

Using the exaggerated care of the thoroughly drunk, he managed to stand upright again. At least he was smart enough to hang on to the back of the booth for support. "Did someone push me?"

When no one immediately confessed, he pushed off in the direction of the bar and muttered, "Sneaky bastards."

It happened again, but this time Melanie grabbed his arm and wrapped it around her shoulders while she put hers around his waist. After two steps, the two of them settled into a steady rhythm.

Yeah, that was better. Definite progress being made here. Their friendly neighborhood bartender stood waiting for them at the bar. She kept one arm around Spence and used her free hand to dig in her purse for her wallet. "How much do we owe you?"

Liam waved her off and held out a receipt. "Your soldier gave me his credit card number, so I put everything on his tab. Figured he should foot the bill."

Spence immediately nodded like a bobbleheaded doll and looked proud of his own generosity. "Right. My treat."

Liam followed as they shuffled toward the door. "How is he getting home?"

Spence reached into his pocket and pulled out his keys. Dangling them in the air, he announced to one and all, "I've got my Harley outside. It's a real beauty, too. I'll ride it home."

Then he frowned. "Hey, come to think of it, I don't have a home anymore. I gave it to Callie when I died."

Melanie wasn't sure what to say to that. Where had he been planning on spending the night if he couldn't stay in his own house? Meanwhile, Liam made a quick grab for Spence's keys and then backed out of reach after shoving them in his own pocket. Spence made a futile attempt to steal them back.

The other man stood his ground. "Sorry, Corporal, but you're not driving anywhere tonight. The cops would have my license if I let someone in your condition out on the roads."

Spence looked insulted. "Hey, I'm not . . . What's the word I'm thinking of?"

He addressed that last part to Melanie, but it was Liam who answered. "Impaired, but that is exactly what you are, my friend. Now, let me help you out to the lady's car. I'll make sure your bike is safe. You can pick it up here tomorrow."

Spence was clearly prepared to stand there and argue, but he was looking worse by the second. If they didn't get him poured into her car soon, they'd most likely have to scrape him up off the floor. She did her best to move him off dead center toward the door. Finally, he cooperated enough to get him moving.

Liam opened the door for her and then helped her guide Spence's faltering steps outside. "I'm parked over there."

Outside, the parking lot was bright from the full moon high overhead. How long had they been in there, anyway? Hours upon hours, judging by the nearly empty parking lot. When she got Spence to the car, she propped him against the quarter panel until she had the door unlocked and open.

"Get in, Spence, and buckle up."

He grumbled a bit, but he did as she said. While he got settled, she crossed over to where Liam stood by Spence's bike. He was busy pulling stuff out of the saddlebags. He held out a leather shaving kit and a few articles of clothing.

"Here, this should be enough to do him until tomorrow. Tell him I'll have his motorcycle locked up in the garage out back. No harm will come to it."

She accepted the stack of Spence's things. "Thanks for everything, Liam."

He looked past her toward the car, his eyebrows drawn down low and his mouth set in a hard frown. "Something has been niggling at me all night. It's like his name is familiar, but I know I've never met him before tonight."

How much should she share? After all, there was a lot she didn't know herself. "Spence grew up here in Snowberry Creek, but as far as I know, he hasn't been home for years. I don't know a lot of the specifics about his time serving in Afghanistan other than his vehicle hit an IED. His two friends survived, but there was a second explosion. All they found were his dog tags, and he was reported as killed in action."

She paused, finding it difficult to continue. "Spence saw his own headstone earlier tonight."

"Son of a bitch, no wonder he ended up here." Liam's eyes glittered in the darkness, staring toward her car. Finally, he turned his attention back to her. "Do you have someplace to take him? I've got a cot in the storeroom if he needs a place to crash."

She'd already considered driving Spence to the nearest motel but had rejected it as being too far to go, not to mention how late it was. Maybe dumping Spence on Liam's cot would be the smart thing to do, but she already knew she was going to turn down his kind offer. Spence deserved better than to wake up in the morning surrounded by cases of beer and hard liquor.

"He can stay at my place for tonight."

Liam didn't argue, but he did ask, "Is there someone there to help you in case he gets rowdy?"

No, she was alone, just like Spence. "We'll be fine. Thank you again for everything, but we should get going."

"I hope he appreciates what you're doing for him, Melanie. If he doesn't, let me know, and I'll kick his ass for you."

She laughed. "I'll keep that in mind. Good night, Liam."

By the time she had the car started, their host was astride Spence's Harley and revving the engine. Hoping she was doing the right thing by entrusting the bike to Liam's care, she pulled out of the parking lot and headed home.

"We're going to my house, Spence. Hope that's okay."

A soft snore was his only response.

Chapter 5

❧ ❧

The moment Spence opened his eyes, he slammed them shut again. Thanks to the sunlight streaming in the window, it felt as if his eyes were being stabbed with shards of broken glass while some bastard pounded a bass drum inside his head.

It was a vicious combination that made it impossible to figure out answers to his two most pressing questions. How far was the nearest bathroom? And where the hell was he, anyway? Only one way to find out.

This time he used greater caution and peeked out at the world through narrow slits. Rolling his head to the side, he studied his surroundings. Nothing looked even vaguely familiar, leaving him just as confused about how he came to be sleeping in this bed. Obviously, if he was going to find answers to his questions, he'd have to hunt them down.

Bracing himself for a renewed surge of pain, Spence rolled up to sit on the edge of the bed. His head spun and his stomach lurched, but at least he could take pride in the fact that he'd managed to stay vertical and not puke on the carpet. Progress was being made.

After the dizziness was under control, he slowly stood up. A quick look down showed he was wearing yesterday's boxers and T-shirt. He spotted his ACUs folded in a neat pile on the dresser with his boots sitting side by side on the floor. His shaving kit was there, too, along with a thick green towel, a matching washcloth, and a bottle of aspirin.

Okay, someone else had to be around. If he'd been alone, his clothes would be scattered on the floor, not squared away. Growing more curious by the second, he made his way around the edge of the bed to look out the window. He closed his eyes and then opened them again to verify what he was seeing. Nothing had changed. It was all real, and he now knew exactly where he was.

Wow, somehow he'd spent the night in the Wolfe House, which was on the local historical register and had a sign on the front fence to prove it. Definitely not the kind of place that took in strays like him. How the hell did he get there? He closed his eyes again and tried to recall the events that had brought him to this point.

Rolling the clock back, he remembered riding into town and stopping at the cemetery. That's right. Melanie Wolfe had found him standing over his own grave. He shoved that WTF moment to the back of the line and kept going. They'd left for the church, where he'd watched Callie marry Nick. Skipping over the details of that disaster, he concentrated on what had happened next.

He'd left the church, looking for the closest watering hole. Someone had been there with him—Melanie. Bits and pieces from the rest of the night came pouring back with a vengeance. He had vague memories of a long, double row of beer bottles lined up on the table in front of him. God, no wonder his head was so fucked up. He hadn't consumed that much beer at one time in years.

He had more questions to add to his list. Why had Melanie decided to keep him company instead of going to her friend's wedding reception? And why would she drag his worthless ass home with her?

All things considered, he was surprised that her mother hadn't come after him with a rolling pin for daring to cross their threshold. Hell, Mrs. Wolfe and her husband had never had much use for him back when Spence and Melanie were in high school. He could only imagine her reaction to the sorry condition he'd been in last night. The woman he remembered would've tossed him out to sleep in a ditch somewhere.

Well, he couldn't hide in this room all day. He also probably owed Melanie an apology—or maybe a dozen—as well as his thanks for sticking with him last night.

He picked up his pants and yanked them on. Grabbing the towel and his kit, he headed out the door. Before he faced anyone, he needed a hot shower to clear his head. Once he was presentable, he would collect his boots and the rest of his gear, make his apologies, and disappear.

Except how would he do that? He was pretty sure his Harley was still back at the bar. He had vague memories of the bartender lifting his keys to keep Spence from driving drunk. Smart of him. He had no need to risk his livelihood for a soldier on a full-out bender. If he'd let Spence ride out of there, he could've been held liable if anything had gone wrong. Even so, Spence was grateful.

He'd thank the man when he got there to retrieve his wheels. How he'd even get there, though, was another problem in itself. Right now he was in no shape for a forced march across town, although he hated asking Melanie for another favor.

He could always stop to refuel at the Creek Café with one of Frannie's jumbo breakfast platters. A gallon or two of her ridiculously strong coffee would do the trick. That would have to be his fallback plan, though. His return to Snowberry Creek had caused enough of a stir last night, and he'd barely survived the experience. Postponing any further public appearances until after he was back in top form only made good sense.

His plans made, he opened the door as quietly as he could and headed down the hallway in search of a bathroom.

Twenty minutes later, he was back in his temporary bedroom and unsure what to do next. That was one good thing about life in the military: What needed to be done at any given moment was rarely in doubt. Standing there having to figure it out for himself felt wrong somehow.

He stared at his own image in the mirror over the dresser. "One step at a time, Corporal. One step at a time."

Those were the words the counselor had forced him to repeat from the first time they met after Spence had been rescued. Even now, he could hear Terry's voice in his head, speaking in that maddening slow, Southern drawl of his. During their first few visits, Terry had done everything he could to get Spence to open up, to cough up all the gory details about the hell he'd been through. Spence had fought him tooth and nail, but he'd ended up spewing it all out anyway.

Afterward, he'd felt as if he'd been turned inside out

and upside down, but he'd been able to sleep through the night for the first time in months. The next visit was only marginally easier, but he'd come to trust Terry and the process. Although the man had used all the correct mumbo jumbo of his profession, in the end he'd boiled his advice down to a few words: *Don't rush. Don't run. Take it easy. Better to take one slow step back toward normal and get it right than to run like hell only to fall on your face.*

Last night definitely qualified as a face-plant episode. It was time to take that next slow step. Gathering up his gear, he left the sanctuary of the bedroom and went in search of his hostesses.

Out in the hall, he paused to listen. The house was strangely silent as he headed down the staircase that led down to the main floor. The enticing scent of fresh coffee led him around to the back of the house, where he found Melanie sitting alone at the kitchen table.

As soon she spotted him, she immediately closed the folder she'd been reading. "Good morning."

He nodded, still unsure how to proceed. "Good morning."

Then she glanced at the clock on the wall behind him. "Or I guess I should have said good afternoon. The coffeepot is on the far counter, and the mugs are in the cabinet right above it. I made a run to Bridey Roke's new coffee shop and picked up half a dozen of her best muffins. Pile your stuff on the counter and help yourself."

"Thanks, Mel."

Was it just him or was her smile looking a bit forced? As he rattled around fixing his coffee and picking out a couple of the muffins, he noticed her eyes kept straying back to that folder. If he had to guess, he wasn't the reason behind whatever had her so worried. What was going on?

He sat down across the round table from her and took his time peeling the wrapper off the first muffin. "I hope your mother wasn't too upset about me crashing here last night."

Melanie flinched. "Not a problem. She doesn't know."

Interesting. "So maybe I should go before she and your father come home and find out. I don't want to cause you any problems. And before I forget, thanks for hanging out with me last night. I know I wasn't the best company."

Her smile brightened a bit. "Believe it or not, I rather enjoyed myself."

He looked up from his coffee to see if she really meant that. It wouldn't have surprised him if she was yanking his chain, but her smile now looked more genuine. "Really? Sitting in a dive watching me try to drink the place dry was a good time? You must not get out much."

Okay, he'd meant that last part as a joke, but she took him seriously. Melanie's smile faded as she explained, "You might not have heard, but my father passed away unexpectedly last summer. I came back to help my mother get things settled, so it's been a while since I've had time for much of anything other than work. By comparison, hanging out in a bar for an evening was a vast improvement, not to mention Liam serves a mean burger."

Okay, then. He got that. It wasn't as if his life had been filled with grins and giggles lately, either. As good as the burger had been, if he were to choose the high point of the evening, it would have been dancing with Melanie. Especially during that slow song there at the end.

The memory of how it had felt to hold her in his arms

came rushing back. It left him hungry for more of the same, especially since he'd always had a weakness for leggy redheads. The downside was that this was Melanie Wolfe. He didn't need her mother to tell him that Mel was off-limits, especially for damaged goods like him.

Despite Spence's best intentions, his dick chose that moment to surge back to life for the first time since ... hell, he couldn't remember. A lot of things had gotten scrambled when that IED had ... No, he couldn't think about that day and what had come afterward. He also ignored his body's interest in the woman seated across from him as he shifted, trying to find a more comfortable position. After everything he'd been through, maybe he should be grateful that the damn thing still worked, but now wasn't the time or the place. And God knows, Melanie wasn't the right woman.

He needed to hit the road before he did something stupid. With that in mind, he stuffed the final bite of muffin in his mouth and swallowed hard. After washing it down with the last gulp of his coffee, he put his mug in the dishwasher. "I should get going before your mom gets back. I don't want to cause you any trouble, not after everything you did for me last night."

"She's not coming back."

Melanie looked as if she'd just bitten into a lemon. He returned to the table and sat back down. "As in not today or as in not ever?"

She shrugged and let out a long breath. "To tell the truth, I don't really know. Mom took my father's death hard, and everything else that's happened since has only made it worse."

Melanie gave that same folder another worried look before continuing. "After he died, I took a leave of absence from my job in Spokane to come stay with her, but I never expected to be here this long. My boss at the library was pretty patient, but I eventually had to resign. When that happened, I gave up my apartment and put all my stuff into storage."

She looked around the kitchen and sighed. "Sometimes it feels like I'm living in one of those extended-stay places."

Not that it was really any of Spence's business, but right now Melanie looked as if she was carrying the weight of the world on her slender shoulders. "So where did your mom go?"

"About three weeks after the funeral, she packed a bag and drove down to Portland to visit her older sister. That was months ago. My aunt keeps me posted on how she's doing. It's not good."

Well, shit. Last night Melanie had stood toe-to-toe with him, refusing to back down an inch. She'd bullied him into eating his hamburger and into getting into her car. He might have no memory of how he came to be in that bed upstairs, but he'd bet his last dollar she'd been beside him every step of the way, nagging him into taking care of business.

Right now Mel looked as if a stiff breeze would blow her away. He might not know her all that well, but he recognized desperate when he saw it. It had to be lonely rattling around in this behemoth of a house all by herself.

Speaking of which, "Is it the help's day off or something? I haven't heard anyone else moving around."

"Our housekeeper retired right after Mom left, and the maid only comes once a month to do the heavy cleaning. With just me living here, things don't get very messy."

There had to be more to that story than she was telling him. Why else would she be biting her lip as if struggling to hold back something?

"Is there anything I can do to help?"

To give her credit, she hesitated a few seconds before shaking her head. "Not at the moment, but thanks for the offer. The main problem is that I've had to learn the family business from the ground up and on the fly. I've made progress, but it's been a lot to absorb all at once. I'm trained to do research, so gathering the pertinent information is easy. It's figuring out what to do with it that's the problem."

Spence leaned forward to rest his arms on the table and stared her straight in the eye. "You will call me if there's anything I can do."

He put enough emphasis in his words to make sure she understood not only that he meant it, but that he also expected that call. Before she could argue, Spence changed the subject. "I hate to ask, but can you give me a ride to the bar? I need to get my motorcycle back from that guy Liam so I can start looking for a place to live."

She was already up and moving. Without being asked, she got him a small backpack to dump his gear in and then dug her keys out of her purse. "So it sounds like you're back in Snowberry Creek to stay."

"I'm back, but that's as much as I can say at this point. I'm not going to reenlist in the army, but I haven't had time to make any solid plans. I just need a place to roost temporarily."

She bit her lower lip and studied him for several seconds. "There aren't a lot of rentals here in town, and the nearest motels are all the way back out on the interstate. What kind of place are you looking for? An apartment or a house?"

Something else he hadn't thought much about. He supposed by rights he could move back into his family home, but that didn't feel right. Either way, it hurt to think about Callie and Nick living there together. He wasn't ready to poke that nest of snakes yet.

Melanie was already heading out the back door. He slung the strap of the pack over his shoulder and hurried after her. Outside, he stopped to think about what he did want. Hell, he had no idea. He ran his hands over his head in frustration and found the familiar feel of his military buzz cut soothing. "I'm not picky. Got any suggestions?"

"Yeah, actually I do."

A set of keys came flying over her shoulder right at him. "What are these?"

"The keys to the housekeeper's cottage. It has a separate driveway off the street that runs behind our property. It's probably in need of a thorough cleaning, but it is furnished. You can stay there for as long as you want."

He didn't know what to say. "Are you sure, Melanie? How much is the rent?"

Not that it mattered. It didn't sound as if he'd have many other choices here in town. She named a figure that had him shaking his head. "That's not nearly enough, Melanie. I might not have lived in the area for a long time, but I do know rents are higher than that."

She didn't answer until they were both in the car. "Fine. I'll drop you off at the bar and then run some errands. You check out the house and see what you think. If it will suit your needs, stop by later and make me an offer."

"It's a deal."

Even sight unseen, he already knew he was going to take it. Just like she said, there were never many rental properties in Snowberry Creek. Even if he could find an apartment on such short notice, he'd have to spend a lot of time and money buying even the bare essentials to make the place livable. Part of getting his life back on track involved deciding if he could stand to live in the same town as Callie and his other former best friends.

Just thinking about Leif and Nick had him wanting to punch something. Yeah, the chances of making Snowberry Creek his permanent home seemed pretty slim. Renting the cottage from Melanie would be the perfect short-term answer.

Now if only he could find such easy answers to all of his other problems. Rather than dwell on things he couldn't change, he turned his attention to studying the small business district that formed the core of his hometown. He smiled as they drove past the Creek Café. Some things never changed, including Frannie's menu. Her prices might go up, but the food stayed the same. She never got any complaints about it, either.

There were a few new businesses, but the character of the town was the same. People waved, most likely at Melanie. He wasn't sure if anyone recognized him, although he'd guess by now the news of his return had spread like wildfire.

At the next stoplight, she asked, "Did you ever think you'd end up back here?"

Interesting question. He gave it some thought. "I don't know. Maybe eventually, but not this soon. I'd planned to stay in the army long enough to earn a pension. That's not going to happen now, but I haven't had enough time to make other plans."

He glanced in her direction. "I guess neither of us meant to end up back in Snowberry Creek, but here we are."

She grimaced. "Yeah, lucky us."

Before he could think of how to respond, they'd reached the bar. Melanie looked around at the empty parking lot. "I didn't think about it being Sunday or that the bar might not be open. I'll wait to make sure Liam's around so you can get your motorcycle back."

Spence got out and headed for the door. Sure enough, it was locked. He pounded on it a few times with his fist. He waited a few seconds to see if there was any response and then tried again. This time, he heard someone on the other side of the door. Luck was with him, because it was Liam who opened the door.

"You survived, I see. I had my doubts."

"So did I." Spence laughed. "Thanks for taking my keys."

"Anytime. I'll go get them."

While Liam disappeared back into the bar, Spence jogged back over to where Melanie was waiting for him. He leaned down to look at her. "He's getting my keys, so you can go. Thanks again for everything, and I'll let you know about the cottage this afternoon."

"Sounds good. I should be home in a couple of hours."

He patted the top of the car. "See you then."

Spence started to walk away but immediately turned back. "If you don't have plans for dinner, why don't I pick up something for both of us? Do you have a preference?"

She didn't even hesitate. "I'm not picky, especially when I don't have to do the cooking."

He'd made the offer on impulse, but it pleased him more than it should have that she accepted. "Okay, then. I'll drop by around six."

"See you then, Spence. Tell Liam hello for me."

Spence stood back out of the way as she drove away, the whole time debating whether he'd actually deliver her message. He had no claim on Melanie. She was only being friendly, so there was no reason to be a jerk about it. It wasn't as if this dump was the kind of place she'd start hanging out in on a nightly basis.

The man in question reappeared. Liam tossed Spence his keys. "It's in the garage in back. Come on, and I'll unlock it for you."

As he unfastened the old-fashioned padlock on the door, Liam gave Spence a sheepish look. "I have a confession to make. It's been a while since I've been on a Harley that nice. I took it for a couple of laps around the block before I put it away."

Spence wanted to be mad, but he owed the guy for how he'd treated both him and Melanie the night before. Liam had gone above and beyond for the two of them. "Not a problem. I would've done the same."

He climbed on and started the engine. "Thanks again. And Melanie said to say hi."

Liam nodded. "Your lady is good people. Stop in again sometime."

"Will do."

Spence revved the engine and headed back toward Melanie's to check out the cottage. As he did, he realized he should've told Liam that Mel wasn't his. Next time, maybe he'd do that. But then again, maybe not.

Chapter 6

✤✤

Melanie let herself into the corner office, one of several that made up the second-floor interior balcony. It used to be her father's, and it still felt strange to think of it as hers. It didn't help that the factory down below was eerily quiet. During the workweek, a constant cacophony of machinery echoed throughout the two-story structure as the employees made the custom-order doors, cabinets, and other wood products that were the company's mainstays. As a librarian, she was used to working in relatively quiet conditions. Here in the small millworks that had been in her family for generations, silence was a rarity.

Since taking over the company after her father's death, Melanie had slowly become more accustomed to the endless racket made by power saws, nail guns, lathes, and forklifts, but some days it was still too much. Whenever she really needed to concentrate, she came in on weekends, when the crew was off.

At least today, she didn't plan to stay long. The payroll

report was finished, and Melanie just needed to review it before signing off so the paychecks could go out on Wednesday. It was one of the jobs she always saved for when she was alone. Reading the numbers always left her feeling a bit sick. No matter how many different ways she looked at them, they all added up to an ugly truth she could no longer deny. The time was coming when she was going to have to start laying off employees if she couldn't create a better balance between the red ink and the black on the bottom line. Once that happened, it might be only a matter of time before Wolfe Millworks would have to close its doors for good.

"Dad, how could you have let it all get this out of hand?"

Her one-sided conversations with her father were the other reason she liked to be alone when she worked on the company's books. She knew the downturn in the building industry wasn't Edmond Wolfe's fault. However, as far as she could tell, he'd ignored the harsh reality of the changing economy until it was far too late. That part was all on him.

She'd never bad-mouth her father in front of the employees, but in private she had plenty to say to him. Not only had he let the business nearly go broke, but he'd exhausted most of his personal savings and then borrowed against the family home in an effort to make ends meet.

The only reason she could continue to pay the bills at all was that he hadn't been able to touch the trust fund that her grandmother had left her. If he'd asked, she would've given him the money, but all things considered, it was better that hadn't happened. As much as she hated to say it, he would've run through it and still not gotten the business back on track.

All she could do was keep moving forward. There was no changing the past. With that bit of wisdom, she opened up the file Bertie had left for her. She didn't bother double-checking the bookkeeper's figures. Bertie might do everything the old-fashioned way, but she did it right. The only trouble was that her system was decades out of date, just another of the problems that Melanie needed to deal with.

Somehow the company had to be dragged into the twenty-first century, but it was slow going and not just because of the financial issues. The sudden death of Melanie's father had come as a shock to everyone, especially the long-term employees. Most weren't ready to accept Melanie as the new face of the company leadership. It didn't help that a lot of them had watched her grow up.

Their attitude would have pissed her off, but she couldn't really blame them. She was out of her comfort zone, and they all knew it. If there had been enough money, maybe she could've hired someone to step in to take over. Well, that wasn't happening. No one worth having would work for the pittance she could afford to pay right now.

She scanned the report, initialed the paperwork, and then signed the stack of checks. The whole process took her less than an hour but left her right hand cramping from holding the pen too tightly. Tension did that to a person.

When she was finished with the last one, she gathered up all the papers and locked them in the safe. With that job out of the way, she reviewed the work orders they had lined up for the week and sighed with relief. There was enough to keep everyone busy, a welcome improvement over the winter months. The number of new jobs still wasn't great, but it was definitely better.

Done for the day, she locked up and headed downstairs and out to the parking lot. At least it was sunny outside. At this time of the year, the rain the Pacific Northwest was famous for could blow in with no warning. She'd been planning on working out in the yard that afternoon.

And now there was something else to look forward to: Spence was bringing dinner. Even before her father's death, her social life had been pretty much nonexistent. She'd been dating a nice guy, but a year ago he had been transferred to another state. They'd kept in touch for a while, but their relationship hadn't been strong enough to survive the separation.

Since coming back to Snowberry Creek, she'd been happy to renew her friendships with Callie and Bridey, getting to know one another again after living in different states for the past few years. However, both of them had new men in their lives. Other than the wedding shower for Callie a couple of weeks ago, Melanie hadn't had a night out with her friends in ages. All in all, she was in sore need of some fun.

Granted, the debacle in the parking lot after the wedding hadn't been any picnic, but hanging out at the bar with Spence had had its moments. His smile had definitely been the same, but it rarely banished the weariness in his eyes. She knew that look. The cause might be different, but she saw the same tired expression in her own gaze every morning when she put on her business suit and headed off to another day at the office. Pretending everything was okay was exhausting.

Other than seeing a few close friends, she did her best to avoid most people in town. All of their questions and comments might be well meant, but they'd quickly grown tiresome. She spent far too much time saying the same things over and over. *My mother is fine. Yes, it was a shame about my father. No, the company isn't for sale. No, I don't know how long I'll be in town. Yada yada yada.*

At first, she'd appreciated the concern. Now she really wished they'd leave her alone. Bad attitude and all that, but it was how she felt.

She suspected Spence would run into the same thing once people found out he was back. They'd all want to know every little detail, even those he didn't want to share. Maybe especially those. If anyone found out that she'd spent the evening at the bar with him, they'd be after her, too. Well, they wouldn't learn anything from her. It was Spence's story to tell or not tell; his choice, not hers, and definitely not theirs.

It had even been a bit risky going to Something's Brewing that morning to pick up muffins. However, since Bridey had been Callie's maid of honor at the wedding last night, it was a safe bet Bridey would have arranged for her assistant to cover the shop. Earlier, Melanie had discovered she had a voice mail from Callie. Evidently, she'd called during the time Melanie was at the bar, and asked why she hadn't shown up at the reception. In return, Melanie left a brief message for Callie apologizing for not being there, but keeping the details vague. The happy couple would already have left on their honeymoon in Hawaii, but at least Callie would know Melanie had tried to return her call.

She hoped no one asked that question again, because she didn't have a good answer. But rather than dwell on things she couldn't control, she planned to finish her errands and then go home to work in the garden. The flower beds had always been her mother's joy. Keeping them weeded and watered took time Melanie didn't really have to spend, but to give up on the gardens felt like giving up on the idea that her mother would ever come home.

She gripped the steering wheel hard enough to make her joints ache. Here she was, a grown woman, one who had held down a well-paying job and lived a life independent of her parents. Now all she could think about was having her mother come back home and be the adult in the family. Shoving that idea back into the dark recesses of her mind, she concentrated on happier thoughts.

Like spending more time with Spence. Yeah, he was only coming over because she'd offered him a place to live and maybe out of gratitude for making sure he'd had a place to sleep last night. That didn't change a thing. Regardless of his reasons, she was looking forward to the evening.

On the way back to the house, she stopped at the store and picked up milk, bread, some soft drinks, a few other things. After a moment's hesitation, she went back and added a six-pack of the same beer that Spence had been drinking at the bar. After all he'd consumed last night, she couldn't imagine him wanting more. If he didn't want it tonight, maybe he would the next time.

Twenty minutes later, she turned down her street to see her father's truck parked on the street in front of the house. She hit the brakes and waited for her pulse to slow down. In her head, she knew he'd sold that red pickup right before he died. But for a few seconds, her heart had forgotten. She'd spent so much time talking to his memory, it was as if her father was really back.

After dragging a deep breath into her lungs, she wiped

her sweaty palms on her slacks and drove the rest of the way down the block. She had heard Leif Brevik had bought the used truck, so it meant he was waiting to see her.

She spotted him leaning on the railing at the far end of the porch. Normally, she liked the man, but today he looked pretty grim. No surprise after what had happened last night. Having Spence show up unannounced must have thrown him for a loop, not to mention Nick and Callie. Some wedding gift that was!

He'd spotted her and straightened up. There was no way to avoid him now, but this was not going to be any fun. She waved as she drove past the house to park in front of the detached garage in back. If not, she'd let him in the front door after she got the groceries inside. She grabbed the bags out of the trunk and started toward the house.

Leif was waiting for her by the bottom of the steps. "Here, let me take those for you."

She handed off the bags and led the way up the stairs and into the house. "Just set it all on the counter. Help yourself to a beer if you'd like one."

She made quick work of putting the perishables away and then fixed herself a glass of iced tea while Leif stood at the window, staring out into the yard. "Want to sit out on the front porch?"

He turned to face her, his dark eyes flat and his usual smile missing. "Sure. I stopped by because—"

She cut him off. "You've got questions about Spence and want to know if I have answers."

"Yeah, that pretty much sums it up."

The chairs on the patio out back were more comfortable, but she chose the front porch to give Spence some warning if he were to show up early. He might not be ready to face his friend again.

As she and Leif walked through the house, she was uncomfortably aware of the unhappy man walking right behind her, the sound of his footsteps uneven as he favored his left leg. From what she understood, he'd almost lost it at the same time Spence went missing. All three men carried scars from their time in the army.

Outside, she plopped down in the closest chair and motioned him toward the other one. Instead, Leif leaned against the railing right in front of her. He stared down at her for several seconds before twisting the cap off his beer. After taking a quick swig, he set it on the railing and crossed his arms over his chest.

"How long have you known Spence was alive?"

He packed a lot of suppressed pain and more than a hint of angry accusation into that one question. She understood how he felt, but none of this was her fault.

"I didn't, not before last night. I was at the cemetery to take a picture of my father's headstone for my mother. She wanted to make sure it had been done right. She's still at her sister's in Portland and was worried about it. I e-mailed it to her."

Okay, she was babbling. Leif didn't care about any of that. "I was about to leave for the wedding when I spotted a soldier standing over where Mr. and Mrs. Lang are buried. I thought he might be another member of your squad in town for the wedding who had stopped at the cemetery to pay his respects to Spence. I walked up behind him and offered to show him the way to the church."

"Son of a bitch!" Leif winced. "Wheels saw his own headstone?"

Assuming Wheels was a nickname for Spence, she nodded. "Yeah, he did."

And she'd nearly fainted once he turned around and she recognized him. Luckily, Spence had caught her in his arms and held her close until her head cleared, but that would be their little secret. "God, Leif, I can't imagine what that was like for him. What I don't get is why wouldn't the army have told someone that Spence was alive? If they did, why wasn't the headstone immediately removed?"

Leif's face looked as if it had been carved out of stone. "The army would have bent over backward to make sure the next of kin was notified."

Then he let loose with a string of curses. "I'm betting they did let Spence's uncle know, and the old bastard couldn't be bothered to tell anyone else. I know for a fact that he didn't say anything to his son, because Austin has been staying at Spence's house with us. A while back, Vince caused some real trouble for the kid, and Gage Logan, the chief of police, intervened. Gage told him to stay the hell away from the kid or else."

That matched up with what Spence had said. Back in high school, Callie had hated the way Vince treated Spence after he became his guardian. Vince had no use for him then, and it sounded as though that hadn't changed.

Even if it made sense, it only added to her confusion. Spence knew better than to trust Vince to do the right thing and let everyone know the good news. At the very least, she would have expected him to call Callie. The two of them had been close since they were kids. She knew for a fact that he often spent his leave time from the military visiting Callie wherever she was working at the time.

"You never made it to the reception last night. Callie was looking for you, but you didn't answer your phone."

Leif's blunt statement brought her thoughts to a screeching halt. She lifted her gaze to meet his. "I know I missed her call."

Something she planned to apologize to Callie for in person after she and Nick got back from their honeymoon. "I did try to call her this morning, but last night there was someplace else I needed to be."

He wasn't buying it. There was no getting around telling Leif the truth. "I'm the one who brought Spence to the wedding. We got there too late to be seated, so we watched from the narthex. When it was over, Spence bolted back outside, and I went with him."

She closed her eyes as the memory of those awful moments came flooding back. "When I first talked to him, he acted like his old self. Friendly. Normal, you know what I mean? That lasted until the service started. One minute he was fine, and the next he was so angry."

Leif jerked his head in a quick nod. "No surprise there. A lot of us come back from deployment with a few anger issues. What happened after that?"

She frowned as she tried to replay the events in her head. "That dog found him. Spence seemed really happy to see him."

Leif stood with his shoulders slumped and his eyes closed, as if the memories hurt. He didn't speak again until after he took another drink of his beer. "Spence was the one who adopted the dog after he saved us from walking into an ambush. The mutt likes me and Nick, too, but Mooch really belonged to Spence. The two were inseparable."

The former soldier opened his eyes and stared off into

the distance, his jaw tight, and with a death grip on his beer. "I just wish Spence had been as happy to see me and Nick."

What could Melanie say to that? She wished she knew some way to ease the bewildered pain in Leif's dark eyes, but he was right. Spence's fury had been impossible to miss.

Leif finally spoke again, his voice sounding rough. "You left the church to follow him."

Again, not a question, but she answered anyway. "Yeah, I did. Considering how upset he was, I was worried about what he'd do next. It took me a while, but I finally found him at that bar on the outskirts of town. I don't know the name of the place, but it's a cinder block building."

For the first time since they'd come out on the porch, Leif smiled just a little. "Nick and I just call it BEER because that's what the only sign on the whole place says."

She'd noticed that, too. "Yeah, that's the right one."

How much more should she tell him? "Spence made it clear he didn't particularly want my company, but I ignored that and stayed anyway. At the rate he was downing beers, I didn't think he should be alone."

Leif's expression was a little less grim. "That was nice of you, and I'll let Callie know why you were MIA at the reception. She'll be glad to know he wasn't alone."

He drained the last of his beer and set the bottle aside. As he did, he said, "I don't suppose he told you anything about what happened, you know, over there. Where he's been all this time. Hell, even where he is now."

Melanie rose to her feet to stand next to Leif. She didn't know him all that well, but it hurt to see him in such pain. Putting her hand over his on the railing was not much to offer in the way of comfort, but it was the best she could do. "No, he didn't talk about what happened to him, and I didn't ask. At closing time, Liam, the owner, offered to take care of Spence's motorcycle for him, and I brought him back here for the night since he didn't have any other place to stay."

Leif's temper slipped loose. "Damn him, that's bullshit! He could've stayed at his own house. Did he think we would've kicked his ass to the curb?"

She so didn't want to get caught in the middle of this mess. "I'm sure he didn't think that, Leif. To tell the truth, I didn't even think about dropping him off there. It was my idea to bring him here."

That much was true, and Spence had been in no condition to argue.

"I honestly don't know where he is right now, but I'll tell him you stopped by when I see him again."

Leif went on point, his dark eyes boring into hers. "So you will be seeing him again?"

She cursed herself for letting that slip, but too late now. "Yes, he's supposed to stop by later. Do you want me to give him a message for you?"

"Damn straight I do. Tell that idiot to come see me or I'll come hunting for him. I don't know what's going on in that thick skull of his, but he owes me that much."

His anger drained away just as quickly as it had come. His voice was thick with emotion as if he could barely get the words out. "Damn it, Melanie, I thought he was dead. We all did. Obviously he's got issues with us right now, and maybe he has a right to be angry. Tell him . . . tell him I'll be around if he wants to talk."

"I will, Leif."

"Thanks for being there for him last night. I'm glad he

wasn't alone. I just wished he would've given us a chance to be there for him, too."

Leif charged down the porch steps. She watched as he climbed into her father's truck and drove away. The poor guy was clearly hurting, but then so was Spence. God, what a mess.

She had no idea what to say to Spence about Leif's visit. Yes, he really should talk to his friends, but it wasn't her call. She also didn't want to get caught in the middle of it all. On the way into the house, she checked the time. At least there was still time to work in the garden. And who knows, maybe she'd be hit with inspiration while pulling weeds.

Stranger things had happened, not the least of which was having Spence Lang back from the dead.

Chapter 7

Spence started to slow down but immediately sped up again to zoom past the driveway that led to his family home without stopping. Rather than dwell on the past, he gunned the engine on his bike and tried to put some distance between himself and everything he wasn't ready to face.

It was almost time to pick up something for dinner and head back to Melanie's house. He hoped she hadn't changed her mind about renting the cottage to him, because living in an apartment held little appeal. The thought of having other people right on the other side of a thin wall where he could hear them moving around at all hours made his skin crawl. It would be too much like being back in that cell again.

The wail of a police siren jerked Spence back out of the past. He backed off on the accelerator and checked his rearview mirror. Damn, less than twenty-four hours back in town and he'd already drawn the attention of the cops. How fast had he been going? He had no idea, but no doubt the cop would be only too happy to tell him.

After pulling off onto the narrow shoulder, he shut off the engine and removed his helmet. Based on a lot of experience, he assumed the officer would want to see Spence's driver's license. He got it out and waited to see how much trouble he was in.

"Put that away, Spence. Even I'm not a big enough bastard to give you a ticket on your first day back in town."

It took Spence a second to match the cop's face with a name. He dismounted and stuck out his hand. "Gage Logan? Well, I'll be damned. When did you get back in town?"

Gage gave his hand a firm shake. "After I lost my wife to cancer, my daughter and I moved back to town. I took over as the chief of police after Chief Green retired."

"I'm sorry about your loss."

Gage nodded as he studied Spence. After a few seconds, he slowly grinned. "You're looking pretty good for a dead man. You caused quite a stir at Nick and Callie's wedding last night."

Spence tried to laugh but wasn't very successful. "Leave it to you not to pull any punches, Gage. I take it you were there?"

"Yeah, I was." Gage took off his sunglasses to give Spence a hard look. "Showing up unannounced like that came as quite a shock to folks. I don't know where you've been, but I'm guessing they had phones there."

Okay, so the man liked to play hardball. "Yeah, they did. I just didn't have anybody I wanted to call."

He waited for the man to rip into him over that, but he didn't. Instead, Gage slowly nodded. "That's what I thought. Look, I'm going to tell you the same thing I told your buddies Nick and Leif when they came to town. The pastor at the Community Church has organized a veterans' support group that meets on Saturday afternoons. I don't know what happened to you over there, but I'm guessing it wasn't any picnic. If you find yourself having trouble dealing with stuff, come to a meeting."

Great, someone else who thought Spence needed help getting his head back on straight. He got up in Gage's face. "How would you know what I need?"

Gage stood his ground, his friendly lawman persona gone, replaced with hard-ass cop. Even so, his voice remained calm and controlled. "You might have had it worse than most, but you're not the only one who's been through hell and lived to tell about it. Sharing some of it with others who've been there, done that, and earned the fucking T-shirt might help reduce the size of that chip on your shoulder."

Spence hated to back down, but he did. Then he said the first thing that came to mind. "I get it, Gage. One step at a time."

Raising one eyebrow and looking a bit puzzled, Gage said, "Huh?"

"That's what the counselor told me to say to myself when things get to be too much." He brushed some dirt off his helmet. "Despite what you've seen, I do try not to be a complete jackass. Maybe things will get easier once the dust settles a bit."

Somehow he doubted Gage believed him. He was proven right when Gage said, "Do us both a favor and keep those meetings in mind. And if you need someone to walk through the door with you the first time, give me a call. I still go once in a while."

Gage held out his hand for a second time. "It's good to see you, Spence. Real good."

After they shook hands, Spence's own smile felt more natural. "Thanks, Gage. It sure as shit feels strange being here after everything that happened. Seeing a few familiar faces helps. I could use a good, strong dose of normal about now."

He climbed back on the motorcycle. Before he put on his helmet, Gage moved in front of the bike, blocking his way. "One more thing, Spence. If I catch you ripping down the street that fast again, I'll personally nail your ass to the wall for it. Are we clear on that?"

Again, some things never changed. Spence had enjoyed the same kind of friendly adversarial relationship with Gage's predecessor. "Perfectly, sir."

Gage waited for him to pull out onto the street before following, which forced Spence to keep to a more sedate pace. When he reached the next intersection, Gage drove up next to him in the right turn lane. He waved one last time and then drove off.

Just for grins, Spence gunned his engine and tore across the intersection but immediately reined it back in. He could see Gage shaking his head and laughed. Having had his fun for the day, Spence headed for Gary's Drive-In to pick up burgers, fries, and two of Gary's amazing shakes. Probably not the easiest meal to carry on his motorcycle, but the shakes should ride all right in his saddlebags. He could prop them up with his clothes for the short distance back to Melanie's house.

If not, oh well. He needed to do laundry anyway.

Dinner in hand, Spence knocked on Melanie's front door. As he waited for her to answer, he spotted an empty beer bottle sitting on the porch railing. There was no telling how long it had been there, but it definitely looked out of place. He tucked the two shakes he'd bought into the crook of his arm and held the bag of food with the same hand. Then he picked up the beer bottle and held it out so it was the first thing Melanie saw when she opened the door.

Her eyes went right to it. "Come on in."

As he walked past her into the house, the flash of worried guilt in her expression told him he was right. The only question was which one of his friends had come calling. On second thought, he knew, because Nick and Callie had no doubt left town on their honeymoon.

"So, what did Leif want?"

Melanie glanced back over her shoulder. "He wanted to know how long I'd known you weren't—"

She cut herself off midsentence, but he knew what she'd been about to say. "I think the word you're looking for is 'dead,' Mel. What did you tell him?"

"I told him the truth. That I ran into you at the cemetery. That I thought another member of the squad the three of you served in had come for the wedding. That I was as shocked as everyone else was to find out you were back."

He followed her the rest of the way to the kitchen and divvied up the food. "He didn't give you any grief, did he? Because this is between me, him, and Nick. I won't have him hassling you."

She sat down and reached for her burger. "No, it wasn't like that at all. When I didn't show up at the reception, they eventually figured out that I had gone after you. Leif wanted to make sure you were all right. That's pretty much the sum total of our discussion except that he asked me to tell you that he'd like to talk. You know, whenever you're ready."

Yeah, like that was going to happen anytime soon. What did Leif think they had to talk about? The depth of their treachery burned straight through him. The self- ish bastards had no right to be living in his house with his dog and his woman.

As the ranting and raving inside his head wound down, he realized he'd tuned out while Melanie was try- ing to tell him something. The only reason he noticed now was that there was an increasing note of urgency in her voice that hadn't been there only seconds before.

"Spence, I said put that down and stand still while I get the paper towels!"

What the fuck was she talking about? Before he could ask, she was back and trying to take something away from him. "Give me the cup."

He had to actually look down to see what she was talking about. Holy hell, he'd crushed the Styrofoam cup that had held his shake. Right now what little that was left of it was oozing through his fingers to join the rest on the table and floor.

"Son of a bitch!"

He grabbed a wad of paper towels from Melanie and used it to wrap up the broken chunks of Styrofoam. He carried the mess over to the trash and tossed it. Could he look any more like a crazy person?

Struggling to sound calm when all he wanted to do was howl, he growled, "Sit and eat while I clean this up. There's no use in letting your dinner get cold."

When he softened his order with a "Please," Melanie silently handed him the roll of towels and retreated to the other side of the kitchen. He didn't blame her for wanting to put some distance between them. Maybe he should just leave. She hadn't signed on to put up with his rapid-fire mood swings.

Kneeling down to wipe up the melting mess, he fought to keep his voice low and soothing. "If you want me to leave, don't be afraid to say so."

Please don't be afraid, Mel, he added silently. He couldn't stand it if the war had changed him to the point that he couldn't trust himself to be around innocent civilians like her.

Her feet appeared in his peripheral vision. Good. She set the trash can down within his reach. "Did you have a chance to check out the cottage?"

Bless her for changing the subject. This was embarrassing enough without having to discuss it. "I did. It's perfect for what I need."

He looked up when she snickered. "Really, Spence? You like doilies, not to mention that lovely pink and white tile in the bathroom? Maybe the war did more damage than you thought."

Holy crap! Did she really just tease him about the war? Maybe he hadn't screwed up things completely. He finished wiping up the shake and tossed the towels in the trash. "Okay, so maybe I'm not much into doilies, and the three identical sets of cat wind chimes are a bit over-the-top."

When she laughed, he added, "However, I have to admit that the shower curtain with the pink poodles on it is a perfect match for the tile. I can't pass up a chance to live surrounded by such excellent taste in decor."

She held up her hands in surrender. "Okay, if you're

sure. We can hammer out all the details later. I'll call the woman who cleans house for me and ask her to give the place a quick polish."

Spence sat down at the table and unwrapped his burger. "No need. I'm actually pretty handy with cleaning supplies."

"Fine, but for the sake of your reputation, you should at least let me spring for a new shower curtain."

As she talked, she got a glass out of the cabinet and dumped half her shake in it and slid it across the table toward him. "What if your army buddies found out you were showering surrounded with all that froufrou?"

Spence didn't know which he wanted to protest more: that he didn't have any buddies left who were likely to see the inside of the cottage or that she'd shared her shake with him. In the end, he settled on saying, "I think you're just jealous of the poodles, but I'll pick up a new one since I have to shop for a few essentials anyway. Most of my stuff is still in storage, but I don't want to send for it until I know how long I'm going to be staying in town."

"Just deduct the cost from the first month's rent."

The cost of a stupid shower curtain wouldn't break him, but he didn't want to argue the point. He held up his glass as if offering a toast to thank her for sharing. "So, what fun things did you do with your day?"

Melanie's smile melted away. Obviously that wasn't the right topic of conversation. "I'm sorry. I guess I hit on a sore subject."

She toyed with one of her fries, using it to draw a circle in her ketchup. "No, it's fine. I spent part of the afternoon at the office when I'd rather have had more time out in the sunshine."

That last part sounded like an excuse and not the real reason why she'd hated going into work on a sunny Sunday afternoon. He'd bet good money on that.

"It must be tough dealing with your father's death and having to take over the company at the same time. At least you grew up around the business."

She finally ate that poor fry. "Yeah, it's been rough. The main problem is that I grew up *around* the business. I didn't grow up *in* the business, if that makes sense."

Interesting. "But you used to work there summers just like I did."

Melanie's answering sigh was filled with pure frustration. "Yeah, Dad let me work there, but the job didn't teach me anything about running the business. All I did was file work orders and things like that. He wouldn't even let me answer the phone." She shrugged. "To say that he was old school when it came to the roles women should play would be to put it mildly. Dad saw it as his job to take care of Mom and me, which meant making all of the financial decisions for the family. That way we didn't have to worry our pretty little heads about things like paying the bills."

Spence leaned back in his chair and studied the woman across from him. Back in high school, she'd been one of the top students. Mel had always been on the quiet side, but she'd still been a leader in their class. He seemed to remember she'd won full-ride scholarships to two top-rated liberal arts colleges, one here in Washington and the other somewhere in the East. Everyone had been surprised when she'd chosen to accept the second offer. Based on what she'd just said, maybe they shouldn't have been.

"I'm guessing that's why you moved to ... Spokane, wasn't it?"

She nodded. "Yes, I wanted to be close enough to visit but far enough away that I could live my own life."

Melanie paused to sip her shake. "I don't mean to bad-mouth my father. He meant well, but it was a major fight when I finished my master's degree and decided to take the job in Spokane. Both of my parents expected me to come right back here and become a clone of my mother."

"I'm sure he was proud of you, Melanie, even if you didn't always see eye to eye on things."

"I know." Not that she sounded convinced of that fact. "But I'm having to learn the business from the ground up. It doesn't help that all of the bookkeeping and accounting methods he had in place are hopelessly out of date. One of the things at the top of my list is to transfer all the records to an accounting system that's more current. I also think a lot of the machines in the plant need a major overhaul, if not actual replacement. The trouble is that we can't afford to take any of them offline long enough to work on them. The company is barely scraping by as it is."

No wonder she looked a bit fragile. "Is there anything I can do? I worked part-time during the school year and full-time in the summer with old Mr. Cosgrove, the maintenance guy at the plant. Early on, I mostly handed him screwdrivers and listened to him cuss at the machines, but eventually he trusted me to do the routine stuff on my own. I'd have to read the manuals first on the newer equipment, but then I could help whoever is in charge of maintaining the machines now."

She laughed. "I hate to tell you, but old Mr. Cosgrove is still in charge of maintaining all of our equipment."

Spence was stunned. "That man was older than dirt fifteen years ago!"

"I wouldn't tell him that, not unless you want him to come after you with one of those big wrenches he leaves lying around the place. A year or so ago, my father hired an assistant for him, maybe in the hope the guy would eventually take over for Mr. Cosgrove. But the guy quit after only a few months, and I can't afford to replace him right now."

Obviously all was not well at the Wolfe Millworks. "I don't mean to butt into your business, but I really wouldn't mind helping out. If Mr. Cosgrove is willing, I'd be glad to show up and give him a hand evenings or on the weekend."

"Don't you have enough on your plate right now? You've barely gotten home."

"True, but it's not like I have a lot I need to be doing. I'll probably have to spend some time with my attorney dealing with a few things, but otherwise my schedule is pretty much wide open."

He stood up. "I should get going. I need to pick up a few things at the store. Thanks again for hanging out with me last night, Melanie. Tonight, too."

"You're welcome."

He glanced down at the floor. "And I'm sorry about making such a mess. My control isn't what it used to be."

Melanie came around the table to put her hand on his arm. "Cut yourself some slack, Spence. Accidents happen."

But it wasn't just an accidental spill, and he knew it even if she didn't. In his head, he hadn't been squeezing the shit out of a cup. That had been Leif's neck in that viselike grip. That fool should never have bothered Melanie.

"Well, like I said, I have to hit the store to pick up a few things for tonight. I'll do a bigger shop tomorrow after I figure out what all I need."

When they reached the front door, Melanie asked, "Do you want to borrow my father's car for your shopping expedition tomorrow? I'm guessing the space in your saddlebags is pretty limited."

"Melanie, you've already done enough for me. I can make several trips if I have to."

The stubborn woman wasn't having it. "What are friends for? Just let me know what you decide."

The offer was tempting. "Since I haven't had a chance to make a shopping list yet, how about I call you at the office if I need the car?"

"That'll work. Since I'm your new landlady, you should have my cell phone number anyway."

After he entered the number on his cell, he gave her his in return. "I'll leave you in peace. Don't forget to talk to Mr. Cosgrove. I'd actually enjoy hanging out with the old coot for a while. He never let me get by with anything back when I worked there, but I learned a lot about machinery from him."

"I will." She followed him outside. "Let me know if there's anything at the cottage that needs fixing. As far as I know, all of the appliances work, but they're pretty old."

That was the last thing he would do. It was obvious she was already carrying the weight of the world on her shoulders. She didn't need to add him and his problems to that burden.

"I'll be fine, Mel."

At least he hoped so. Then on impulse, he leaned in to give her a quick kiss. He meant to aim for her cheek, but at the last second he couldn't resist the temptation of those full lips. He kept it quick and friendly, but that didn't lessen the impact it had on him. Melanie felt it, too, judging by the way her eyes flared wide in surprise.

"Good night, Spence. I'll see you tomorrow."

There was a husky note in her voice that he hadn't heard before. He liked it. He brushed a lock of her silky red hair back from her face. "Yes, you will."

Before he could do something stupid like kissing her again, he ran down the steps to where he'd parked his Harley. Giving in to the impulse to show off a bit, Spence gunned the engine and roared out of her driveway.

He was still grinning when he arrived at his new home. For the first time in nearly a year, he had a reason to be looking forward to tomorrow.

Chapter 8

✣ ✣

Leif ignored the crowd milling around him on the lower level of Sea-Tac Airport while he waited for Nick and Callie to find him in the baggage claim area. He'd volunteered to meet their flight when they returned from their honeymoon, but he hadn't counted on their flight being over an hour late. He watched a trio of soldiers making their way through the crowd, laughing and talking as if they didn't have a care in the world. God, had he, Nick, and Spence ever looked that young?

He couldn't remember.

Unable to watch them, he did an abrupt about-face and made yet another trip down the concourse to check the list of incoming flights. Good, Nick's flight had finally reached the gate. He and Callie should make their appearance soon.

He hoped they'd managed to put the fiasco with Spence's reappearance behind them long enough to enjoy their time alone. They deserved that much. Even now, a week after the wedding, Leif wanted to punch

Wheels for showing up with no warning and no explanation. That effing idiot should've known better. Wheels could be thoughtless sometimes, but he'd never been cruel.

In fact, Leif had not even recognized Spence at first. The man had lost a lot of weight, but that wasn't the reason. No, it was all of that crazy, out-of-control fury that had distorted Spence's face beyond recognition. It wasn't until he'd reacted to seeing Mooch again that Leif had seen anything of his friend in the man. Wheels had changed, that was for damn sure, and for the worse.

What was up with letting his friends think he was dead even one second longer than necessary? What made it worse was knowing he'd chosen to screw up what should've been the happiest day of Callie's life. Whatever issues Wheels had with Nick and Leif, surely she had deserved better from him.

Leif finally spotted Nick and Callie heading for him. Before they reached him, she peeled off in another direction, maybe looking for a handy restroom. Leif walked over to wait with Nick. The first words out of his friend's mouth didn't come as much of a surprise.

"Is he okay?"

Nick had been more than a friend to both Leif and Spence. He'd been their sergeant and the one in charge the day that their vehicle had hit an IED. That single instant in time had changed all of their lives profoundly. Even though it wasn't his fault, Nick had been living with the knowledge the life of a friend had been lost on his watch.

There'd been plenty of guilt to go around, and Leif had been struggling to live with his own share of it. He'd come damn close to losing his leg in the explosion. The only reason he was still breathing was that Nick chose to drag him to safety first. If Sarge had helped Spence instead, whatever had happened to Wheels would have happened to Leif.

Nick got right up in Leif's face when he didn't immediately answer. "Well? Is he?"

He fought the urge to shove Nick back a step. Both of them had short tempers these days, but right now Leif needed to defuse the situation. They were in public and didn't need to draw attention to themselves like this. He forced his shoulders to relax and unclenched his fists. "I don't know, Sarge."

His efforts to take it down a notch failed because Nick was practically vibrating with tension. "What do you mean you don't know?"

"I mean that I haven't seen him, and Wheels sure as hell hasn't come looking for me."

A fact that hurt like a bitch. He shared the few bits of intelligence he'd been able to scrape together. "I talked to Melanie Wolfe the day after the wedding. She apologized for not coming to the reception, but she was worried about what Spence would do. After checking out the local watering holes, she finally found him at BEER. He told her to leave him alone, but she stayed with him while he proceeded to get stinking drunk."

"That was good of her." Nick frowned and finally let some of his anger drain away. "He's never been a heavy drinker, so that's not like him. None of this is."

Leif could only agree. "No, it's not like the Spence we served with, but who knows what has happened with him? After talking to Melanie, I went back to the bar and talked to the owner to get his take on the situation. He didn't much want to share details on a customer, but he did admit that Spence had been there until after closing. The only other thing he knew was that Wheels left the bar that night with Melanie."

"What else did she have to say?"

"When I talked to her, she said Spence had crashed at her place that night, but she claimed not to know where he went after that. I might be grasping at straws, but I got the sense she knew more than she was telling. I've driven by her place a few times, but I haven't seen any sign of him hanging around. It would be hard to miss that Harley of his."

He hadn't realized that Callie had rejoined them. "Once we get settled in, I'll call Melanie."

Nick put his arm around his wife and pulled her in close. "Better yet, the three of us will go see her."

Leif considered that idea but rejected it. "No, we don't want to overwhelm her or make her feel as if we're ganging up on her. I'm guessing she's more likely to share what she knows with Callie."

Turning his attention to her, he asked, "You two have been friends since high school, right? Wouldn't she talk to you?"

Callie frowned as she considered his question. That she didn't immediately answer was ominous. Callie looped her arm through Nick's and tugged him toward the luggage carousel. "Let's get our suitcases, and I'll think about how to approach her. For now, let's go home. I'm ready to stop moving for a while."

After they were all in the truck with Callie sandwiched between the two men, Nick looked over her head at Leif. "Maybe we should've asked this earlier. Do we actually still have a place to come home to?"

Leif waited until he turned south on I-5 and merged

into the heavy traffic to answer, "So far no one has come knocking at the door to throw me and Austin out on our asses. I've also glanced through your mail, but there hasn't been anything that looked like some kind of scary legal documents. Even so, I'm thinking you and Callie should check in with Spence's attorney once you have a chance to catch your breath."

"Spence wouldn't kick us out with no notice." Callie sounded sure of that, but then she went on to say, "But if you guys think we should move over to my folks' until we know something definite, I'm sure Mom wouldn't mind."

Nick shuddered. "Sorry, Cal, but I'd check us in at a hotel before I'd move in with the in-laws. I like your folks and everything, but that's a little too much togetherness for me. In fact, that's way too much."

Leif didn't think Callie was wrong. They should be prepared for anything at this point. "I could move my stuff over to Zoe's. I spend a lot of my time at her place anyway, but that would leave Austin in the lurch. He's pretty touchy about accepting anything he sees as charity. There's no way he would let us foot the bill for a room for him someplace until we get this all sorted out, and I don't want him to end up in some dump like the one he was living in before."

"God, what a mess. I've always been able to talk to Spence about anything." Callie clearly sounded frustrated. "I would never have imagined a time might come when I couldn't."

She leaned her head back and sighed. "Which brings me back to what to do about Melanie. She and Spence knew each other in high school. They both used to hang out at my house a lot, although they were never particularly close. I'm glad she was watching out for him that night, but I don't know what to make of it. If he is spending much time at her house, I wouldn't want to risk running into him without warning."

Leif mulled it over. "Maybe you should ask her to meet you for coffee. Bridey's shop would definitely be more neutral territory than Spence's house or even hers."

"That might be a good idea, but right now I'm too fried by the long flight and the time zone change to think clearly."

"Spence has waited this long to let us know he's alive. Finding out what happened can wait another day."

Nick looked over Callie's head to meet Leif's gaze head-on. "We may not like what we learn."

Well, no shit! But Leif kept that comment to himself. Nick looked haunted, and Leif suspected he had much the same expression on his own face. Tonight they'd all go back to the house and crash. But come tomorrow, the mission to reestablish communication with Wheels would begin.

Chapter 9

❧❧

"Damn it, boy, do it the way I showed you!"

Spence winced and bit back the urge to air his frustrations. He prayed for patience, something he was in short supply of these days, and tried again. "Yes, Mr. Cosgrove, I know you told me how to do this, but that was nearly ten years ago. Could you please refresh my memory?"

The old man spit tobacco into the empty soup can he always kept handy. "Fine. Loosen that bolt there." He used a screwdriver to point in the general direction of the one he meant. His advice might even have been helpful if there hadn't been half a dozen identical bolts within twelve square inches of space.

Spence rocked back on his heels to study them for a second. Oh yeah, it had to be that one. Using a socket wrench, he gave the bolt a hard yank. Since Cosgrove didn't start cackling at his effort, Spence had chosen the right one this time.

It had been a long evening, and he was relieved a few

minutes later when they put their tools away, done for the night. One machine all tuned up and ready to go when work started up in the morning. He ignored how many more machines they still had left to do. It wasn't exactly depressing, but he was too tired to count that high. Spence wiped his hands on an oily rag as he looked around to make sure they'd cleaned up their mess. The day crew wouldn't appreciate having to pick up after them.

As they made their way toward the door, Spence automatically shortened his stride to make it easier for his old mentor to keep pace with him. Mr. Cosgrove stopped by a panel on the wall near the door and turned out the lights. "You did good tonight, boy."

That was high praise from the old man. He'd never been overly generous with pats on the back, which made the ones he did give out all the more meaningful. "Thank you, sir. It felt good to get my hands greasy with you again."

That was no less than the absolute truth. As they stepped out into the parking lot, Spence smiled down at his much shorter companion. "Everything I learned from you about engines and machinery is the reason they always put me to work maintaining our vehicles and equipment whenever we were deployed. Hell, I'm embarrassed to say half the guys in our unit didn't even know their way around a dipstick."

In a show of disgust, Mr. Cosgrove spit out the rest of his tobacco and tossed the can in a trash barrel as they walked past. "You were always a quick learner, kid. Not like that idiot that Miss Melanie's father hired a year or so back to help me. He was plumb pathetic. My daughters have both been on my ass to retire for a couple of years now, but I couldn't abandon my machines to that fool's care. If he hadn't quit when he did . . . well, let's just say it wouldn't have been pretty."

They stopped at Spence's motorcycle. "I'll see you here again tomorrow night. Do you want me to wait with you until your daughter gets here?"

Oops, that was the wrong thing to ask. The old man bristled with indignation. "Boy, I don't need no goddamn babysitter. I've been getting along just fine without one so far and don't see that changing anytime soon."

"Well, I'll get going, then." Spence took his time putting on his helmet and starting the Harley. He'd about run out of delay tactics when a car pulled off the street and headed straight for them. Good. Despite the old man's protests, Spence wouldn't have felt right abandoning him to wait alone in a deserted parking lot.

"See you tomorrow night, Mr. Cosgrove."

The older man stepped closer to the bike and put his hand on Spence's shoulder. "Even though he's been gone for nearly thirty years now, 'Mr. Cosgrove' still makes me think you're talking to my father. Don't see no reason you shouldn't be using my Christian name, boy. My friends call me Will."

Another honor. Spence grinned at him. "Okay, then, Will." He stumbled a bit over the name, but he'd get used to it. "I'll see you tomorrow night, and I'll bring some treats to go with our coffee. Maybe a couple of those fancy cupcakes that Bridey Roke bakes at her shop."

"I don't need nothing fancy, Spence, but I wouldn't turn down one of her blackberry muffins."

"It's a deal. I'll see what I can come up with."

Spence waved at Will's daughter on his way out of the parking lot. It was a nice night with a full moon overhead. Rather than drive straight back to the cottage, he took the long way around. His chosen route allowed him to enjoy a little more time on the Harley but also kept him from having to drive through the heart of town. So far, his efforts to avoid contact with very many people had been successful.

Other than with Will, he hadn't spent more than five minutes in any one person's company for the past week, and that was fine with him. Well, there was one other exception—Melanie. She'd come knocking at his door two days ago to let him know that Mr. Cosgrove was willing to take him up on his offer of help to get all of the equipment serviced.

She'd started off insisting on paying Spence some ridiculous amount of money, which he didn't need and suspected she did. They'd finally agreed that he could stay in the cottage rent free for a month in lieu of a salary. He'd pretended not to notice how relieved she was by the arrangement.

While he was glad to have something constructive to do with his time, he had to wonder why she hadn't just called with the news. Was this her way of checking up on him? If so, that would piss him off big-time. He was doing fine, damn it.

Mostly.

On the other hand, they'd ended up sitting out on the front steps for more than an hour talking about nothing in particular. When she announced it was time for her to get back to the house, he'd walked with her, stopping short of seeing her all the way to her door. Somehow that would have felt as if they were crossing into dangerous territory to be something more than just friends.

He didn't want that. Or at least, he shouldn't. He didn't like to think about how he'd been unable to tear his eyes away from watching how her faded jeans showed off the curves of what was one spectacular ass as she walked away. Not to mention how much he wanted to tangle his fingers in that unruly red hair tumbling down her back.

It had been ages since he'd gotten laid, but Melanie Wolfe wasn't the kind of woman a man pursued just to scratch an itch. At least he'd held on to enough of his honor to know that. He was damaged goods, and she deserved better. Not to mention he'd always hoped to come home and convince Callie to spend her life with him.

Thanks to Nick, that wasn't going to happen. The enemy might have stolen months of Spence's time, but it was his friend who had stolen his life. A fresh infusion of anger had him picking up speed as he tore down the back roads. He entered the next turn driving flat out and way faster than the posted speed limit. Big mistake. He and the Harley almost went flying straight into the trees that crowded close to the edge of the road. It took a shitload of luck and every bit of sheer stubbornness he had to muscle the bike back under control without laying it down.

When he successfully reached the straightaway on the other side of the curve, he slowed to a stop on the narrow shoulder. He yanked his helmet off and wiped the sweat off his forehead with the hem of his T-shirt. As he waited for his pulse to slow down, he studied his image in the review mirror. He didn't much like what he saw.

"Damn, man, do you have a death wish?"

He tipped his head back to let the evening breeze cool him down. The familiar burn of adrenaline had left him breathing hard and shaking in his boots. Staring up at the night sky, he counted his lucky stars that he was alive. There'd been times in the past months when he would have greeted death with open arms, but it looked as though maybe he'd turned that corner and put it behind him.

When he had everything back under control, he checked for oncoming traffic and pulled back out on the pavement. This time he kept his speed within spitting distance of the speed limit. There was no use in pushing his luck.

When he made the last turn onto his street, there was an unfamiliar car parked right in front of the cottage. It was tempting to drive right on by, but maybe he was only jumping at shadows. Besides, he was tired. All he wanted was a hot shower and a cold beer, and not necessarily in that order. He sure didn't need uninvited company, but he suspected he was about to get some.

Sure enough, as soon as he pulled into the driveway, the driver got out of the car. Now it would be a footrace to see if Spence could get inside before the guy caught up with him. He would've made it except the other man sprinted directly across the yard to stand on the steps, effectively blocking Spence's way into the house.

"Corporal Lang?"

"Yeah, that's me."

"It's nice to finally meet you, Corporal. I would've been here sooner, but it took me a while to find out where you were staying." He offered Spence a smile and stuck out his hand. "My name is Reilly Molitor, and I'm a reporter for the *Snowberry Creek Clarion*. I'm here to interview you."

The reporter probably thought his grin was all slick and charming. Spence wanted to smack it right off his face. Ignoring the reporter's outstretched hand, he pulled out his cell phone. "You have fifteen seconds to get back in your car and drive away before I tell the police that you're trespassing."

The smile faded a notch, the shark coming out. "I just have a few questions, Corporal."

He had to give the man points for having the balls to stand there when Spence had several inches on him in height and a good thirty pounds of muscle. "I asked you to leave."

The reporter held up a small recorder. "Seriously, man, just a few quick questions is all I need. I can get whatever else I need for the article from other sources."

What article? Spence didn't want his name plastered all over any paper, not even the *Clarion*. "No interview and no article."

The reporter remained unfazed by Spence's growing anger. "Look, Corporal, or can I call you Spence?"

"No." He forced himself to back away, but the reporter's next words brought him to a dead stop.

"It's not often we have a real hero come home from the war, especially one everybody thought was dead. It's your obligation to share the story, and I think your neighbors and friends have the right to hear what happened to you over there. It's an amazing tale."

That did it. Spence latched onto the reporter with one hand and dialed 9-1-1 with the other. The reporter was still fighting like a fish trying to break free of a hook sunk deep in its gut when Gage Logan himself pulled up in front of the house a few minutes later. The police chief strolled across the front yard, the flicker of the blue lights on his patrol car lighting up the yard.

"Hi, Spence. I see you've met Reilly."

The reporter twisted his head to the side, trying to look directly at the lawman. "Chief, I want to press charges against this guy for assault."

Gage ignored him. "Spence, want to tell me what's going on here?"

Not particularly, but he had no choice. "This guy ambushed me when I came home. I told him I wasn't interested in being interviewed and made it clear that if he didn't leave I would call the police and report him for trespassing."

He finally released his hold on the reporter and stepped back, figuring things would go more smoothly if he at least appeared to be in control of himself.

"He refused to leave and prevented me from entering my house." He flexed his hands and fought to calm himself. "Then this little pissant told me that it was *my obligation* to tell him my story, that people have *the right* to know what happened to me over there."

He hated that he sounded desperate. Rehashing the hell he'd lived through would be like ripping the scab off a barely healed wound, one where the infection had run bone deep. To make matters worse, at that moment Melanie came pelting around the end of the house. Son of a bitch, he should've known the sound of the siren would bring her running.

Ignoring her, he kept talking. "He threatened to tell the story one way or the other, and if I wanted to control what went into the story, I'd better cooperate. I don't much like being threatened."

"And that's when you called me?"

Spence nodded. "It was either that or beat the shit out of the little prick."

Melanie gasped.

Gage turned his attention to the reporter. "Are you going to deny any of that?"

"I didn't threaten him, Gage. Hell, look at the difference in our sizes. I'm not suicidal. I did tell him that I was going to run the story whether or not he contributed to it. Neither of you can stop me, First Amendment rights and all that."

Melanie sidled nearer until she was standing close enough to Spence for him to feel her body heat. Damn, he wished she wasn't there. He didn't need her rushing to rescue him again. It might not look like it, but he had the situation under control. Mostly.

Gage got right in Reilly's face. "Spence is a personal friend of mine, so I'm going to tell you this once. He's already sacrificed enough for our country without having to give up his privacy just to satisfy your need to fill the front page of the paper."

"But, Chief, he's a hero!"

Spence started to speak, but Gage cut him off. "Every man and woman who puts on a uniform is a hero, Reilly, not just the few who make for good headlines. The last thing Spence needs right now is the attention you'd be aiming his way, especially when he's been back such a short time."

"But I—"

"No! You're still not listening. Maybe you'd really like to face those trespassing charges Spence mentioned. If that happens, I'll also have your car impounded, so you won't only be spending a night in a cell, you'll be out a couple of hundred bucks in towing and storage fees. It's your call. And if you do bother Spence again in any way or form, well, let's just say it won't be pretty."

Reilly stalked away still muttering under his breath about the Constitution and the public's right to know. It made Spence queasy to think about seeing his life spelled out in black and white for everyone in town to read. He didn't care what most folks thought about him, but there were a few whose opinions mattered.

Even if he wasn't speaking to them.

Gage walked back to his cruiser and shut off the flashing lights. He waved at a couple of the neighbors as if to let them know the show was over for the night and came strolling back up across the yard.

"I'll give the owner of the paper a call when I get home to let her know what really happened here. I'm not saying Reilly would embellish the story, but sometimes she needs to give his leash a good hard yank."

Gage took his hat off, which made him look less like a hard-nosed cop and more like a concerned friend. "I think she'll be reasonable, Spence, but he was right. I can't legally stop him from running the story."

"Yeah, I know." His neck was tight. He rolled his shoulders in a futile attempt to ease the tension. "Maybe I could've handled the situation better, but it's been a long day."

He glanced down at Melanie and then back at Gage. "Do you two want to come in for a beer? I was headed that way myself when all of this started up."

"I'll take a rain check if that's okay." Gage put his hat back on. "I'm actually off duty, and my daughter, Syd, likes me to get home before she goes to bed."

"Thanks for coming, Gage. I'll try not to need your professional services for a while."

He expected Gage to laugh, but he didn't. Instead, his eyes bounced back and forth between Spence and Melanie while he was probably trying to decide how much to say in front of her. "Not a problem, Spence, but here's the thing. You did the right thing by calling us, but your reaction was over-the-top. Hell, Reilly's half your size and couldn't fight his way out of a wet paper bag."

Spence's face flushed hot. The man wasn't wrong, but that didn't mean he wanted to hear about it. Not with Melanie standing right beside him, listening to every word. Did she always have to witness him at his worst?

Gage was still talking. "Next time, walk away. Lock yourself in the house if you have to, and then call us. If he'd insisted on filing assault charges, I would've had to drag both you back to the station to sort it all out. That would not have made me a happy man."

What could Spence do but apologize?

"Sorry, Gage. Like I said, I'll try to stay off your radar for a while."

"See that you do." He touched the brim of his hat. "Good night, Ms. Wolfe."

"Good night, Chief Logan."

As Spence watched Gage pull away, he remained acutely aware of the woman standing beside him. Why hadn't Melanie made an excuse to leave, too? Especially since the only reason she'd come running was that she'd seen the flashing lights. Instead, she'd stayed.

"Would you like that beer?"

He hadn't meant to repeat the offer, but he couldn't think of anything else to say. While he waited for her to answer, he walked up the stairs and unlocked the front door. Reaching inside, he flipped on the outside light, which bathed them both in its soft light.

She followed him up the steps, making the small porch seem crowded. "No, I can't stay. I was on my way over to see how things went at the factory with Mr. Cosgrove when I heard the police siren."

She rubbed her arms as if she were chilly. Didn't she have enough good sense to dress for the weather? He shrugged off his leather jacket and wrapped it around her shoulders.

"It went fine." Realizing how gruff he sounded, he added, "By the way, it's no longer Mr. Cosgrove. I get to call him Will now."

Silly as it was, he was actually pretty proud of that fact. Melanie was clearly impressed, too. "Wow, that's quite an honor. Even after all the years they worked together, my father never got to do that, but then Dad always drew a sharp distinction between management and the people who worked for him."

What could Spence say to that? Both of her parents had always struck him as cold and aloof, which made him wonder how Melanie had turned out to be so warm and approachable. When she looked up at him with those gentle eyes, he was reminded that there were good people in the world, ones who would never betray him. His gut instinct said that once she gave her loyalty, there would be no holding back, no second thoughts.

A man would do well to have someone like her at his side. She'd bring such passion to every facet of their lives.

Not liking where that line of thought might lead, he decided it was past time to put some distance between the two of them. With everything that had happened since he left the factory, his control was about shot. He pulled the door closed and locked it again. "Come on, I'll walk you back to the house."

"You don't have to, Spence. I know the way."

He ignored her protest and used the only excuse he had. "I want my jacket back."

Neither of them pointed out that she could simply hand it back to him right there. As they cut through the grounds toward the main house, she stopped and touched her fingers to her forehead. "I swear half the time I'm lucky to remember my own name. There was something else I wanted to ask you. Didn't you used to drive one of the delivery trucks for my dad?"

Where was she going with this? "Yeah, he had me

cover whenever one of the regular drivers was on vacation or out sick. Why?"

"I got a call right after dinner that one of my delivery guys has to go out of town for a family emergency. He'll be gone the rest of the week. Ordinarily, I could shift a few things around and make do, but he didn't give me enough notice to do that. We've got a full schedule of deliveries to make tomorrow, and I'd rather not ask customers to wait an extra day.

"Please feel free to say no, but I was wondering if you'd be able to drive one of the trucks. You wouldn't have to cover the rest of the days, but it would really help if you could fill in for him tomorrow."

Why not? It wasn't as if he had any pressing engagements on his calendar. "Sure. What time do I need to be at the factory?"

She started walking again. "The trucks are loaded and ready to roll by nine. I'll call your buddy Will and tell him that you won't be able to help tomorrow night."

He so didn't need her doing her mother hen imitation right now. "No, don't. I can handle both."

"That will make for a long day, don't you think?"

Shit, could she not hear the thread of temper in his voice? His bad mood was not her fault, but her concern wasn't helping matters. "Damn it, Melanie. If I couldn't handle the work, I wouldn't volunteer."

She shot him a considering look as if deciding if she could believe him. "Fine, then, but I will pay you for tomorrow. No arguments or the deal is off. Got that?"

He liked that she didn't back down. "Yeah, since you put it so nicely."

They'd reached her patio. She took off his jacket and handed it back. "Thanks, Spence. You're a real lifesaver."

Before he could turn away, she rose on her toes to kiss him on the cheek. "I'll see you in the morning."

She no doubt meant the gesture as a simple thank-you for helping her out of difficult situation, but his body reacted as if he'd stepped on a live electrical wire. He stepped back and waged a hard-fought battle not to gather her into his arms and show her what a real kiss was all about.

He lost the fight.

She'd already started up the steps when he threw his jacket on the ground with a muttered curse and followed after her. Melanie immediately turned around and came back down to the first step, which put her right at his eye level.

"Did you need something, Spence?"

"Yeah, I do."

He grasped her upper arms and tugged her tumbling forward to land hard against his chest, her mouth in the perfect position for a kiss. Melanie immediately opened her mouth to protest or maybe did so simply out of surprise. He didn't care why she did it; he was just grateful for the chance to take the kiss to a whole other level, deep and hot and hungry.

At first she protested and tried to push away from him. He immediately softened the kiss, aiming to coax her into enjoying the moment. Five seconds in, and she was right there with him, taking as much as she was giving.

He might go to hell for this, but right now he was pretty sure it was worth the price.

Chapter 10

❧ ❧

Melanie pried open one eye to make sure she was really kissing Spence Lang. Hot damn, she was! Back in high school, how many nights had she lain awake dreaming of a moment like this? Far more than she would ever admit to anyone. It was everything she'd ever hoped for, possibly the best kiss she'd ever had.

His tongue darted into her mouth and swept across hers, tasting and teasing. Earlier, the temperature had been chilly, but right now the two of them were burning up the night. His arms cocooned her in a powerful grip, one that shut out the rest of the world and made her feel safe and protected.

Clear thinking was nearly impossible. This was no time for second thoughts, only pleasure bubbling out of control. Then Spence's big hand brushed across her bottom and settled there to lift her firmly against his erection. In that instant, the simple kiss transformed into something so much more complex.

As attracted as she was to Spence, she wasn't ready to

take that next step. It was too much and too soon. This time when she pushed against Spence's chest with both hands, he ripped his lips from hers and took a giant step back, looking as stunned as she felt. She grabbed onto the stair railing in part to regain her balance, but mostly to keep from following right after him.

Even if she regretted breaking off the embrace on one level, seeing the panicky expression flash across Spence's face made her glad she hadn't given in to the temptation to invite him inside. She should say something, but what?

She went with the first thing that popped into her head. "I'm sorry."

He went from panicked to pissed in the blink of an eye. "What the hell for? I'm the one that started it."

Would apologizing for apologizing be completely stupid? Yeah, probably. She shut her mouth and left the next move up to Spence. He glared at her, but somehow she sensed she wasn't the real target for his anger. "Go inside. I'll wait here until you lock the door."

"But—"

"Don't push it, Mel. Go now."

Don't push what? Obviously this wasn't the time to ask. She ran up the stairs, each step of the way feeling as if she were making a huge mistake. A few seconds later she was inside with the locked door providing a safe barrier between her and the man still standing in her backyard. What was he doing out there? She had her answer when her cell phone rang. He was already talking before she had a chance to even say hello.

"Look, I'm the one who should apologize. These days my temper rides pretty close to the surface. I shouldn't take it out on you."

He paused as if waiting for an answer. All things considered, she went for the obvious. "Apology accepted."

Watching out the window, she could tell he jerked his head in a quick nod, but it was too dark to read his facial expression. What was going on in that head of his that kept him hanging on the line but not saying anything?

"I'll see you in the morning, Spence." She softened her voice. "Get some sleep. You're going to need it."

He shook his head, but she was pretty sure he was smiling now. After picking up his jacket, he started across the yard still holding the phone to his ear. When he was almost out of sight, she said, "Good night."

His last words before he disconnected stabbed her right in the chest. She was almost, but not quite, sure what he'd said before hanging up was "Good night, Callie."

Maybe she was wrong, but then maybe not. It was all too easy to believe, especially thinking back to the night of the wedding and the look of despair on Spence's face as he watched Callie marry his friend Nick. As Melanie turned off the lights and trudged upstairs to bed, she pondered what had just happened. It was all too clear in her head exactly who she'd been kissing out on the patio: one Corporal Spencer Lang.

The real question was: Who had he been kissing back?

Groaning, Spence rolled over in bed and reached for his cell phone. He'd set his alarm to go off at seven thirty, but it wasn't even six yet. What the hell had woken him up at this ungodly hour?

He stayed right where he was and waited to see if he heard the noise again. A few seconds later, the racket started up again. As near as he could tell, some kind of an animal was raising a ruckus out on the front porch. It sounded as if the damn thing was trying to dig its way under the house.

His sidearm would provide a quick fix to the problem, but he'd promised to stay off Gage's radar for a while. Waking up the neighbors with gunfire just so he could scare off a varmint would no doubt violate that agreement, but he had to run it off somehow. For Melanie's sake, he couldn't let the place be torn apart by some four-legged intruder.

He crawled out of bed and grabbed a pair of sweatpants to pull on. Padding into the living room, he peeked out the front window but couldn't see anything. Things were quiet out there again, so the critter must have knocked off for the moment. Rather than open the front door, Spence headed toward the kitchen to go out the back way and circle around to the porch to do a little recon.

As he rounded the side of the house, his feet stuttered to a stop while he tried to make sense of what he was seeing. At first he couldn't believe his eyes, but the proof was sitting right there staring at the front door, wagging his tail, and whining.

"Mooch?"

The dog froze, his tail stopping midswing. Spence started forward again. "Dog, how the hell did you get here?"

The mutt's only answer was a joyful bark as he came barreling off the porch to bounce off Spence's chest. The blow knocked Spence right on his ass. Landing hard on the gravel driveway hurt like hell, but he didn't care. Not when his arms were full of wiggling canine love, something he'd been missing for months.

The two of them rolled and wrestled with a lot of hollering and barking. Spence fought hard to fend off an early-morning doggy-spit bath while Mooch was just as determined to give him one. Finally, Spence surrendered and conceded victory to his buddy. After all, the dog had been on a mission and successfully captured his target. A soldier, even a four-legged one, deserved to celebrate a victory like that. It was good for morale.

When Mooch draped himself across Spence's chest and sighed in contentment, Spence gave him a thorough scratching. "Mooch, how did you find me?"

There were only a couple of possibilities, and just one of them made sense: Somehow the dog had tracked Spence to the cottage. The other option would mean that either Nick or Leif had dropped Mooch off and then simply driven away. Neither of them would've done that, not without calling first or at least waiting to make sure that Spence was home.

Which meant they probably had no idea where the dog was. As much as Spence didn't want to talk to either of them, he couldn't let his friends worry unnecessarily. He shoved the dog to the side and rolled up to his feet.

"Come on, dog. Thanks to you, I've got a couple of phone calls to make."

Mooch danced around him all way to the back door, nearly tripping Spence again. "Damn it, Mooch, quit it. God, I forgot what a pain in the butt you can be."

The dog didn't care and neither did Spence. Mooch bolted inside and launched an immediate inspection of the tiny house. It didn't take him long to scope out the living room, the bathroom, and the single bedroom. He was back in the kitchen in time to watch Spence start cracking eggs into a skillet.

"You'll have to settle for scrambled eggs with no bacon, Mooch. Be glad you're not getting a bowl of dry cereal. I wasn't exactly expecting company."

Mooch flopped down on the floor right were Spence had to step over him every time he made a move. Some things never changed. The dog had always taken up more than his fair share of space.

Spence scraped half of the eggs into a bowl, filled a second one with water, and then set them both down on the floor. He fixed his own plate and poured himself a cup of coffee. It didn't take long for his uninvited guest to wolf down his breakfast and then assume his official mooching position right at Spence's feet. Since there was no telling how long the dog had gone without eating, Spence caved and set his own plate on the floor.

"That's the only time I'm going to let you eat people food, Mooch. If you're going to hang around here, it will strictly be kibble for you."

If being the operative word there. Logic said the dog had been living with Nick and Callie for some time now. Plus, he needed a stable home, something Spence couldn't offer him right now, when he didn't know where the hell he was going to be long-term.

All of which reminded him that he had no choice but to call Nick or Callie. Drawing a deep breath, he hit Nick's number on speed dial. It rang four times and then went to voice mail. Spence closed his eyes and breathed a sigh of relief as Nick's message played out.

"Listen, Mooch showed up on my doorstep this morning. He's safe and fed."

What else should he say? "I'll be gone until late this evening, but the fur ball can hang out with me today."

He disconnected the call and considered whether he

should give Callie a ring, too. Knowing what a soft heart she had, she'd be worried about Mooch. Who knew how soon Nick would check his messages? On the other hand, they might not even know the dog was gone yet.

Cursing himself for a fool, he dialed her number next. Experience said that it should kick over to voice mail after four rings. Crossing his fingers that his luck would hold, he counted them off in his head. One, two, three—

"Hello?"

Damn, he should've known he wouldn't be lucky twice in a row, but hanging up now would only make him look like a coward.

"Callie, it's Spence. Thought you'd like to know Mooch is with me. Not sure how he figured out where I was staying, but he's okay."

"Hold on for a second, Spence, while I tell Nick and Leif. They've been going crazy looking for him." After a second's hesitation, she added, "Please."

He wanted to hang up, but he couldn't. Not when she sounded as if she knew that's exactly what he'd been about to do. Despite everything, he couldn't bring himself to be that rude. Not to her.

"Okay, but I have to leave for work soon."

She'd already put him on hold, but she wasn't gone long. "Thanks for calling. I'm not sure what we'd have done if something had happened to him. He's all we had left of—"

She cut off midsentence, but he knew what she was about to say. Mooch had been all she had left of Spence. Feeling as if he'd just taken a roundhouse kick to the gut, he said, "I didn't want you to worry."

"I appreciate that." She sniffed as if fighting back some tears. "We all love you . . . your dog."

Her voice cracked on that last part. What could he say to that? The silence dragged on until he reached the breaking point. "Look, I've got to go."

"Wait, Spence. Don't hang up."

"Why?"

She was crying now, which made him feel like a total jackass for hurting his best friend this way. That didn't mean he was up for a long discussion about everything that had happened.

"Look, Cal, I'm sorry you're hurting right now, but I can't do this. I get that it's my fault, that the problem is mine. I really am glad that you and Nick are happy even if most of the time I don't act like it. It's just that ever since I woke up in that hospital, everything about my life has been torn apart. Eventually, I'll make sense of things again, but right now it's mostly still all a jumble. I hope someday you'll find a way to forgive me for being such a jerk."

He drew a long breath as he tried to find the right words to say, to make things go back to the way they were between them. When he couldn't, he settled for saying, "Look, I'll drop Mooch back by the house soon."

Not that he could carry the dog on the Harley. Besides, he wasn't sure if he wanted to give Mooch back at all. Callie had Nick and Leif. Spence had nobody to call his own. Not anymore.

"No, Spence. Keep him. After all, he's yours. The house is, too." Callie got real quiet and then whispered, "And there's nothing to forgive, Spence. You've always been my best friend. No matter what, that hasn't changed. All I ask is that you'll let me know when we can get together and figure all of this out."

What was there to figure out? Did she really think he

wanted to move back into that place after she and Nick had been living in it? The thought made him sick.

"Look, I'll keep the dog. You keep the house. Call it a fair trade," he said.

Then Spence hung up before she could say another word. He ignored it when it started ringing a few minutes later. He might have answered if it was Callie, but the caller ID showed Nick's name. He set the phone aside and leaned forward, elbows on his knees and head in his hands. What a fucking mess!

From the beginning, Mooch had been sensitive to the emotional state of the people around him. It said a lot about how upset Spence was that the dog abandoned the last of his breakfast to lay his head in Spence's lap.

Stroking the dog's soft fur, Spence's fingers brushed across the jagged scar on Mooch's shoulder, another reminder of the ugly circumstances under which they'd met. The dog had come close to losing his life when he warned Spence and the rest of his squad of an enemy lying in wait for them. That event had forged an unbreakable bond between the two of them.

It was the same kind of bond that had existed between him, Nick, and Leif as well. Right now that connection was bruised and battered; only time would tell if the three of them could patch it up.

He stared down into a pair of worried-looking eyes. "So, dog, what am I going to do with you today while I work?"

He couldn't lock Mooch in the house all day, not to mention that he didn't have any more food for him. Maybe he should call Melanie to see if she could give him and the mutt a ride to work this morning. She wouldn't mind if Mooch rode along with Spence while he made deliveries. Later, the dog could hang out with him and Will Cosgrove while they worked on the machines that night.

Glad to have a plan of action, he dialed Melanie's number, but it went to voice mail. He left a brief explanation of what had happened and asked her to call him back. While he waited, he'd take a quick shower and get dressed.

Half an hour later, he checked his phone to see if Mel had called back, only to find she'd texted him instead. Evidently, she'd had to go into the office early, but she promised to leave him the keys to her father's car under the planter on the patio. He was free to use it for as long as he needed it.

Spence stared at the message and frowned. It was a generous offer, one he should appreciate. Instead, what he was feeling was a lot closer to disappointment than gratitude. Not because she hadn't given him what he needed, but because he'd missed a chance to talk to her.

It was his fault. He should've postponed his shower until the phone rang. But then again, she hadn't called, had she? Texting was efficient but impersonal. He hadn't realized how much he wanted to hear Mel's voice, to make sure that last night hadn't changed things between them. God knows he hadn't handled the situation all that smoothly.

But that kiss had been . . . amazing.

He didn't blame her at all for stopping him when he got grabby even if it left him edgy until after midnight. He'd expected the lack of sleep to leave him dragging this morning, but the combination of that encounter with Melanie last night and Mooch's unexpected appearance had left him feeling energized.

"Come on, dog. We've got places to go and things to do." He reached down to pat Mooch on the head. "And if you play your cards right, one of those things might just include a stop at the store for some dog food."

As Mooch trotted out the door, he sneezed three times. Spence laughed at the dog. It might have been purely coincidence, but it sounded more as if Mooch was expressing his opinion on the subject of kibble. While the dog would eat the stuff, he'd always preferred to share Spence's army rations with him. Whoever heard of a dog with a craving for MREs?

Nose to the ground, Mooch ranged back and forth across the yard on the way to Melanie's patio. It was good to see the dog looking well fed and happy. At least one good thing had come out of the time Spence had spent in Afghanistan.

The keys and a garage door opener were hidden right where Melanie had said they would be. He let Mooch into the passenger seat of the station wagon before walking around to the driver's side. After cracking the passenger window for Mooch, he drove out of the garage and headed for the closest grocery store.

An hour later, he and Mooch were in the cab of a fully loaded flatbed truck. The foreman had gone over the list of deliveries with Spence, refreshing his memory on how to match up order numbers to make sure each customer got the right items. One name at the bottom of the list had Spence's stomach churning: Nick Jenkins.

There went his good mood. As tempting as it was to get that particular delivery over with first, he couldn't do it. The various orders were arranged in a specific pattern on the truck that matched the time frame given to the customers as to when they could expect their delivery.

Cursing under his breath, Spence drove out of the parking lot and headed for his first stop. He could do this. He would do this, if for no other reason than he'd promised Melanie he'd get the job done.

Hell, how many times had he walked into enemy fire without hesitation? By comparison, delivering a couple of doors to Nick and Leif should be a piece of cake.

He reached over to pat his partner for this mission on the head. "You distract them while I unload the doors. Once we achieve the objective, we'll retreat to safety and get the hell out of Dodge. How does that sound?"

Mooch sighed and stretched out on the seat. Spence laughed. "Yeah, that's what I thought."

Chapter 11

Melanie stood at the window and watched the truck pull out of the parking lot. She'd deliberately stayed up in her office the whole time Spence was downstairs in the factory. Cowardly? Yeah, maybe, but she wasn't up to facing him yet.

He'd sounded so normal when he called this morning to ask for a ride for him and the dog. She wasn't sure what to make of that. Either he didn't realize what he'd said last night or else he didn't care, which didn't seem likely. There was a third option, she supposed. In the best of all worlds, he had said her name and not Callie's. She wished she knew for sure.

Jealousy was an ugly emotion, and she wasn't proud of herself for giving in to it. After all, Callie was married now to a man who clearly made her very happy. Their love for each other had been forged in the pain of their shared grief over Spence's death and tempered by the peace they found in each other's arms.

Callie wasn't the kind of woman who would have married a man if he was only a substitute for the one she'd lost. Melanie knew her friend better than that, but right now she was flashing back to high school when she'd be at Callie's house and Spence would drop by. God, how she'd envied their easy relationship, the way they'd laugh and tease each other while she sat in the corner and watched.

To be honest, Spence wasn't the only guy who'd left her tongue-tied back then, but he'd been the only one she'd had a crush on during their senior year. At some point she'd realized that part of the attraction stemmed from the fact that in a lot of ways they were both outsiders looking in. People treated her differently because of who her family was. She guessed that was to be expected when both she and the high school they all attended shared the same name.

Spence's problems stemmed from his family, too, but for far different reasons. By all reports, his adoptive parents had been good people, and he'd been happy with them. It was only after their death and his maternal uncle became his guardian that Spence's life had all gone to hell. Vince Locke had a well-deserved reputation as a mean bastard, and he had made life tough for his nephew.

Spence had responded by running wild. Her parents had frequently warned her to stay away from him, and she didn't argue. Fortunately, they never realized how much time he'd spent at Callie's house, and Melanie hadn't told them. As teenage rebellions went, hers had been pretty pathetic.

"Ms. Wolfe?"

Melanie turned away from both her past and the window to face her secretary. These days they were usually called executive assistants, but the job title was one more proof how old school her father had been.

"Yes, Mrs. Cuthbert?"

"Your aunt is on line two. She said it's not an emergency or anything. She can call back later if that would be more convenient."

Did Melanie look too busy to take a call? Or was the woman hinting that she wasn't busy enough? Gosh, she resented feeling as if she had to justify herself to the secretary, but she'd spent her high school summers working directly under Mrs. Cuthbert. Neither one of them was particularly comfortable with the sudden reversal in their roles.

Crossing to her desk, Melanie picked up a stack of folders and held them out to the other woman. "I finished reading through the correspondence and signed all the letters, so you can have them back. I also completed that additional paperwork the bank asked for. They said to fax it to them since that's faster and easier than mailing it."

She regretted making the suggestion as soon as the words were out of her mouth. They had a fax machine now because Melanie had bought it out of her own pocket. The older woman avoided using it as much as possible because she wasn't comfortable with new technology of any kind. Melanie bit back the need to point out that she never would be if she didn't even try.

Mrs. Cuthbert backed toward the door, her mouth a flat slash. "I'll take care of it, Ms. Wolfe."

Melanie waited until she was gone before reaching for the phone. Even if it wasn't an emergency, an unexpected call from her aunt couldn't be a good thing. She took a deep breath and hoped for the best. "Aunt Marcia, how are you?"

Her mother's sister was never one to mince words. "Fine, but I'm calling about your mother."

What else was new? Melanie leaned back in her chair and stared up at the ceiling. "What's happened now?"

"She wants you to send more of her things. I told her to make a list and e-mail it to you tonight."

The other woman had hesitated before continuing. Then her words ran together as she spoke as if she couldn't get them out fast enough. She probably suspected they would upset Melanie. She wasn't wrong. It was tempting to refuse, but what good would that do? If she didn't send the stuff, her mother would most likely go on a shopping spree. Neither of them could afford that right now.

She pinched the bridge of her nose and tried to wish away the headache that was coming on. "I assume this means she has no immediate plans to come back home."

Her aunt's voice softened. "I'm sorry, Melanie, but I don't see that happening anytime soon, if ever. We both know that without your father, she's like a boat without a rudder. She doesn't understand what happened to all their money."

The image fit, except maybe the boat was also sinking. "She won't believe me when I tell her it's gone no matter how many times I've tried to explain it all to her. She blames me even if I'm only the messenger. If it wasn't me who lost it all, she'd have to admit that it was Dad."

It was same discussion they'd had several times in the past few weeks. "I hate to speak ill of my own sister, but sometimes I want to shake some sense into her. Your father was a good man, but he wasn't infallible, especially when it came to money. He treated her like a princess and spoiled her rotten in the process. He didn't do her any favors, and now you're having to play the heavy because of it."

At least with her aunt, Melanie didn't have to pretend that everything was all right. "Tell her to send the list, and I'll ship everything as soon as I have time to pull it all together."

"I'll do that." Her aunt sighed heavily. "Hon, I know it's hard for you having her all the way down here while you try to deal with everything on your own, but we both know that Sandra wouldn't be any help at all. It's better that she's down here transforming my yard into a thing of beauty."

It was nice to know her mom was interested in something. For the first three weeks after her husband's death, all she'd done was sit and stare at their wedding portrait over the fireplace. "Working in the garden was always her great love. Tell her I'm doing my best to keep our yard up to her standards."

Her aunt laughed. "Good luck with that. I swear Sandra manicures my grass with scissors, and any weeds that dare to pop up end up running for their lives."

Melanie laughed. It was that or cry. "Well, I should get back to work. Hug Mom for me, and I'll transfer some more money to her account at the end of the week."

"I've got plenty for both of us, Melanie, so hold on to that money if you need it."

Evidently, Melanie's father wasn't the only one in the family with too much pride to ask for financial help. "I'll send it, Aunt Marcia. She'll feel better if she has her own spending money."

"All right, but the offer stands. I'll keep you posted on how she's doing."

"Thanks. And it really helps to know you're looking out for her."

"It's the least I can do. Tell me, and I want an honest answer about this. Are you doing more than rattling around in that house by yourself? Don't sacrifice your own happiness for the sake of your family name."

Melanie debated whether or not to tell her aunt about Spence moving in to the housekeeper's cottage. Considering how her mother had always felt about Spence and his uncle, maybe it was better to keep it to herself until she knew how long he was going to stay. There was no use in getting her mom all worked up over it if he was only staying a short time.

"I'm mostly doing fine, but I'd better get back to work. Hugs to you both."

After hanging up, she yanked open the bottom drawer of her desk. If there was ever a time to dig into her secret stash of dark chocolate, this was it. Not even the milk chocolate would do. She grabbed a handful and dropped them on the desk. After staring at the small pile for a few seconds, she counted out five pieces and put the rest back. Over the months after having her whole life turned inside out, she'd developed her own chocolate-to-crisis ratio where really bad days went as high as ten to one. It was a stretch to say that finding out that her mom wasn't coming home anytime soon warranted even three.

But if she threw in her doubts about last night and Spence, surely she was justified in taking two extras. Unwrapping the first one, she popped it in her mouth and took the time to savor the soothing flavor on her tongue. After that, she unwrapped another one and opened the next folder on her desk.

While she started through the facts and figures in front of her, she spared a second to wonder how Spence was doing on the deliveries. Was he like her, falling into old routines and feeling as if he'd never really been gone? She'd have to ask him sometime, but for now she really had to get back to work.

*   *   *

Spence pulled into the driveway and stopped. This would be the first time he'd seen his family home in nearly two years. His parents had been gone since his early teens. No matter how many times he reminded himself of that fact, somehow he always expected to see them sitting on the front porch whenever he came back.

He ought to be embarrassed by how run-down he'd let the place get over the years. Certainly, Callie's folks shouldn't have to live next to a complete dump. For him, though, the overgrown grass and faded paint served as a reminder of all that he'd lost and that his parents weren't waiting there for him.

However, back when he was in the hospital in Germany, he'd carefully studied the Web site Callie had created to showcase her plans for the bed-and-breakfast. Intellectually, he knew that they had done far more than mow the grass. That didn't mean he was ready emotionally to witness the changes firsthand.

"Damn it, dog, I so don't want to do this."

Mooch had been dozing in the seat beside him until Spence slowed to make the turn into the driveway. Now he had his nose out the window and was yipping softly as he waited impatiently for Spence to drive the rest of the way to the house.

"Okay, fine, but don't think we'll be hanging around for any length of time. We'll drop off the doors and then head back to the factory to meet up with Mr. Cosgrove. I promised him treats from Bridey's place, which I still have to buy. You'd better be ready to leave when I am, dog, or you're on your own."

He put the truck in gear and rolled forward. As soon as he saw the house, he slammed the brakes on again, sending his poor companion scrambling for purchase on the slick vinyl bench seat. Spence grabbed Mooch by the collar and hauled him over onto his lap.

The place had been . . . Transformed was the only word he could come up with. The grass had been recently mowed, the flower beds were neatly edged, and the bushes had all been trimmed. His eyes burned as he studied the house itself. The sagging gutters had been replaced or at least repaired, and someone had been scraping the peeling paint off the siding.

The house was far from perfect; it was obvious there was a ton of work left to be done. Yet it was clear that someone cared about the place again, something that had been missing for years. It made him feel ashamed that he'd let it get so bad in the first place.

As he pulled around the circular drive in front of the house, Nick stepped out on the porch. Leif wasn't far behind. The only one missing from the party was Callie. Spence really hoped she wouldn't put in an appearance. There was no telling how this was going to play out, and she didn't deserve to get caught in any cross fire.

"Come on, Mooch. You owe them an apology for worrying them so much."

The dog shot him a look that clearly said *Look who's talking!*

Maybe that was Spence's conscience talking, but maybe not. The dog always seemed to understand far more than he should. Neither of them was going to accomplish anything by hiding in the truck. He climbed down out of the cab and stood back to let Mooch hop down after him.

The two of them rounded the front of the truck but made no attempt to join the other two men up on the porch. "I've got your doors."

Nick ignored him and glared at the dog instead. "I

should kick your flea-bitten ass from here to hell and back for worrying Callie like that."

Mooch broke formation and trotted up the steps to sit in front of Nick and Leif. He didn't move an inch, not even to wag his tail, until the two men finally gave up and welcomed him home. So maybe Spence hadn't needed to buy that dog food after all.

"Where do you want me to put the doors?"

Leif straightened up and crossed his arms over his chest, his feet planted wide. There wasn't even a hint of a smile when he said, "Wheels, do you really want me to tell you where you can stick those?"

Spence didn't rise to the bait, mainly because it felt too much like old times. Meanwhile, Nick had squatted down to pet Mooch. "Anywhere is fine. I'll give you a hand."

Spence wanted to refuse. He couldn't bring himself to be that petty, especially when he realized Callie had just stepped out of the woods that separated his place from her folks' yard.

"Fine."

He hated the feel of those three pairs of eyes boring into his back as he vaulted onto the back of the truck. He did his best to ignore them and began untying the two cardboard containers that held the two doors. The truck lurched to one side as Nick climbed up to help him.

They worked in silence. When they were done, Nick climbed back down to catch the box as Spence slid it over the side. Leif came down off the porch to help, his gait uneven as if his left leg was stiff or something. Then Spence noticed the cane leaning against the column on the porch.

What the hell had happened to him?

Nick met his gaze over the small expanse of cardboard that separated them. "He almost lost his lower leg in the explosion. Some days are worse than others."

Shit, Spence hadn't meant to ask that out loud, but he knew exactly which explosion Nick meant. So he wasn't the only one whose life had gone to hell that day. He wanted to ask more questions, but he couldn't find the words.

Nick and Leif picked up the first door and carried it up onto the porch. God, it hurt to see Leif hobble up the steps, always leading with his right leg and dragging the left one up more slowly.

As soon as they had the door stowed, they came back for the second one. Spence started to pick up one end, but Leif shouldered him aside. "We'll take care of it. You've done enough."

Enough what? It was tempting to argue, but Nick caught his eye and shook his head. Fine, if Sarge thought it was that important, Spence would concede the point, at least for now. He pretended to look through the stack of papers on the clipboard, gripping the damn thing so hard his hand ached. One signature was all he needed, and then he could leave.

Callie had taken her own sweet time coming across the yard. Maybe she was hoping he'd be back in the truck and on his way before she got there. More likely, she thought if she moved too fast he'd bolt whether they were done unloading the doors or not.

"So you're working for Melanie now."

Spence forced himself to look his friend in the face but couldn't stop himself from taking a step back to put more room between them. He hated the quick flash of hurt that crossed Callie's expressive face. "A little. Nothing permanent. She was shorthanded today."

"Where are you staying?"

How much did he want her to know? But then, why keep it a secret?

"I'm renting the old housekeeper's cottage on the back of the Wolfe House property."

Callie tilted her head to the side and narrowed her eyes as she studied him. "I didn't realize that you and Melanie were such good friends."

The question might have sounded innocuous, but there was a note in Callie's voice he didn't much like. Why would she care if he and Melanie hooked up? "Is that a problem?"

"No, not at all. You just never mentioned keeping in touch with her."

Nick moved up beside Callie with Leif not far behind. At least Mooch decided to stand beside Spence. If the dog had chosen to take their side, it might have been more than he could take right now.

"I didn't," Spence said.

"Didn't what? Keep in touch with her or bother telling me you had?"

Seriously, with everything that had happened, this was what had Callie spoiling for a fight? He'd hoped their phone conversation had eased some of the tension between them. "Look, I need to go. I've still got a long evening's work ahead of me."

Nick stepped between him and the truck while Leif moved to block any avenue of retreat. Son of a bitch, he didn't want to do this right now. Actually, ever.

"Nick, not now. I'm on the job and don't have time for this."

His friend gestured at the now empty flatbed. "Looks like you're pretty much done making deliveries."

"Yeah, so?"

"So, if you don't have time now, Corporal, when will you?"

"Time for what, Nick?"

The former sergeant breathed in slowly, his nostrils flaring wide. "Callie, do me a favor and go inside. Take Leif with you."

She was already shaking her head. "But we need to talk things out. I want—"

"Please, Cal, let's not gang up on him. I'm guessing he's feeling cornered right now, which pretty much guarantees Wheels won't be reasonable." Nick spared her a quick glance, his fierce expression softening just for her.

Spence wanted to punch him, partly out of jealousy and partly because Nick could read him so well. Maybe he would let a fist fly once Callie was out of the line of fire. He watched as Leif put his arm around her shoulders and tugged her toward the porch. She hesitated before climbing the steps to disappear into the house. Leif mirrored her action, but after aiming a hard look in their direction, he went inside and closed the door.

Meanwhile, Nick studied Spence as if he found him to be an interesting specimen. He could look all he wanted. "I'm assuming you didn't run them off just to stare at me."

To his surprise, his old friend actually laughed. "God, Wheels, no wonder I used to have to thunk you on that hard head of yours once in a while just to get your attention."

Then he leaned against the side of the truck, clearly in no hurry to get to the point. Spence didn't buy it for a minute. Sarge might look relaxed, but he was perfectly capable of going on the attack with no warning.

"Okay, I was talking about you making time to talk to us. Time to explain what the hell happened to you. Why you're acting like you hate us." Nick straightened up, his eyebrows riding low over a rock-hard gaze. "I made some calls and got the basic facts, but that's not the same as hearing it from you. I'm guessing whatever happened was fucking damn ugly. I'm sorry about that, but keep in mind that it wasn't any picnic for me and Leif, either. He damn near lost his leg, and it's taken multiple surgeries and a helluva lot of therapy to having him walking even that well. I hate that for him, and there's not a day that goes by that I didn't wish it had been me and not him."

He took a step toward Spence. "But that was nothing compared to living with the knowledge I got you killed. Now you're back, but it's like I'm talking to a total stranger wearing your face."

As tempting as it was to lash out, Spence couldn't bring himself to even make a fist. "That's how I feel, Nick. Maybe it's better for you to go on pretending the man you knew did die that day."

Nick's shock was painfully clear. "God, Wheels, don't even say that!"

Spence looked around the yard, trying to focus on something other than the mix of anger, guilt, and hurt feelings standing right there in front of him. Right now it felt as if he were back in that cell with the walls closing in on him. He wanted to scream, but if he gave in to the impulse he feared he might never stop.

"I've got to get out of here, Nick. Tell Callie I'm sorry. I don't mean to keep hurting her. I've already told her that the problem is with me, not her."

Nick didn't move. "I'm not going to let you get in that fucking truck until you agree to sit down with me and hash this all out. Name the time and place, and I'll be there. Leif, too."

As it turned out, Spence wasn't into taking orders anymore, especially from Nick. "No. Now get out of my way."

He didn't wait to see what Nick would do. He shoved his friend out of the way and reached for the door handle. Before he got a good grip on it, his friend charged right back. They grabbed onto each other and took the discussion to the ground, each one trying to get in the first good punch.

Spence could hear shouting coming from somewhere. Maybe it was him and Nick, but then Mooch's barking drowned it out. The dog danced around them, pitching a fit. Still struggling to pin Nick, Spence growled, "Mooch, get back."

But Mooch wasn't having it. Instead of retreating, he went on the attack, nipping first at Spence and then at Nick. He didn't draw blood, but it was close. The sharp pain broke through the red haze of anger.

Spence released his hold on Nick and rolled to the side, covering his face with his forearm. It wouldn't have surprised him if Nick planted his fist right on Spence's face, but he didn't.

They lay side by side, both breathing hard. Nick let loose with a colorful string of words, ending with "Well, I'm going to catch holy hell from Callie for this."

Spence dropped his arm down onto the ground and looked over at Nick. "Why? I started it."

"Yeah, like that's going to make a difference."

Nick sat up, wincing a bit as he did. Spence followed suit, mentally taking inventory of a few aches and pains. As much as he hated to admit it, Nick was right. They both needed to clear the air, but he wasn't ready. On the other hand, maybe he'd gotten a step closer to when he would be.

Mooch plopped down on the grass and kept a wary eye on both of them. Spence reached out to pet him, but the dog snapped at him again. Okay, so he owed more than one apology right now.

"I promise we'll talk, but don't corner me on this, Nick." He forced himself to look his friend in the eye. "I'm pretty twisted up inside right now. It should be pretty obvious that I can't be rational on the subject yet."

Nick crossed his legs and rested his elbows on his knees. He supported his head with the palms of his hands on his forehead. "I wish I could say it gets easier, but some days—"

"Yeah, I get that. Tell Callie I promise not to be such a total asshole, but I really do have to get going."

He didn't really owe Nick any explanations, but he offered one anyway so that he'd know Spence wasn't just blowing him off. "I'm doing some maintenance work on the machines at Melanie's factory in the evenings after the day crew leaves."

Nick looked up. "Sounds like the perfect gig for you. You always did like getting greasy and playing with engines. Do you plan to take a job there permanently?"

Spence poked and prodded that idea. "Too soon to tell. Right now I'm just helping out."

He braced himself for another bout of pain and stood up. "Damn it, Sarge, did you have to knee me in the ribs?"

Nick was rubbing his jaw where Spence had clipped him. "It seemed like a good idea at the time."

Spence didn't want to laugh, but he did. He held out his hand and pulled his friend up to his feet. It wasn't the same as a handshake, but it was close.

"Call when you want to talk, Spence. If you don't want to come here, maybe we can meet at that bar you went to the other night and share a few beers. I'll even buy the first round."

"You'll buy more than that, but I'll think about it." He forced himself to look at the house again. "You guys are doing good work."

"Yeah, we've got to talk about that, too."

Something else Spence didn't want to deal with but knew he'd have to sometime soon. He opened the truck door and looked around for Mooch. "Well, dog, are you coming with me or staying here? It's your choice."

Mooch slowly stood up and walked over to Nick. He licked his outreached hand and then hopped up into the truck. Spence tried not to show how relieved he was. Right now he needed the dog's undemanding company.

Nick knocked on the window and waited for Spence to roll it down. "I'm assuming Callie knows the place you're staying. We'll drop by Mooch's stuff this evening while you're gone, if that's okay."

Spence wanted to refuse the offer, considering he didn't know how long Mooch was going to stay with him or even how long he himself would be sticking around Snowberry Creek. On the other hand, maybe Nick needed to do something for Spence. "That would be nice. Just leave it on the front porch."

He risked one last look back toward the house on his way out of the driveway. Callie and Leif had come back outside. He waved. It was the least he could do.

Chapter 12

❧ ❧

Melanie hesitated before walking into Something's Brewing. It was far from the first time that she'd met Callie there for some quality girl time. However, there'd been something different in the way Callie sounded when she called to extend the invitation. Melanie had a good idea what was at the root of the hint of tension in her friend's voice.

Or rather, who was behind it: Spence.

Callie no doubt had questions about how Melanie had come to offer Spence not only a place to live but also a job working for her family's company. The real question was how Callie felt about all of that. In a perfect world, she ought to be happy Spence had found a place to stay and something to do with his time.

Unfortunately, this wasn't a perfect world. Chances were that Callie was unhappy about the situation. Melanie reminded herself there was only one way to find out. Trying to look calmer than she felt, Melanie opened the door and walked inside.

Bridey was behind the counter. As soon as she spotted Melanie, she offered her a smile that was more of a wince and nodded toward the back of the shop. Sure enough, Callie was sitting at the far table, facing away from the door. Rather than heading straight for her, Melanie stopped at the counter to place her order.

"I'll have a tall black iced tea and one of those double chocolate brownies. No, make it two." She lowered her voice. "What kind of mood is she in?"

Bridey set the tea on the counter and used tongs to pick out the brownies. When she added a third to the plate, Melanie started to protest. Bridey waved her off and even refused her money. "My treat. You're going to need all the chocolate you can get."

She'd been afraid of that. "Is it too late for me to make a fast escape?"

Bridey's smile was sympathetic. "Yeah, it is. Even if Callie is pretending not to have noticed, I'm sure she knows you came in. Go talk to her. You'll both feel better if you do. Let me know if you need me to referee."

Melanie hoped that wouldn't be necessary, but Bridey was right. To run and hide wouldn't help anything. She and Callie had known each other for too long, and their friendship was important to her. That didn't mean the next few minutes would be easy to get through.

The shop wasn't large, but a growing sense of dread made the small expanse of shiny tile seem more like the Grand Canyon. By the time she reached the table and sat down, her hands were shaking hard enough to rattle the small plate of brownies. "Sorry I'm late. I got tied up with a call from one of our suppliers."

She took the seat next to Callie that faced the wall and away from the rest of the room. They were the only two customers in the shop right now, but that could change any second. She'd rather have the small amount of privacy the position offered.

Callie eyed the three brownies, and her mouth twitched just a little. She was familiar with Melanie's rules about eating chocolate and no doubt thought stress was the driving force behind her ordering extra.

"Okay, so I asked for two. It was Bridey who decided I needed three. I'm hoping the extra one was for you."

When she started to move it to the empty plate in front of Callie, her friend blocked access with her hand. "No way. I've already had two cupcakes. Any more sugar and I'll be bouncing off the walls."

Melanie put it back on her plate. If all else failed, she'd wrap it up and take it back home with her. She'd seen Spence out walking with his dog late last night, but they hadn't spoken since the morning he'd left her the voice mail about needing a ride two days ago. She shouldn't need an excuse to seek him out, but she wanted one anyway. It would make it seem less like she was stalking him.

She sipped her tea and waited for Callie to call this meeting to order. When the silence continued beyond the time it took her to enjoy the first nibble of her brownie, she took charge.

"Look, we both know why we're here today. You're worried about Spence, so ask your questions, Callie. I'll answer what I can."

Her friend had been staring into her cup of coffee as if it held the answers to the universe. Callie's eyes came up to glare at her with anger and hurt. "Why is he with you?"

Melanie flinched at the cold chill Callie had packed into that one question. Where did she think he should be staying? Did Callie really think Spence would've been comfortable moving in with her and Nick? Then there was the fact that in addition to Leif living there, so was Spence's cousin. Unless things had changed, the two of them were hardly on speaking terms. If Spence didn't know his cousin had moved back into the house, she didn't want to be around when he found out. It had taken the police to throw Austin and his father out of Spence's house the first time.

She kept her answer simple. "He needed a place to stay. The cottage was available."

Callie was busy shredding a napkin, watching intently as the tiny pieces floated down onto her empty plate. When she reached for a second one, Melanie took another bite of her brownie and waited for Callie to continue.

"You skipped my wedding reception to go with him." She looked up briefly before turning her attention back to her new hobby. "I understand why, but I'd like to hear what happened from you."

"I told all of this to Leif."

Callie nodded. "You know men. He laid out the bare-bones facts, but that was all. Spence is . . . was my best friend, Melanie."

Then as if realizing how that sounded, she added, "Guy friend, anyway. I'm worried about him."

Melanie had to wonder how Spence would feel about her sharing confidences about him, especially with Callie. If he wanted her to know what was going on in his life, wouldn't he have told her himself?

But she and Callie were friends, and her friend was hurting. Hoping she was doing the right thing, Melanie repeated much of what she'd already told Leif and then added a few more details.

"He's renting the cottage until he decides what he's going to do long-term. Meanwhile, he's helping out at the millworks on a special project servicing all the machines. When Spence worked for my father back in high school, he used to help maintain the equipment in the factory."

Without waiting for Callie to respond, Melanie continued. "He's made a few deliveries because I'm down a driver. Other than that, I don't know what Spence's plans are. He hasn't said."

That much was the absolute truth. It wasn't as if he'd gone out of his way to confide in her.

Callie shoved the remains of the napkins to the center of the table. "I knew about him driving for your company because he delivered the doors we'd ordered for the house. Talk about awkward. There he was, bringing us the doors for his house, paid for with his money, and us living there instead of him."

Suddenly, that brownie wasn't settling very well. "I'm, sorry, Cal. If I'd known your order was on that truck, I would never have asked him to deliver it. He should've said something."

Darn the man, anyway! She was sure the foreman in charge of shipping had gone over the list with Spence before sending him out. Granted the foreman wouldn't have known that particular delivery might cause problems, but Spence sure as heck did. What had he been thinking?

On the other hand, maybe it did make perfect sense. "I'm guessing that on some level, he used it as an excuse to approach you, Nick, and Leif. You know, without having to call ahead or anything."

Now she was the one ripping up a napkin. "So, if you don't mind me asking, how did it go?"

Callie rolled her eyes. "Not well, but it could've been worse, I guess. Nick and Leif were unloading the doors when I came back from my folks'. I suspect Spence felt a bit cornered by all of us being there. He had that deer-in-the-headlights look going on."

Her mouth settled into a sad smile. "It helped that Mooch was with him. We're still not sure how the dog found Spence. All we knew was that he disappeared, and we couldn't find him anywhere. We feared for the worst until Spence called to tell us that the dog had shown up on his doorstep. God, that was a huge relief."

"I've seen him out walking the dog a couple of times."

Callie nodded. "From what Nick and Leif have told me, Spence and Mooch were inseparable in Afghanistan. On the one hand, I'm grateful Spence isn't alone right now. On the other, I'm frustrated with him for not sitting down and talking to Leif and Nick. He's already apologized to me, but that's not enough. It almost destroyed them to think that Spence had been killed. Doesn't the jerk realize that?"

Yeah, Melanie would guess he did, but it was Callie's other statement that stuck out. Spence wasn't alone, and not just because Mooch had moved in with him. She'd been there for him, too, even if he didn't seem to remember that right now.

Her friend was still talking, but Melanie hadn't been listening.

". . . and soon. Tell him that, will you?"

"I'm sorry, Callie. I didn't catch the first part of that. Tell Spence what?"

"That he needs to tell us what really happened to him over there, and what he wants to do about the house. We're still working on the place, but we're not sure we should be. It's the not knowing that's driving us all crazy. If he wants it back, that's fine. It's his, after all."

She took a sip of her coffee before adding, "Nick deserves that much from him. We both do."

Melanie had never thought of Callie as selfish, but this was too much. "What about what Spence deserves? God knows what all he went through. Try seeing it through his eyes. When he comes home, you're marrying his friend and living in his house. Heck, you even had his dog. Granted there are good reasons for all of that. None of this is your fault, Callie, but you and Nick need to cut Spence some slack. I'm sure he's doing the best he can under the circumstances."

And she'd just revealed more than she meant to. "Look, I'll pass along your message to Spence if I see him. I've got to get back to work."

She lurched to her feet with her eyes welling up with tears, making it hard for her to gather up her empty cup and plate. As soon as she managed to pick them up, the shreds of napkins went fluttering to the floor like so many flakes of snow.

"Shit, shit, shit!"

Callie gasped, most likely because Melanie rarely cursed and absolutely never did so in public. That much of her mother's teachings had taken hold at an early age. Right now she wanted to shout the worst words she could think of at the top of her lungs, but it wouldn't accomplish anything.

She stood absolutely still for a count of five to regain control. When that didn't do the job, she counted to ten. Feeling only a tiny bit better, she knelt down to start scooping up the bits of napkin.

Bridey appeared at the edge of her peripheral vision

with a broom and dustpan. "That's okay, Melanie. I'll take care of it."

Another five-count allowed her to stand up. "Sorry about the mess."

"That's okay. It happens."

Her friend meant well, but she was wrong. Members of the Wolfe family never made public spectacles of themselves. It wasn't done. Granted, shouting a curse word in a small coffee shop wasn't exactly the end of the world.

But that one crack in her control scared her. Since her father's death, she'd been working so hard to hold everything together for the sake of her mother and the people who depended on the millworks for their living. She couldn't afford to fall apart. Not now. Not ever.

Bridey was still talking. "How about I wrap up your brownies to go and fix you another iced tea?"

Melanie drew a slow, deep breath and forced a smile. It felt brittle, but it was the best she could do. "Thanks, Bridey. That's really nice of you."

She was well aware that Callie was watching her every move. "Like I said, I'll pass along your message, but I'm Spence's landlady, not his keeper."

Rather than wait for a response, she followed Bridey over to the counter and waited for her drink. Proud of the facade she'd managed to piece back together, she thanked her friend again when Bridey held out the small bag and the tea.

"These are delicious, Bridey. And you were right, this is definitely a three-brownie day."

Once she was out on the sidewalk, Melanie automatically turned to the right and kept walking. Rather than return to the office, she headed home. On the way, she called her secretary and lied, saying she had an appointment and wouldn't be back.

She'd left her car at work, but she could pick it up later if she needed it. For now, the walk home would help her burn off the last vestiges of agitation. Tomorrow would be soon enough to go back to being the stoic representative of the Wolfe family who took care of everyone else.

She'd even call Callie to apologize for . . . well, in truth, she wasn't quite sure if she actually regretted anything. Of course she should have been more tactful with Callie, but she'd meant every word she'd said.

Also, she should at least thank Bridey again for the treats and the tea. The three of them had been friends for years, and this wasn't the first time they'd hit a rough patch. Somehow they'd find a way to get through it all with their friendships intact. At least she hoped so.

For now, though, she had her own plans for the afternoon. Once she was behind the safety of locked doors, she'd indulge herself with a bubble bath, a bottle of wine, and those decadent brownies. Her plans made, she turned onto her street and cut across the lawn to the front porch.

After unlocking the door, Melanie stepped inside and kicked off her shoes. It took every bit of strength she had to take even one step farther into the oppressive silence that filled the house. God, she missed her cozy apartment in Spokane. Right now, even the tiny cottage with the poodle shower curtain where Spence was living would be preferable to this dinosaur of a house. Maybe it used to be filled with life, but right now it just felt dead.

Padding in her stocking feet to the kitchen, she picked out a bottle of wine from the fridge. As she headed back to the staircase, her mother's voice whispered in her ear that she also needed a glass. After all, a real lady would never guzzle wine right from the bottle, not even in the privacy of her own bathtub. Well, too bad.

Melanie held up the bottle and shouted, "All the rules and regulations are hereby suspended for this one afternoon."

She toasted the announcement with the first sip of the wine. The small rebellion did nothing to improve Melanie's mood, but it did serve as a reminder of how close she was to losing it right then. As she trudged up the steps, she added one more thing to the afternoon's activities: a good cry.

Chapter 13

❧❧

Mooch growled and stared at the front door. Some-one was approaching the house. Spence had al-ready put in a long day making deliveries and an even longer evening helping Will rebuild a lathe at the factory. The last thing he wanted was company, but the lights made it clear he was home.

When the soft knock finally came, he yanked the door open, half expecting it to be that damn reporter again. Instead, it was Melanie standing there with her hand still raised as if she were about to knock again. He took a step back, unsure whether or not to invite her in. They hadn't been face-to-face since the night they'd kissed, and he was fairly sure that was a deliberate choice on her part.

And to tell the truth, he'd been relieved. That kiss had packed quite a punch, one that had been occupying his dreams ever since. He would have been tempted to go for a repeat performance, but she'd been acting skittish around him. He didn't blame her. More than anyone else, she'd been witness to how unpredictable his behavior had been since he returned to Snowberry Creek.

Rather than invite her in, he stepped out on the porch with her. "Hi, Mel, what's up?"

"I was just, uh, wondering how things went with you and Mr. Cosgrove tonight."

On the surface there was nothing wrong with what she'd asked, but his gut instinct was that she wasn't really all that interested in how much better the lathe would be running tomorrow when the day crew showed up for work. He leaned against the porch railing and crossed his arms over his chest.

"It went fine. Will and I figure on having the rest of the machines serviced and tuned up over the next three weeks. After that, we'll set up a regular schedule to make sure they stay that way. Once everything is caught up, he should be able to handle most of the routine stuff on his own, but he'll call me in for the big jobs if he needs help."

Melanie nodded. "That's great, Spence. Be sure to keep track of your hours and add them to the time you've spent driving the truck. Turn them into Bertie in payroll every week so you can get paid."

What the heck? "That wasn't the deal, Melanie. You're already letting me live here rent free for the month for helping Will. That's enough. Besides, working for you gives me something constructive to occupy my time with. I'm not used to sitting around with nothing to do."

Mooch had come outside with them. Melanie watched his every move as if riveted by the sight of the mutt poking his nose into every bush and plant, woofing softly when he found a particularly interesting smell.

"Aren't you afraid he might run off?" She glanced

toward Spence. "I mean, there's nothing holding him here. No fence or anything."

"Not really. Mooch knows where his food bowl is and who keeps it full for him. After growing up scrounging scraps in the streets, he's got it good living here with me." Spence inched closer to Melanie. "Besides, he's been microchipped. If he did get lost, they'd be able to track down either me or Nick and return him."

"That's good. Really good. He seems like a nice dog."

Spence snickered. "Yeah, right. He snores, leaves his toys lying around right where I'm most likely to step on them in the middle of the night, and has questionable personal hygiene. Other than that, he's the perfect roommate."

She laughed, which was what he was hoping for, not that he was exaggerating. Just the night before he'd damn near killed himself when he stepped on one of the fool dog's rubber bones with his bare foot on the way to the bathroom. He'd bounced off the dresser while he was hopping around and cursing the dog's entire lineage.

As if sensing he was the topic of conversation, Mooch trotted back across the yard and up onto the porch. Softy that she was, Melanie immediately sat down on the top step and let Mooch sprawl across her lap. As she stroked his fur, the damn dog looked up at Spence with his tongue lolling out of his mouth in a big canine grin, no doubt sensing his serious jealousy.

He joined the pair on the step. Something was definitely going on that had Melanie all tied up in knots. If she didn't start talking on her own, he'd have to find some way to drag it out of her. After working a double shift, he was pretty much worn out, but for her he'd hang in there for as long as it took.

Finally, she sighed. "I didn't really come down to ask about the lathe or argue about what I'm paying you."

Spence leaned over close enough to bump her shoulder with his. "I kind of figured that out on my own."

Still focusing all of her attention on the dog, she said, "I saw Callie today. She asked me to meet her at Something's Brewing because we hadn't seen each other in a while. That much was true, but it wasn't the real reason she wanted to talk. She wanted to pump me for information about you."

He wrapped his arm around Melanie's shoulder and gave her a quick squeeze. "I'm sorry she put you in such an awkward position, Mel. I know she's worried about what's going on with me, and I haven't been very forthcoming about it. But that's no excuse for making things hard for you."

Melanie leaned into him, her head coming to rest just below his chin. "I suspected going in that you'd be the main topic of conversation. I told her the same stuff that I'd told Leif about why I followed you to the bar that first night and that I was renting you this house and why you were working for me right now."

She seemed to need him to respond, so he said, "All that's okay. No big deal. Besides, she already knew that much."

But instead of calming her, his comment seemed to send a new surge of tension through her. "What else did she say?"

"She thought you owed it to Nick to explain what was going on with you." Mel lifted her head to look at Spence directly for the first time. "That's when I lost my temper and told her that whatever had happened in Afghanistan wasn't your fault and that nowhere is it written that she and Nick were the center of the universe. Then I told her to cut you some slack because you were doing the best you could under the circumstances."

The words poured out in a rush as if a dam had broken. As soon as she reached the end of her explanation, she pushed Mooch off her lap and started to stand up. "I just thought you should know. I'm sorry if I've made things worse for you."

He caught her hand and tugged her back down beside him. "You didn't do anything wrong, Melanie. It's hard to be caught in the middle. And I don't mean to make things difficult for you, especially when you've already got so much on your own plate right now. If you want me to find another place to crash, just say the word."

As much as he hated it, honesty made him add, "And Callie's not wrong. I do need to figure out what to do about the house and everything. I've been letting it all slide, and that's on me. I'll call my attorney and make an appointment to find out what my options are. Once I've talked to him, I'll get in touch with Nick and Callie and try to work it all out."

Melanie offered him a small smile. "You'll be glad you did, Spence. Believe me, I would rather keep my head buried in the sand, but ugly realities have a way of only getting worse when you ignore them. As bad as things are with the company, people are still getting paid on a regular basis. That's something."

And she was carrying that burden alone. By comparison, his own problems were pretty minor. The only one depending on him to keep food on the table was Mooch, and kibble was cheap.

"If I haven't said so, I really admire what you're doing, Melanie. You could have taken one look at the mess your father left, shut down the factory, and walked away.

Instead, you're doing everything you can to keep the place running, not to protect your family's legacy, but because you know Will and the others depend on the millworks for jobs."

Her eyes were so damn sad. "But what if I can't figure out how to save the company?"

The fear in her voice made him ache, but she didn't want platitudes or empty sympathy. "You'll at least know you tried, Melanie. No one can ask more than that. Hell, you've put your whole life on hold to try to save the company. Not many people would make that kind of sacrifice."

She let out a slow breath and shook her head. "All things considered, it's a pretty small sacrifice, especially compared to what you've been through. Nick and Leif, too, for that matter. I might have had to give up my librarian job, but you three almost lost your lives."

Melanie entwined her fingers with his and stared down at their hands. "God knows I have nightmares thinking about what you might have gone through before you were rescued."

God had nothing to do with what had happened to him, and the last thing he wanted was to fill Melanie's head with the actual details. It was bad enough he had to live with them. "Don't let what happened to me bother you, Mel. I survived it. That's all that matters."

"Sometimes I have to pinch myself to remind myself that you're really back." She glanced at him out of the corner of her eye. "The day of your funeral was one of the worst days of my life, far worse even than when we buried my father."

What could he say to that? It still seriously creeped him out to know that they'd buried an empty coffin. He hadn't gone back to the cemetery to see if they'd taken down his tombstone. Hopefully, someone had taken care of that chore for him.

He was still trying to think of what to say when he noticed Melanie was blinking a lot. Oh, hell, was she crying? Yeah, there was a silvery trace of tears on her cheek. It took all he had to stand his ground instead of giving into the typical guy reaction of wanting to run for the hills.

"Aw, Mel, don't cry. I'm right here." As if that fact would do anything to fix her real problem.

She swiped at her eyes with the back of her hand. "I'm sorry, Spence. I don't mean be such a downer. Sometimes things just pile up, and today was a tough one."

Yeah, he could relate to that. "If you want to go to the bar and consume an unhealthy number of beers, I could keep you company. I'll even be the designated driver this time. I'm sure Liam would be glad to see you again."

It was a relief to hear her laughter ring out across the yard. "That's quite an offer. As tired as I am, it wouldn't take more than a beer, maybe two, to knock me out. At least you managed to walk out of the bar on your own, mostly, anyway. You'd have to carry me out."

Now, there was an image. He hadn't forgotten how good it had felt to hold her in his arms that first night when she fainted. Placing his hand over his heart, he solemnly vowed, "It would be my honor to carry you out of the bar, Mel. I bet Liam would even hold the door for us."

She was still chuckling. "Can you imagine the scandal if it got out that I ended up passed-out drunk at the local roadhouse? It would send shock waves right through the country club crowd for sure. Especially if they found out I'd already drunk most of a bottle of wine by myself today."

Melanie leaned closer to whisper, "I didn't even bother

with a glass. Just swigged it straight from the bottle while I took a bubble bath. Who knows, maybe the scandal might even be enough to convince my mother to come back home. Protecting the sanctity of the Wolfe name was always her number-one priority, you know."

Meaning the needs of her only daughter took a back-seat to what best served the family name. Anger on Melanie's behalf warred with the image of her in that old-fashioned claw-foot tub, chin deep in bubbles. Damn, he wished he'd been there.

"You're looking pretty fierce there, Spence."

He wasn't about to admit that he had a raging hard-on, thanks to her innocent remark about the bubble bath. "It makes me mad that your parents didn't appreciate you enough. They couldn't have asked for a better daughter."

"That's sweet of you to say, Spence. They weren't mean or anything. They just had such high expectations for me to live up to all the time. They worried a lot about who my friends were and what we were doing. Reputation was everything to them."

"I'm guessing they didn't want you hanging around with the likes of me."

"And you'd be right. Of course, they didn't know how much time you used to spend at Callie's, and I sure didn't tell them. I was afraid they'd tell me I couldn't hang out there anymore."

So Callie's house had been a refuge for more than just Spence. He'd been so caught up in his own problems with his asshole uncle at the time to wonder why Melanie always seemed to be lurking in the background whenever he showed up at the Redding house. It would never have occurred to him that she'd been just as unhappy as he was.

If she could share, so could he. "Mr. and Mrs. Redding were a big part of the reason I survived those years. They stood with me when I had to have the police evict my uncle. I joined the army because I wanted to make something of myself so they would be proud of me."

Melanie nodded. "I was so jealous of Callie sometimes for having such terrific parents. They never seemed to mind having extra mouths to feed or the constant sleepovers."

Spence acted put upon. "I ate more than my fair share of meals there, but for some strange reason I never got invited to the sleepovers. That doesn't seem fair."

"If it's any comfort, you were always a topic of conversation, accompanied by a lot of giggling."

Odd that Callie never mentioned that little fact. "Really?"

"Yeah, you and Callie were always good friends, but some of the rest of us had secret crushes on you."

Okay, now he knew she was pulling his leg. "So, if that's true, how come I had only a handful of dates the whole time I was in high school? I had to beg Callie to go to the senior prom with me, and she made me wait until the last minute to make sure she didn't get a better offer."

She looked at him in total disbelief. "Seriously? She never told me that. I would've gone with you in a heartbeat!"

So, did that mean she was one of the ones with a secret crush on him? The idea had him fighting the urge to grin, but he wouldn't embarrass her by asking. It was hard to bring that image into focus. When he looked down just in time to catch Melanie fighting the urge to yawn, he realized how long they'd been sitting there. As much as he was enjoying this trip down memory lane, they both had to work tomorrow. Glancing at his watch, he grimaced. It was well past midnight.

He pushed himself up off the step and tugged her up after him. "Come on, Mel. We'd better get you home before we both end up falling asleep out here on the porch. What would the neighbors think?"

She fell into step beside him. "I'm not sure I care."

Spence put his arm around her shoulders. "That's the spirit."

Mooch ranged out ahead of them, scouting for any possible threats from squirrels in the area. Every so often, he'd stop and glance back to see what was taking the two humans so long. Despite knowing it was past time for Melanie to be back home and tucked into bed, Spence wasn't going to hurry the process along any more than absolutely necessary. They'd both touched on some painful subjects, but talking about them left him feeling better, not worse. He hoped it was the same for her.

All too soon they reached the steps that led up to her back door. Was it too late to take another lap around the yard? Probably.

Melanie took that first step up but then turned around to face him. "I should've called before coming over tonight, Spence. I promise not to drop in unexpectedly again."

"You can drop by anytime, especially if you're going to stroke my ego by telling me that some of Callie's friends thought I was hot."

He tilted his head to one side and stepped right up to the edge of the step, leaving her at his eye level with only a few inches of space between them. "Okay, I promised myself I wasn't going to put you on the spot, but I've just got to know. Were you one of them?"

Although he couldn't see her face clearly in the darkness, he was willing to bet his last dollar that she was blushing right now. Her reaction answered the question without her saying a word. "Never mind. Forget I asked."

Her hand fluttered up to rest on his chest. "I can still remember how my heart would race whenever you went roaring by on that big motorcycle. It was as if you were riding on the wind, all wild and free. I was so jealous."

"You should've said something. I would've gladly taken you for a ride. I still would." His voice sounded deep and rough to his own ears, especially because he wasn't sure if he was just talking about the two of them riding double on the Harley.

Her tongue darted out long enough to lick her lower lip. "I'm not sure I'm brave enough."

He caught her hand in his and brought it up to press a soft kiss right in the center of her palm. "We'd take it as slow and easy as you want, Mel."

Her soft moan was almost his undoing. If he didn't back off right now, he wasn't going to be able to. Rather than give in to an impulse they might both regret, he ran through the list of reasons they shouldn't continue to flirt with temptation. She was his employer, not to mention his landlady. She didn't need any more complications in her life and neither did he.

None of that mattered in the grand scheme of things. The truth was that he wanted her touch, needed it, in fact. He'd give anything to take her to bed and lose himself in the sweet welcome of her arms. It was a craving that had been growing in strength since that very first night. While he was arguing with his conscience, she stood there, staring up at him with those huge eyes.

He couldn't walk away. Not now. That didn't mean following her up those steps would be the smart thing to do, especially for her. But maybe there was one thing he could do.

"Wait here for me, Mel."

She blinked at him, looking confused. "Okay, but where are you going?"

He was already backing away. "I'll be right back. I promise."

When she finally nodded, he took off at a run. "Come on, Mooch. You need to come with me."

The dog hesitated briefly but then broke into a run, keeping pace with Spence. When they reached the cottage, Mooch followed Spence inside.

"Sorry, buddy, but you can't come with me. Guard the house, and I'll be back in a little while."

Spence grabbed his old helmet and the new one he'd bought since he got back. He'd let Melanie wear it and use the old one himself. Back outside, he straddled his Harley and started the engine. Rather than drive around the block to Melanie's house, he drove across the property to save time, because he wasn't sure how long she would wait for him.

But as he tore across the yard, there she was, a huge smile slowly spreading across her pretty face. Unable to resist showing off a little, he gunned the engine. The neighbors might not appreciate the racket, but right now he didn't give a damn. He had a woman to impress, and that was all that mattered. He brought the bike to an abrupt halt just short of the staircase where Melanie was still standing.

He held out the helmet. "Well, Mel, ready to ride the wind?"

Chapter 14

✣ ✣

It was all Melanie could do to nod and reach out to accept the helmet dangling from Spence's hand. Was she really going to do this? Apparently so, because she was already pulling the helmet on over her hair and fumbling to snap the chin strap. Spence grinned at her and motioned for her to come stand beside him. "Let me fix that for you."

He made quick work of adjusting the straps to fit her. When he was done, the helmet felt more comfortable, although she suspected she looked ridiculous. He took her right forearm and helped her climb onto the bike behind him. She had to straddle the seat, which left her sitting snuggled up tight against Spence's hips. Although she was no innocent, there was something a bit shocking and intimate about the position. He reached back to take her hands and wrapped them around his waist, which pulled her flush against his back.

Her mother would disapprove, which only left Melanie even more determined to enjoy the experience.

"Hold on tight."

Before she could respond, Spence revved the engine and set the bike in motion. She squealed in surprise, but Spence only laughed and kept going. For the first few blocks, he kept up a slow pace, giving her a chance to adjust to the strange sensation of riding behind him on the bike. She closed her eyes and leaned her head against his back, feeling the vibration of the motorcycle's powerful engine beneath her. The cool night air provided a sharp contrast to the warmth of his body.

She loved it.

At the next stop sign, he turned his head to ask, "Ready to cut loose?"

Swallowing hard, she said, "Yes! Go for it."

His grin was wicked. "Okay, wild thing, but if it gets to be too much, squeeze my ribs, and I'll slow down."

Then they were off and running, tearing down the back roads through the night. She suspected Spence was still holding back, keeping the bike to a more sedate pace than if he'd been alone, but it was plenty fast for her. Still, with her heart pounding in her chest, she held on tight and lost herself in the moment.

They mostly had the road to themselves, which reminded her how late it was. She didn't care. It might make for a long day tomorrow, but she was sure she wouldn't regret one moment of this time. It wasn't often a person got a chance to live out an old fantasy.

After a few miles, she risked loosening her hold on Spence enough to sit up straighter. She smiled up at the clear night sky where the moon was nearly full and painted the world with its silvery glow. For the first time in months, maybe even years, her spirit soared with the stars overhead. It was as if the worries about her responsibilities toward her mother and the company, which were her constant companions, couldn't keep up with the speeding motorcycle. She didn't want the ride to end, but she knew that eventually Spence would turn back toward her house and her two-wheeled magical coach would morph back into a pumpkin.

But for the time that it lasted, she savored the sweet taste of joyous freedom, and the moment was magical.

An hour later, Spence brought the bike to a halt about a block from her house. He looked down the street that led to her driveway and then down the cross street that would take him directly back to the cottage. It was as if he couldn't make up his mind which way to go.

"Spence, is something wrong?"

He shook his head. "No, just thinking."

Up until they stopped, he'd seemed relaxed and appeared to enjoy the ride as much as she did. But now he felt tense and stiff as they finally turned into her driveway. He drove around to the back steps, maybe intending to cut across the back of the property to the cottage once he dropped her off. Maybe he was worried about how little sleep he was going to get.

When he stopped the bike, she climbed off. Her legs threatened to collapse after the long ride, but she managed to catch herself. While she fumbled with the strap on the helmet, Spence set the kickstand on the bike and joined her standing on the patio. He took her helmet and his and set them both on the bike.

He looked so serious when he asked, "You okay?"

"I'm way better than okay. That was wonderful."

She gave in to the impulse to hug him. "I should be exhausted, but I feel great. I don't know what made you decide to take me for a ride, but it was a wonderful idea."

After staring down at her for the longest time, he finally answered, "I'm glad you enjoyed it."

That tension she noticed before was running hot again. "Spence? Is something wrong?"

He pulled her closer with one arm. "No, the problem is that something is too right."

Before she could ask what he meant, he used his free hand to tilt her head back. His mouth came down on hers hard and fast. As he kissed her, he lifted her up and carried her across the patio to press her back against the side of the house, trapping her between the cool feel of the wood and the burning heat of Spence's body.

She caught his face with both of her hands and broke off the kiss long enough to whisper, "What's my name?"

He frowned but answered, "Melanie."

Okay, then. She smiled and kissed him this time, using the tip of her tongue to tease him into deepening the kiss. He groaned and lifted her higher, guiding her legs around his hips, bringing her core directly against his erection. She rocked against him, needing to get closer to him any way she could. As their tongues continued to dance, Melanie tugged his T-shirt up and splayed her hands directly on his back, loving the feel of all that warm skin and flexing muscle.

When his hand slipped between them to cup her breast, she smiled against his mouth as he kneaded and squeezed the soft flesh. As good as it felt, it wasn't enough. Too many layers of clothing separated them. She wanted to get skin to skin with him, and the sooner, the better. But not out here. The big wall that ran along the side of the property provided a certain degree of privacy, but it wasn't in her to throw all sense of propriety to the wind.

She reluctantly broke off the kiss again. "Spence, can we take this inside?"

But rather than immediately starting for the staircase, he froze, his eyes wide and wild as he slowly lowered her to the ground. "Shit, I never meant for this to get so out of hand."

So much for romance and passion. Melanie tugged her blouse back down into place and tried to tame the tangled mess her hair had become. The last bit of joy left over from the motorcycle ride turned into a knot of pain in her stomach. "Sorry, Spence. Forget I said anything. You'd better go. We both have to work tomorrow."

When she tried to slide past him to make her escape, he caught her arm. "Don't go, Mel. Not yet. Damn it, I'm making a royal mess of this."

She blinked back the burning in her eyes. "Don't worry about it. We'll just pretend the evening ended when I got off the bike and call it good."

Although what had come after had actually been the icing on the cake—or at least she'd thought so. Obviously, Spence had a different opinion.

He muttered an obscenity and ran his hands over his close-cut hair in obvious frustration. She tried once again to reach the steps that led up to the back door, but he quickly planted those heavy boots he wore firmly between her and her one means of escape.

"Melanie, let me explain." He lifted his hand to caress the side of her face. "Please."

The simple touch threatened to stir the embers of passion back to a full burn. She stepped back to give herself space to breathe. "I'm listening."

"First off, believe me when I say there's nothing I'd like more than to take this to its logical conclusion. My whole life went off the rails in Afghanistan, and what came afterward was a hell like I could never have imagined. Until I can put it all behind me, I've got no business getting involved, and especially with a woman like you. A lot of the reason I've even come this far back toward normal is our friendship. I don't want to risk messing that up or hurting you."

She wanted to say that he wouldn't, but her heart told her that he could, despite his best intentions. It might even be inevitable, considering how attracted she was to him. Why couldn't he quit being so damn noble and finish what he'd started? But that stubborn streak of honor was at the core of who he was. On the surface, he looked so strong and self-assured, but every instinct she had said that underneath that brave exterior was a man who needed her.

Deciding actions spoke more than words, she closed the small distance between them and slid her arms around his waist. She kept the hug gentle and friendly, careful to keep those embers carefully banked. "You're a good man, Spencer Lang. Now you'd better head back to the cottage and try to get some sleep. I'll see you at the factory tomorrow."

His arms tightened around her, nearly squeezing the breath out of her. "Good night, Mel. I enjoyed . . ." She felt him press a soft kiss to the top of her head. "Everything."

"So did I."

He stood watch while she made her way up to the landing by the back door. Before she stepped inside, she had one more thing she wanted to say. "Spence, when you're ready, I hope we can finish what we started."

Then without waiting for him to respond, she closed

the door and turned the lock. Standing in the dark kitchen, she watched Spence start up the Harley and disappear into the night. After a quick drink of juice, she went up to her room to get ready for bed. She had to be up in less than four hours, but she didn't care. She'd enjoyed everything, too.

Just as she pulled up the covers, her cell phone buzzed to tell her she had a new message. One glance at the screen had her grinning like a fool. It was from Spence, and all it said was Me, too.

She was still smiling when sleep finally claimed her.

Morning came brutally early. The foreman at the millworks had called Spence at six thirty to tell him that he didn't need to come in until eleven. Something about a rush order that they wouldn't have ready to go until then. Despite his most determined efforts to relax, he remained awake after letting Mooch out, staring up at the ceiling and thinking about what it would have been like if he and Melanie had finished what they'd started last night. Hell, if his conscience had kept quiet, he could have spent the remaining few hours of the night making love with a beautiful woman. He could just picture Melanie beneath him in the bed, her fair skin flushed with passion. She'd made it clear that she was willing, so the only thing standing in the way was him.

What an idiot!

Except that he wasn't talking about some random woman. This was Melanie Wolfe, the last heir to the Wolfe family legacy. She deserved better than a broken-down soldier with no idea where he'd come from. He'd been placed in foster care at age two after being abandoned by his mother, and the space for his father's name on the birth certificate had been left blank. He'd been damn lucky to be adopted at all. It might have hurt when Uncle Vince called him a mongrel, but the man hadn't been wrong.

Most of the time, none of that bothered him, but right now he could use some deeply set roots, the kind other people took for granted. The war and all that had happened since had left him blowing in the wind. Once he got things settled about the house, he wasn't even sure he wanted to stick around Snowberry Creek, the only home he'd ever known.

All of this thinking was getting him nowhere. He threw back the covers and rolled out of bed. Maybe a shower would clear his head. In the bathroom, he winced at the sight of the hot pink poodle shower curtain. He really should replace the hideous thing, but that would make it feel as if he was starting to think of the cottage as more than a temporary haven. He'd left all the doilies in place for the same reason.

After stripping off his boxers, he stepped into the stinging spray of the shower. Oh yeah, that felt good. He set the temperature just shy of scalding and let the steaming water work its magic. When the hot water was almost gone, he shut off the shower and toweled off. He had to go into work later, so he shaved and trimmed his buzz cut before pulling on his favorite jeans and a clean shirt.

After heading into the kitchen, he considered his options for breakfast and settled on the last two pieces of a pepperoni pizza with a large glass of iced tea to wash them down. He took it all out onto the front porch to read the paper while Mooch sniffed around the yard, returning occasionally to make a halfhearted effort to see if Spence was willing to share.

"Here, dog." He tossed the last piece of crust to Mooch and then unfolded the paper. Every time it showed up on his porch, he grimaced and prayed Reilly Molitor hadn't made good on his threat to write about Spence's experiences in Afghanistan. He breathed a sigh of relief when his name wasn't splashed across the front page of the *Clarion*.

His luck might not hold forever, but the longer Reilly held off on running the story, the more emotionally prepared Spence would be to deal with it. At least that's what he kept telling himself. He was about to start the crossword puzzle when a car slowed to a stop on the street in front of the cottage. At first, he thought he might have conjured Reilly up just by thinking about him.

When he saw who was really climbing out of the car, he almost wished it had been the reporter dropping by for another visit. Callie, Nick, and Leif weren't the only people Spence had been avoiding. Callie's parents were also on that list, but his luck had just run out. At least it was only Mrs. Redding. He wasn't sure he could have faced her husband, too.

He set the paper aside and stood up. Mooch barked and wagged his tail like crazy the minute he spotted the woman crossing the lawn. She stopped to let the dog come to her and held out some kind of treat for him. Spence noticed she was careful to keep the plastic bag in her other hand out of Mooch's reach. Hey, maybe she'd brought him a batch of his favorite chocolate chip cookies, not that he deserved them.

When she finished petting Mooch, Spence stepped off the porch and right into the comfort of her embrace. It felt like coming home. She held him tight, and he was pretty sure she was crying. Shit, why was nothing ever easy?

"I'm sorry, Mrs. Redding."

"Apology accepted." She stepped back to study him, her cheeks stained with tears. "But since when have you called me anything other than Mama R.?"

A lump of cold pain in the center of his chest started melting, but if anything, her easy acceptance made him feel worse. "All things considered, I wasn't sure I still had the right. In fact, I'd feel better if you yelled at me or maybe punched me in the nose, especially after how I acted at Callie's wedding."

Her hazel eyes, so like her daughter's, filled with tears again. "Aw, Spence, honey, I'm not mad at you. Coming home to find her marrying Nick had to come as a shock. They know that, too. I'm just so glad you're back home and in one piece. Given time, I'm sure we'll fix whatever is wrong between you, Callie, and your army buddies. Right now all that really matters is that I got my boy back. God knows, thinking we'd lost you almost killed us, too."

Then she hugged him again. "Welcome home, Spence."

When she released him and stepped back, he made a show of eyeing the bag in her hand. "I don't suppose that's for me."

Mrs. Redding handed it over. "You know it is. I baked my chocolate chip cookies, but I also stuck in some oatmeal raisin and some snickerdoodles, too. Gotta fatten you up a bit." He picked her up and swung her around and around. "You, lady, are a goddess among women! I've missed all those goodie boxes you and Callie used to send me."

After setting her back down, he peeked into the bag and did a quick count. There had to be at least six dozen cookies, and all just for him. Well, good manners dictated that he offer to share with Mama R., but no one else was going to get any. Not even Mooch.

"Come on inside," he said. "I'll make a pot of coffee, and we can break out the goodies."

She followed him into the cottage. As soon as she stepped across the threshold and got a good look around, she started laughing. "I love what you've done with the place, Spence. If I'd known you liked doilies this much, I would've mailed you some with every goodie box I sent you. Just imagine how cozy they would've made your barracks. I'm sure all the other guys would have loved them, too."

"Yeah, right." Spence grinned back at her. "Check out the poodle shower curtain in the pink bathroom. It's so me."

He left her to explore the small house while he ground the beans for the coffee. When he was filling the coffeemaker with water, he heard the front door open and close. Where had she gone? After hitting the ON button, he stepped out on the porch to see Mama R. standing by the open hatchback on her car. She was in the process of picking up a pair of cardboard boxes. From the effort she put into it, he had to guess they weren't exactly light.

He loped across the yard to help. "Let me get those for you."

She surrendered her burden and then closed up the car. "I brought more than cookies. Once I got started baking, I got to thinking about all your favorite things. I hope you have some freezer space. I'm afraid I went a little overboard."

He let her lead the way back to the house so she could open the door for him. "Don't worry about that. Home cooking never goes to waste around me. I'd tell you that you shouldn't have, but I'm not that noble, especially when it comes to your cooking."

Inside, she helped him unpack the two boxes, which contained a dozen different casserole dishes, all carefully labeled with what each one contained along with instructions on how to cook them. He'd be eating like a king for the foreseeable future.

"I can't thank you enough for doing this. Nobody cooks like you do, Mama R., and I should know. I'm surprised you never asked the attorney who watched over my inheritance for regular cash donations to your food budget."

She didn't appreciate the humor. "Your parents were our best friends. The least I could do was make sure you got some decent hot meals. Looking back, I should've insisted on feeding Austin, too."

How did that jerk enter into this conversation? Mama R. knew how he felt about his cousin. Rather than say anything, he got out a plate and put a few of the cookies on it. After pouring each of them a mug of coffee, he offered her a seat at the small kitchen table.

"Don't think I missed your reaction to the mention of Austin's name, Spence. Now isn't the time to talk about him, but just know that he's working hard to turn his life around, which is another miracle in itself. You'll like the man he's becoming."

He didn't see that happening. "I'll have to take your word for that."

"All I'm asking is that you give the boy a chance. You know full well how hard a time he's had because of that awful father of his."

Yeah, he did, but he didn't want to hear about it. The kid could've made different choices. Rather than argue,

Spence nodded, letting her think he was conceding the point.

When they were settled at the table, she accepted one of the cookies but set it down without even taking a bite. "So, Spence, tell me what you've been up to since you came back to town. I'm guessing you're probably not ready to share what happened over in Afghanistan after the explosion and may never be. I'd just like to know how you came to be living here among the doilies and poodle prints, and what your long-term plans are if you have any."

He sipped his coffee and considered how much to share. Maybe she wouldn't notice him dancing around the tougher issues if he gave her enough detail on the easy stuff. He started off with running into Melanie that first night at the cemetery and kept going right up to working last night with Will Cosgrove. He stopped short of telling her about his late-night adventures with Mel.

But Mama R. had always had an uncanny knack for knowing when he was being evasive. She studied him over the rim of her cup several seconds. "Okay, I knew about Melanie following you to that awful bar, which really came as a surprise to all of us. I wouldn't have expected her to do something so impulsive, but I'm grateful that someone was watching over you that night. I also appreciate why you wouldn't have felt comfortable moving back into your family home under the circumstances, and it was nice of Melanie to offer you this place instead."

She set the cup down and leaned closer. "I do want to point out that you could have stayed with us. Although I also understand why that might have been awkward for you, too. Having said that, I'd like you to come to dinner soon. It would be just me and Mr. R. Bring Melanie with you if that would make it easier for you. I haven't had a chance to spend much time with her since she's moved back home. It would be nice to get caught up with her."

Sneaky woman. She had him cornered and she knew it. There was no way he could turn down her invitation without hurting her more than he already had done. It probably wasn't fair to Melanie to drag her along as a buffer, but he wasn't sure he could face the Reddings alone, not for an entire evening. What if Callie and Nick decided to drop by, even though they weren't invited? He wouldn't put it past them.

He swallowed hard. "I'll ask Melanie what her schedule looks like and give you a call to set a date."

She beamed at him, her relief obvious. "That's really great, Spence. Make it soon, though. The longer you put it off, the harder it will be for you. It's just one little step back toward reconnecting with more of your past."

She was right. "I'll try to make it in the next couple of weeks. I'm working a lot of evenings right now at the millworks, so it will have to be on a Saturday or Sunday."

"That will be fine. Just let me know. My calendar is clear for the foreseeable future. Even if it wasn't, I'd change my plans to be able to spend time with my boy again."

She finally ate her cookie and then finished off her coffee. "Well, I'd better get going. You probably have things you need to be doing."

He walked outside with her. Mama R. slipped Mooch another treat from her pocket before giving Spence another rib-crunching hug. "I thank God every night for sending you back home to us, Spence. Find some way to make peace with your friends soon. You'll all feel better."

Then she patted him on the cheek and gave him a soft smile. "I suspect you'd always thought when it was time for you to come back home to live that Callie would be part of it. She is, just not in the way you were thinking. I would have been proud to have you as a son-in-law, Spence, but you two were always more like brother and sister than anything else or something would have happened between you years ago. I think in your heart, you probably know that's true."

While he struggled to come up with something to say, she got in her car and closed the door. After starting the engine, she rolled down the window. "One more thing, Spence. Judging from what you didn't say, I suspect that you're feeling anything but brotherly toward Melanie Wolfe. If so, I approve. The two of you have so much in common."

She pulled away from the curb, leaving Spence stunned and staring after her. She waved one last time before making the turn at the corner and disappearing from sight. How was he supposed to react to that last bombshell? What could he and Melanie possibly have in common other than that they were both back in Snowberry Creek and weren't particularly happy about it? As he walked back inside, he shook his head and grinned. Mama R. always had been able to read him like a book, so maybe she was right. And speaking of Melanie, it was time to get ready for work.

Chapter 15

Melanie made it to lunchtime without falling asleep at her desk, but it was a close call. She'd make it through the day if it killed her, and right now she was afraid it just might. On the other hand, she couldn't bring herself to regret a single second of the time she'd spent with Spence: sitting on his porch and talking, her first ride on a motorcycle, and, well, the kiss that had come afterward. What an amazing night!

Too bad she didn't have anyone to confide the details in right now. Talking to Callie was clearly out of the question, and she couldn't involve Bridey without putting her in the awkward position of having to keep secrets from Callie.

A knock on her office door snapped her attention back to the present. "Come in."

Mrs. Cuthbert stepped into the room, clenching a file folder in her hand, her expression grim. "I'm sorry, Ms. Wolfe, but there's a problem with the paperwork we sent to the bank."

Melanie frowned. "Did I make a mistake when I filled it all out? I double-checked all the figures before I gave it to you to fax back to them."

"No, that's not the problem. They say they never got the paperwork at all, and now we've missed the deadline."

Being tired didn't stop Melanie's temper from flaring hot. "But we sent it over in plenty of time. Get me the confirmation from the fax, and I'll call the loan officer myself."

If anything, Mrs. Cuthbert looked even more upset. "I don't have a confirmation."

"Why not? If you didn't get one, you should've just resent the whole package to the bank. Better that they get duplicate copies than none at all."

The older woman was already shaking her head. "I couldn't get the fax machine to work even though I tried. Since the mail carrier was due in a few minutes, I stuck the paperwork in an envelope and sent it to the bank that way. It should've gotten there the next day."

Okay, they'd deal with the fax problem later. Right now Melanie needed to find some way to salvage the situation. "Did you asking for tracking on the envelope so that we can prove when the paperwork reached the bank?"

She knew the answer before the woman even opened her mouth, but she let her speak. "I'm sorry, but we've never had trouble with the mail before. There was no reason to spend the extra money for special handling."

Melanie fought the urge to throw something. "It costs less than a dollar to include tracking, Mrs. Cuthbert. Considering the importance of getting that paperwork to the bank on time, I think we could've sprung for that much. If I'd been told there was a problem, I would have faxed the paperwork myself or even driven the damn things to the bank. At the very least, you sure as hell should've said something at the time."

Mrs. Cuthbert gasped. "Melanie Wolfe, you should be ashamed of yourself! Your father never uttered one curse word in all the years I worked for him."

Enough was enough. "And I'm not my father, Mrs. Cuthbert! I know you'd rather he was sitting in this chair. To be honest, so would I. However, he's also the one who left this mess for me to clean up. Believe it or not, I'm doing the best I can, and the paperwork that didn't reach the bank was a big part of the plan to save this company."

Clearly the woman wasn't willing to believe anything Melanie told her. "Your father never said that the company was on shaky ground. He had no trouble making payroll, and I know for a fact he never had to borrow money from the bank to do so."

The last thing Melanie wanted to do was get in a shouting match with an employee, but maybe it was time they all did a reality check. "That's because he borrowed the money against our family home, not the company. Without the new financing, I'm not sure I'll be able to keep this place running for even another six months. I'd be glad to let you look at the spreadsheet yourself if you don't believe me."

Mrs. Cuthbert flushed red and then went pale. "I won't stand here and let you bad-mouth your father, Ms. Wolfe. He was a good man and a great boss. Everyone loved him."

From the odd note in the other woman's voice, Melanie was beginning to suspect that the feeling Mrs. Cuthbert had harbored for Melanie's father had gone far beyond that of an employee for a boss. But she so didn't want to go there.

It was time to play hardball. "Mrs. Cuthbert, if you can't deal with the new circumstances around here, you might want to consider tendering your resignation."

"Maybe I will."

Melanie didn't hesitate. "I'm sure you know what paperwork needs to be filled out to make that happen. Leave it on my desk, and I'll sign it. I would appreciate two weeks' notice."

From the shocked look Mrs. Cuthbert gave Melanie, she hadn't expected her to accept her resignation. Well, she wasn't going to beg her to stay, not when she wasn't willing to meet Melanie halfway on the changes that needed to be made to drag the company into the modern age.

"For your father's sake, I'll stay that long."

"Thank you, Mrs. Cuthbert. Now, I assume that file in your hands is the paperwork for the bank. Give it to me, and I'll see what I can do."

The secretary dropped the manila folder in the center of Melanie's desk and disappeared back out to her own office. Chances were news would spread through the plant like wildfire that Melanie had ordered Mrs. Cuthbert to retire. In the long run, they'd both be happier, but it was clear who was going to be the villain in this farce.

Rather than dwell on it, she reached for the phone to call the man at the bank she'd been dealing with and sent a prayer skyward that he'd have some suggestions on what she should do next. If not, her trust fund was going to take another hit, one that would leave it nearly depleted. If she couldn't pull off a miracle this time, Mrs. Cuthbert wouldn't be the only one retiring or looking for a new job.

She pinched the bridge of her nose, hoping to hold off the headache that felt imminent, as she waited for the banker to come on the line. Hoping she sounded cheerier than she felt, she said, "Hello, Mr. Lunt. This is Melanie Wolfe calling, and I understand we have a little problem with our paperwork."

When Spence got back from making his final delivery, the usually talkative foreman barely said more than the absolute minimum to give Spence his orders for the next day. "That's it for today. Tomorrow should be a full day, though. The regular driver will be back after that."

Then he settled back in his chair and went back to studying the paper he had spread out on top of his desk. Spence noticed he was reading the Help Wanted ads. "Looking for work?"

He'd meant it as a joke. Like most of the employees at the millworks, the foreman had started working there right out of high school and only had a few years left until he could retire. The thought of him moving on to another company seemed unlikely. However, from his reaction, Spence was obviously wrong about that.

"All things considered, I might not have any choice. Ms. Wolfe started laying people off today."

What? That couldn't be right. If things had gotten that bad around there, surely Melanie would've said something last night. He'd known there were problems, but he'd thought she was making good strides toward pulling the company back from the edge. He glanced up at the second floor of the factory, wishing he knew what to do.

His first impulse was to go running up the stairs to see what he could do to help.

On the other hand, he had been making a real effort to avoid anyone getting the idea that he and Melanie were anything other than old acquaintances who had gone to high school together. With things going to hell around her, the last thing she needed right now was to have her name linked to his. He didn't know for sure, but he suspected that many of her employees still thought of him as that wild Lang boy even though he'd left that kid behind years ago.

He knew it would be better to wait until everyone had gone home before he approached her directly. At least he could text her without anyone being the wiser. "I'm going to grab a quick bite in the lunchroom. Will you let Mr. Cosgrove know that's where I am if he comes in looking for me?"

"Sure."

Luckily, Spence had the small lunchroom to himself. He bought a pop from the machine and sat down to text Melanie.

R U OK?

She answered within seconds. I'll survive. :-}

Anything I can do?

No. Well; unless you happen to stumble across a pile of $$ lying around somewhere.

He smiled and texted back, I'll keep an eye out.

After a slight hesitation, he added, What happened today?

This time it took longer for her to respond. Nothing I can explain in a text. Can you stop by the house after you get done tonight?

> I'll be there. I'll even bring some of Mama R.'s fresh-baked cookies to share.

She sent back a happy face followed by You are my hero. Thank you.

> You're welcome. Now I'd better get back to work before the boss finds out I've been flirting on company time.

> Good idea. I hear she's on a real tear today.

> She doesn't scare me. I'm a trained combat soldier. I'll bust out some of my best moves if I have to.

> If they're anything like the moves I saw last night, I'm all for it.

> **blush**

> Yeah, right. It would take more than that to embarrass a big, tough guy like you. Now we'd both better get back to work. See you later.

> Yes, ma'am.

"Boy, what's on that fancy phone that has you looking like a kid in a candy shop with ten dollars to spend?"

Spence nearly jumped out of his skin. How had he not heard Will come in? He looked around to make sure no one else had slipped into the room when he wasn't looking. What if they'd looked over his shoulder and learned that he'd been flirting with their boss? Meanwhile, Will was still waiting for an answer.

"A friend sent me a link to a joke. It was pretty funny."

"All that texting crap is a waste of time, if you ask me. If you're done fooling around, those machines out there could use our attention, and I'd like to get home before eleven o'clock for once."

Considering his plans to meet up with Melanie, Spence clapped his old friend on the shoulder. "Let's aim for ten."

The phone call with the banker hadn't gone as well as Melanie had hoped it would, but it hadn't been a total disaster, either. They wouldn't have to start over from scratch to restructure the company's debt load, but there was no guarantee what the interest rate would be when they finished the process. Under the circumstances she supposed she should be grateful for even that much. She'd spent the rest of the afternoon updating the paperwork. It might have been cowardly of her, but she'd waited until Mrs. Cuthbert had left for the day to fax the paperwork to the bank herself. Afterward, she'd gathered up the other files that needed her immediate attention and headed home.

That had been four hours ago, three of which she'd spent poring over reports at the kitchen table. The only concession she'd made to working at home was to exchange the suit she'd worn to the office for a pair of flannel pj bottoms and a tank top. When all the numbers started to blur, she decided that enough was enough. She set it all aside and fixed herself something to eat and started to top off her wineglass but then stopped herself. She was already tired, and her head was foggy enough without adding more alcohol. Besides, Spence had promised to stop by. The last thing she wanted was to be passed out on the couch when he got there.

The poor guy had enough problems of his own without having to deal with hers, but he was the only one she could be totally honest with about everything. At work, she had to pretend she knew what she was doing even when she didn't. Dealing with the bankers was even worse. Numbers didn't lie, but she still had to try to put a positive spin on the millworks' bottom line. Nobody was that good a liar.

She was considering diving back into the files when she heard a low rumble coming from outside. A single headlight lit up the front window as a motorcycle turned into her driveway. Spence! It wasn't even nine thirty, far earlier than she'd expected him, not that she was complaining. Just that quickly, her depressing exhaustion disappeared.

She practically skipped to the kitchen to open the back door for him. He'd already parked the Harley and was headed up the steps, taking them two at a time.

"You finished work early." That came out wrong. "Sorry, Spence. That came out sounding like a boss. What I meant to convey was how happy I am to see you."

"Will and I got an early start on the two machines we wanted to do tonight." When he reached the top step, he gave her a worried look and brushed a lock of her hair back from her face. "I heard about Mrs. Cuthbert, but I'm guessing your version of what happened will be closer to the truth. Are you all right?"

"I'm better now that you're here. We can talk about

what happened if you want to, but I'd really rather wait until after you've had a chance to catch your breath."

"It's a deal as long as you remember I'm willing to listen." Then he held up a quart-sized plastic bag crammed full of cookies. "Cookies as promised. I brought both chocolate chip and oatmeal raisin. I had snickerdoodles, too, but I couldn't bring myself to share those. Call me greedy."

She couldn't even pretend to be disappointed. "Don't worry about it. You don't see me offering to share my secret stash of dark chocolate, do you? Come on inside. Have you eaten? I have sandwich makings if you're hungry."

"Nope, I'm good. I grabbed a burger on the way home." Inside the kitchen, he added, "However, I wouldn't turn down some ice cream to go with the cookies if you have any."

"I do."

She started for the freezer to get it, but Spence caught her arm and spun her back to face him. "There's something else I want first, though."

The greedy gleam in his eyes made it clear exactly what he wanted: her. Her whole body came alive as he gathered her into his arms for a hard, full-body press even as his lips settled against hers. The slide of his tongue across hers immediately sparked a fire deep inside her, leaving her breasts feeling full and heavy and a hungry ache throbbing at her core. She felt the hard evidence of Spence's own response to the embrace pressed against her stomach. Clearly they were picking up right where they'd left off the night before.

It might not be smart, but darned if she could come up with the strength to resist him. When Spence began nuzzling her neck, she shivered and arched her head to the side to give him easier access. "Oh yes, just like that," she murmured as she dug her fingertips into the hard muscles in his shoulders.

Once again it was Spence who banked the fire, but only a little. This time he stayed right there in front of her, breathing hard and his eyes a darker shade of green. "Mel, my life is still screwed up with no end in sight. I can't tell you how long I'll be here in Snowberry Creek or even where I'll end up when I leave."

No surprise there. "Spence, I understand all that. You've never made any claims otherwise, and my own situation isn't much better. If I can't save the company, I won't be staying in town, either. I won't ask you for promises you can't keep, not when I can't make any myself."

He stroked her cheek with the tips of his fingers. "So we're good?"

She gave him a heated look of her own, eyeing him from the top of his head all the way down to his boots and back up again, pausing at a few favorite stops along the way. "I just know we're going to be."

Was he blushing? It was hard to tell, but the thought made her smile. He nodded in the direction of the plastic bag he'd tossed on the counter. "I'm thinking the cookies and ice cream can wait. You know, we can save them until afterward."

She arched an eyebrow. "Better yet, let's plan on having them in between."

His eyes widened, and his mouth quirked up in a big grin. "Well, okay, then. Guess I've got my marching orders."

His response had her feeling far bolder than she'd ever been with a lover before. "That's right, soldier. The only question is where you want to start this party."

Spence reached over to give the kitchen table a quick shake and then did the same with the counter. "These both seem plenty sturdy."

Two could play at this game. "I should point out that the couch in the den is more comfortable than the one in the living room. Then again, if you're a traditional kind of guy, the bed in my room is king-sized."

Rather than continue the conversation, in a surprise move Spence lifted her up and set her down on the kitchen counter. She squeaked in surprise but happily let him make room for himself between her knees. He stroked his fingers up her legs and the outside of her thighs to grip her ass with both hands as he kissed her hard and deep. She clamped her legs around his hips and rocked against his erection. Better, but not nearly enough to satisfy either one of them.

She jerked the hem of his shirt up. "Get rid of this."

Spence was only too glad to do Melanie's bidding. After tossing his T-shirt over his shoulder, he retaliated by peeling off her tank top and issued an order of his own. "Lie back."

As soon as she did, he leaned down to kiss her midriff. From there, he moved up to scatter kisses along the top curve of her breasts. With a flick of his fingers, he unfastened the front clasp of her bra and shoved the lace out of his way. He paused for a long second to stare down in wonder at her full breasts with their dusky tips that begged to be kissed. God, he'd dreamed about this moment, but his fevered imagination hadn't even come close to the realty.

He cupped her breasts and gave them a soft squeeze, then a second one with a little more pressure. Oh yeah, she liked that. Melanie arched up, pressing them more firmly into his hands. Her expression was looking a bit desperate, which pleased him to no end. He didn't want to be the only one feeling that way.

She looked up at him with those smoky gray eyes. "Please, Spence!"

He captured one nipple with his mouth and suckled hard. He'd never tasted anything so sweet and warm. Melanie wrapped her arms around his neck and held him close, making it clear that she wanted more of the same. He gave equal time to the other breast, using his teeth and tongue to coax the nipple into a tight bud.

As he did, he slipped a hand between them to press against the juncture of her legs. The soft flannel did little to disguise the damp heat gathering there, but even the thin layer of fabric was too much. On impulse, he lifted her legs high to rest on his shoulders while he pressed a kiss right where his hand had just been. Melanie's eyes widened in surprised shock. When she didn't protest, he did it again, this time swirling his tongue hard enough to leave her moaning. It was almost his undoing.

They needed to get naked. Right now.

He could take her right there on the counter or even the table, but Melanie deserved better than that. Her bed would be best, but right now he was running too close to the edge to make it upstairs to her bedroom. Hadn't she mentioned something about the couch in the den? He muscled her up off the counter and started down the hall with her holding on for dear life.

He managed to open the pocket doors. Enough light spilled in from the hallway to make it unnecessary for him to mess with turning on the lamps. He set Melanie back on her feet and immediately tugged her pj bottoms down past her hips while debating whether to leave her lacy panties in place for the moment. No, there was no time for that.

Holding on to his shoulders for balance, she kicked off her flip-flops before stepping out of her pants. As soon as she was done, she reached for the buckle on his belt. When he tried to help her, she batted his hands aside. "Let me."

He was pretty sure waiting for her to undo his belt and then his zipper was the road to insanity. Finally, she got them both undone and started working his pants down his legs. As soon as his penis sprang free from the confinement of his jeans, she smiled and took it in a gentle grip. His eyes nearly rolled back in his head. One stroke of her hand snapped what was left of his control. Once again, he picked her up, this time to settle her down on the cool leather of the couch. He managed to remain vertical long enough to pull a condom from his pocket, something else he'd picked up when he stopped at the cottage to get the cookies.

After stripping off his pants and boots, he stretched out on top of Melanie and settled between her legs, skin to skin at last, as he held himself poised right at the threshold of her body and kissed her softly. "How can I make this good for you?"

Her smile was a siren's song as she brought her knees up, settling him more firmly against her. "Just keep doing what you're doing."

He wanted to give her more than a frantic coupling. It took every bit of willpower he could muster to back off enough to restore a bit of his control. He kissed her mouth, her pretty lips already swollen with passion.

From there, he slid farther down her body to pay homage to her breasts.

Melanie's hands fluttered down to hold his head as her own tossed back and forth in the same rhythm while his mouth tugged on first one breast and then the other. After a few seconds, he continued on his journey, kissing the soft curve of her belly before finally reaching the damp curls below. As he tongued her clit, he slid first one finger and then a second deep inside her, trying to prepare her for when he finally claimed her with everything he had.

When she keened out in release, he surged back up her body, holding back for a moment before thrusting deep and hard inside her. One of them hollered, most likely him. He tried to give her a minute to adjust to the abrupt invasion, but when her nails dug hard into his backside, all bets were off. He raised himself up to support his weight on his arms, then let his hips swing hard and fast, the slap of his body against hers the most erotic thing he'd ever heard.

The ride was fast and sexy and over way too soon. Melanie panted his name as a second, more powerful climax rolled through her, shoving him right over the cliff at the same time. He shouted and shuddered as he rode out the storm with her, loving the feel of his body pouring out every bit of his passion deep within this one woman.

When the last of the tremors faded away, he realized he was crushing her. He immediately pushed himself up to use his arms to support his own weight while leaving their bodies connected.

"Melanie, that was ... wow."

Her eyes lit up. "Yeah, that's the very word I was looking for. 'Wow' is good."

He ducked down to kiss the tip of her nose. "I only have one question for you. Well, actually two."

She stroked his back with her hands. "Which are?"

"What flavor is the ice cream? Second, do we eat it down here or take it up to your room since you said it was for in between?"

Melanie's giggle sent a vibration through to a certain part of his anatomy, which immediately stirred to life again. She knew it, too.

"I have chocolate, strawberry, and chocolate chip mint, and I vote for upstairs." Then she rocked her hips just a little. "However, I'm thinking there might not be enough time in between for ice cream. We may need to save it for afterward after all."

And that's what they did.

Chapter 16

🌿🌿

Melanie had never eaten ice cream in bed naked with a man before. Before coming upstairs to her room, Spence had filled his bowl with strawberry ice cream and grabbed the bag of goodies he'd brought from home. What was that old expression? Oh yes. She definitely wouldn't kick him out for eating cookies in bed even if he did sneak a bite from her bowl every chance he got.

When he tried again, she smacked his greedy fingers with her spoon. "Quit it! You could've had chocolate if you had wanted it. In fact, you still can if you want it that much."

He held out his bowl. "Or you could share yours."

"Not happening. I don't share chocolate. Not ever." She scooted a little farther away from him. "Ask anyone who knows me."

"Fine, I get it. No sharing." Spence settled back against the headboard of her bed. Just when she let her guard down, he snagged the bag of cookies and tossed it out of reach on the table on his side of the bed.

She rolled her eyes. "Real mature, Spence."

He shrugged and kept eating his ice cream. After a bit, he relented and put the bag back within her reach. "So, what happened with Mrs. Cuthbert?"

Melanie wasn't sure she wanted to spoil this peaceful moment talking about work, but venting would feel good. "I shouldn't tell tales about an employee outside the office, but the truth is that the strain between me and Mrs. Cuthbert has been building for some time now. A lot of the procedures my father had in place are hopelessly out of date, but she doesn't see it that way. That would mean he wasn't perfect. Believe me, he wasn't."

She paused to eat another bite of her ice cream and gather her thoughts. "Okay, maybe that was uncalled for, but if we're going to stay in business, something has to change. The trouble is that there is a certain element among the employees who are resistant to any kind of change at all. Perhaps it's because I'm a woman, and the building industry is still pretty much male dominated. Maybe they don't see me as an authority figure because they knew me when I had skinned knees and braces on my teeth."

He was already nodding. "I've heard a few grumblings along that line. On the other hand, the guys in the factory are happy that you're making the effort to get the machinery back into good shape. They figure you wouldn't bother if you were going to close the doors for good."

That was something. At least she'd done one thing right. Setting her bowl aside, she drew her knees up and wrapped her arms around her legs. "Most of the problem is on the administrative side. Hardly anything is done by computer, which translates to inefficiency. Things get lost in the process, and there aren't any backup procedures in place to act as a safety net."

He kept prodding. "So what fell through the cracks this time?"

"I've been working with a local banker in an effort to restructure the company's debt load, and some crucial paperwork went astray. He went on vacation for a week, and the guy who was covering for him got busy and didn't follow up on it. However, the real problem was on our end. I'd hoped to lock in a lower interest rate if the loan was approved, and each day's delay means that much more of our already limited funds is going to pay some pretty-high-interest payments. My biggest worry is that this screwup was an indication that the Wolfe Millworks is no longer a company they would want to do business with."

Even her favorite brand of chocolate ice cream wasn't going to make this conversation more palatable. "I can't blame Mrs. Cuthbert entirely for all of it falling apart. Obviously it wasn't her fault the banker was gone or that the envelope got lost somewhere between the office and the banker. As important as those papers were, all things considered, I should've faxed them over myself."

Spence set his bowl aside to pull her into his arms. "You can't expect to do everything all by yourself, Mel. If that woman was having problems, she should've told you. That's her job."

"*Was* her job. She gave her two weeks' notice. She definitely didn't like it when I lost my temper and cursed in front of her. Evidently, my father was too much of a gentleman to ever have done such a scandalous thing. I feel bad that she'll be leaving angry after all her years of service to the company, but I honestly don't know what

I could've done differently. Her loyalty to my father and his memory is commendable, but she'll never truly accept me as his replacement. I can't function if my staff is fighting me every step of the way."

She snuggled closer to Spence's warm strength. "I don't know how to make everyone see me as something besides Edmond Wolfe's little girl."

"I guess the need to put our pasts behind us is something else we have in common." His laugh rumbled through his chest. "Try living down a reputation like mine. I'm the first to admit that I ran wild after my parents died and Uncle Vince moved in. Hell, I probably wouldn't have survived at all if it hadn't been for the Reddings. Thanks to them, I finally got my act together. Yet every time I run into someone who hasn't seen me since I left town, all I hear about is my exploits. One asshole even hinted that my being reported killed in action was just another prank."

She bolted upright. "Seriously? What jerk said something that stupid? Is it someone I know?"

Spence gathered her close again. "Down, girl. When I run into idiots like that, I just remind myself that stupid can't be fixed."

"True enough, but that doesn't keep their idiotic comments from being hurtful. He'd kick himself if he could see the marks your service has left on you."

It hadn't been until they were in the kitchen to dish up the ice cream that she was actually able to see the evidence of the various wounds he'd suffered along the way. They still gave her the shivers. It was painfully obvious how close they'd come to having lost Spence for real. Most of the scars were faded, but one in particular still looked painful. She trailed her fingers across the puckered jagged scar that started on his chest and followed the curve of his rib cage.

"God, Spence, I can't stand to think about what you must have gone through. I hate the people who did this to you."

He caught her hand in his and brought it up to his lips for a quick kiss. "I'm sorry my scars bother you. I'll put my shirt back on."

"No, don't." She rolled over to straddle his lap. "They bother me because it means you were hurt, Spence, not because they repulse me. As far as I'm concerned, each and every one of them is a badge of honor."

To make sure he knew she meant every word, she sought out each scar on his powerful body, no matter how small, and kissed it. As she progressed downward, Spence kicked his head back to watch her, his eyes at half-mast while he tracked her every move. That he liked what she was doing was very apparent by the time she worked her way down his ripped six-pack. The mood shifted from healing to something far more primal.

When she flicked her tongue along the ridge of his hipbone, Spence's legs moved restlessly. She smiled, taking great pleasure in using her feminine power to bring her lover to full arousal. After stretching out beside his thigh, she met his gaze as she captured his cock with her hand and gave it a long, slow stroke. He rolled his hips toward her, clearly asking for more. She gave it to him, this time using her tongue in a series of quick strokes.

He gripped handfuls of the sheets, his big body rigid with tension. "You're killing me here, Mel."

"Is this better?" she asked as she took him in her mouth. His hand came down to tangle in her hair in unspoken encouragement. She worked him slowly, managing to drive them both crazy in the process. The instant it was too much for Spence, he begged her to stop.

She froze. "You don't like what I was doing?"

"On the contrary, I like it too much."

She looked up to see if he meant that. There was such an amazing expression on his handsome face: a potent mix of pleasure, hunger, and something else she couldn't quite define. He caressed her face with his fingertips. "I just want to finish this together, and I'm thinking we should try out that big claw-foot tub while we're at it."

"Great idea. I'll go start the water."

As he followed her into the bathroom, neither of them wearing a stitch of clothing, it occurred to her that she'd never been so comfortable being naked with any other man. With Spence, she was blissfully unselfconscious. And other than his momentary concern about his scars, he seemed to feel the same way. She was glad, because she loved having the freedom to explore his body, learning what he liked and what he liked even more.

After turning on the water, she asked, "How do you feel about making it a bubble bath?"

Rogue that he was, he glanced down at his body with a wicked grin. "I'm up for it."

She laughed and tossed a towel at his head. "Don't blame me if the guys give you a bad time tomorrow for smelling like lavender."

"Not going to be a problem." He swept her up in his arms and gently lowered her into the frothy bubbles and then slid in behind her. "After how great tonight's been, I can't imagine anything could spoil my mood."

All things considered, she thought he might just be right about that.

*   *   *

Spence pushed his motorcycle across Melanie's backyard, waiting until he'd gone some distance before starting the engine to ride the rest of the way back to the
cottage. There was no use in making it obvious where
he'd spent the night. He felt bad about leaving Mooch
alone so long, which was the only reason he was sneaking across the yard long before the sun crested the
mountains to the east.

God knows he hadn't wanted to leave Mel's bed at all.
It had felt too good to have her incredible body cuddled
next to him, that fiery red hair spread out against his
skin. If he could have, he would have lingered there long
enough to count the scattering of freckles across her
shoulders. But for the sake of her reputation, as well as
for poor Mooch, he'd shaken her awake long enough to
tell her why he was leaving.

Temptress that she was, she'd responded by coaxing
him into an early-morning quickie. At this rate, he'd be
dead by the end of the week and for real this time. At least
it would be a far better way to go than what his captors
had had planned for him, which was the last thing he'd
ever expected to joke about. He was still chuckling when
he let himself into the cottage. Mooch bolted past him in
a rush to get outside. Poor fur ball. Spence would make it
up to him with scrambled eggs and bacon for breakfast.

He gathered up the ingredients and quickly made a
four-egg omelet for the two of them to share. As they ate,
he considered Melanie's financial problems. Maybe he
could do something about that. His parents had left him a
tidy nest egg. He'd barely touched it since taking full control of his inheritance. The house was paid for, and so was
his motorcycle. If Melanie needed money, he had it to
lend. Hell, he could give it to her outright and not miss it.

Thinking about her problems made him realize that he needed to confront his own. Even if he wasn't sure about what he wanted to do with his life, it wasn't fair of him to leave Callie, Nick, and even Leif living in limbo. It was too early for his attorney to be in the office, but to make sure he didn't chicken out, Spence left a message for him to call. Even that small step felt good. Once he knew where he stood on the legalities of everything, he'd contact Callie and Nick and have that long-overdue sit-down with them.

He hoped the attorney's office would be able to set up an appointment for him within the next couple of days. Now that he'd taken that first step, he wanted things to move along rapidly. Rather than pace the floors until he had to report to work, he went outside to tinker with his motorcycle's engine. Considering how long it had been since he'd ridden the Harley regularly, it could use a tune-up. He'd picked up everything he needed a few days ago and just hadn't had time to do the work.

Naturally, the minute he got his hands greasy his phone rang. After wiping his hands on a rag, he checked to see who was calling. Good, it was his attorney, Troy Nash. That was quick service.

"Hey, Troy! Thanks for calling me back." He glanced at his watch. "Especially so early. Isn't this before office hours?"

"Yeah, it is, but I have to be in court and came in to pick up some files. When I heard your message, I wanted to get right back to you. The truth is that I'd expected to hear from you long before now, Spence. Are you doing okay? Really?"

The man had always been a straight shooter. The concern in his voice was genuine, so Spence gave him an honest answer rather than the bullshit response he gave most people. "I won't deny seeing my own headstone was a total freak-out moment, but I'm doing okay. And, yeah, I should've gotten in touch with you as soon as I got back, but . . . well, I just wasn't up to dealing with anything complicated."

"And now?"

There was no easy answer. "I can't make any long-range plans until I get everything straightened out. Besides, there are other people who will be directly impacted by any decisions I make."

As usual, Troy didn't pull any punches. "Callie and Nick have called a couple of times."

"I figured as much. Sorry if I've put you in a tough position."

To his surprise, the other man just laughed. "That's why you pay me the big bucks. Is there anything you want me to tell them?"

"Not yet. I need to know my options and what kind of fucked-up tangled mess my lack of being dead has created for everybody."

He meant that last part to be a joke, but Troy didn't take it that way. For the first time, there was a thread of ice-cold anger in his voice. "Not funny, Spence. No one gives a rat's ass how tangled things are. Not me, not Callie, and for damn sure, not your two buddies. All that matters is that you came home. Got that?"

Well, shit. "Sorry, Troy. I really do know that. Sometimes my mouth goes out of control, but then that's always been a problem for me." He drew a slow breath. "What I should've said is that I can't fix things with Callie and Nick until I know what my options are."

After a brief silence, Troy said, "Apology accepted. So, what does your schedule look like?"

"After today, it's wide open. Pick a time that works for you, and I'll be there."

"How about nine o'clock tomorrow morning? We can start later, if you'd rather, but I want to make sure we have plenty of time to go through everything."

"I'll be there."

"Damn, it will be good to see you, Spence. I've missed you. After we get all this legal crap settled, we should hit the lodge for a steak dinner, my treat."

One of the reasons Spence had always liked Troy was his down-to-earth attitude about everything, even though he could play legal hardball with the best of them. "Sounds good, Troy. Now I should let you go and get ready for work. See you tomorrow."

After Troy hung up, Spence forced himself to make the next call on his list. It rang twice before Callie answered, "Spence?"

"Yeah, it's me." As if she didn't know that from the caller ID on her cell phone. "I wanted to let you know that I'm meeting with my attorney tomorrow morning. Not sure how that's going to play out, but I thought you'd want to know."

"I appreciate that." There was a brief silence before she spoke again. "You might not want to hear this, but I really miss you. I miss what we had. Do you think we'll get past all of this?"

He pinched the bridge of his nose, trying to ward off the pain that came with the truths he needed to share with her. "I hope so, Callie. I really do. I know now that what we shared is different than what you have with Nick. I guess I'd hoped that's what the two of us would have someday. I am trying my best to be happy for the two of you. He's a good soldier and a good man."

"He really is. He misses you, too, you know."

"Yeah, I do." Kind of, anyway.

Callie's voice perked up. "Do you want to talk to him? He's right here."

Hell no, but at least he had a better excuse than simply not wanting to talk to Sarge right now. "I can't, Callie. I'm on my way out. If I don't leave now, I'll be late for work."

He was relieved to finally disconnect the call. Obviously he'd been wrong about nothing dulling his good mood after last night. The thought of wading through piles of papers and making one hard decision after another made him queasy. At least having to drive the truck all day followed by another evening of getting greasy with Will would help distract him.

"Mooch, come on, buddy. It's time to leave for work."

At some point, he would text Melanie to check on her. He hoped she would have a better day than she'd had yesterday. They hadn't made any plans for tonight after he got off, but maybe he could coax her into sharing some more of her ice cream. Smiling at the prospect, he headed for the millworks, his good mood back in full swing.

It had been one of those days when there simply weren't enough hours to finish everything Melanie needed to get done. At least that meant the hours had flown by, something to be grateful for. It hadn't come as much of a surprise that Mrs. Cuthbert had called in sick for a second day. And who knows, maybe she really wasn't feeling well. Recent events had to have come as a shock to her.

Melanie was relieved not to have to face her when she was running on so little sleep. The emotional high from the night she and Spence had spent together had given her enough energy to carry her through the morning and well into the afternoon. Unfortunately, she'd finally hit the wall long before she could go home, at least not without carrying a big load of guilt with her.

There was one more decision to make before she could leave. She picked up the envelope emblazoned with the name of the local country club and studied it. Her family had been members from the day the place had opened its doors. Who knew how many rounds of golf her father had played there with his buddies? And her mother had headed up at least one of the major committees every year.

The Wolfes had also financially supported the winter charity ball and auction every year. She had a sinking feeling that's what the letter was about. Using her father's silver letter opener, she slit the top of the envelope and pulled out the thick piece of paper. After scanning the brief note, she dropped it on the desk before walking over to stare out the window. The contents didn't surprise her. It was only reasonable for them to ask the Wolfes for their usual annual donation.

Her mother would expect her to make the donation, even if the company couldn't afford it this year. Melanie was surprised by her own urge to reach for her checkbook—and it wasn't simply to delay the rumors that would be sure to fly around town about the fragile state of the family finances.

It had nothing to do with the family image. Instead, she considered how many people benefited from the charity ball. Her trust fund would take a hit, but it was all for a good cause.

Her decision made, she sat down and wrote out a

check, wincing at the number of zeros she had to write. This might be the last year the Wolfe family would participate, but she'd reach out to help her neighbors as long as she possibly could. It was the right thing to do, and she felt good when she signed the check and put it in the envelope to go out in the morning's mail.

The last of the machines in the factory below had gone silent half an hour ago, and the offices in the upper balcony had emptied out shortly afterward. Now she could leave in good conscience, turning off the lights before making her way downstairs.

As soon as she reached the main floor, a familiar bark rang out, accompanied by the scrabble of a dog trying to get traction on the slick concrete floor. Knowing what—or who—was coming, she set her laptop and purse down on a handy worktable and braced herself for some serious doggy love.

Sure enough, Mooch came charging straight toward her at a dead run, only pausing to detour around the clutter of machines, carts, and tools when he was too tall to go under them. From somewhere on the far side of the factory, she heard Spence mutter a curse and something about how good a doggy skin rug would look on the front porch.

Both she and the dog knew he was all bluff and bluster. She retreated to sit on the steps and waited for Mooch to join her. Two seconds later, he was sprawled on her lap and panting as if he'd run a mile. A couple of slurpy doggy kisses washed away the last bit of strain from her long afternoon. When Spence finally arrived on the scene, she and Mooch each offered him a grin.

She jingled Mooch's army-style dog tags. "I can't believe you threatened to skin a fellow veteran, Corporal Lang."

Spence stood there with his hands on his hips and glared at the unrepentant dog. "He disobeyed a direct order. I told him the only way he could come with me tonight was if he stayed right where I was working."

She patted the dog on his head. "You'd better get back where you belong, Mooch. Besides, I'd like a moment alone with your owner."

As soon as she shoved the dog off her lap, he trotted back across the factory. About halfway across, he stopped to bark, sounding for all the world as if he were telling Spence to get a move on.

"Sounds like you got your marching orders, too." She gathered up her things. "I'll get going and let you get back to what you were doing. The sooner you get done here, the sooner we can . . . well, I'm sure we'll think of something to do."

She was surprised the answering flare of heat in Spence's eyes didn't set off the overhead sprinkler system. "We'll be there as soon as we can."

As they walked back across the factory, he shoved his hands in his back pockets. She liked to think he was doing it because he was having a hard time keeping them off her. She was glad to have her own full with her laptop and purse for the same reason.

When they reached the door, he stared up at the evening sky. "I just met with my attorney this morning to get the ball rolling on straightening everything out. I also called Callie to let her know."

She knew those hadn't been easy calls for him to make. "Good for you, Spence. I'm sure you don't believe it now, but you'll feel better when you get it all figured out and know what to do. I could go with you next time if it would help."

He leaned down and pressed a quick kiss on her lips. "Thanks for the offer, but this is something I need to do on my own. See you soon."

Melanie watched as he disappeared back into the factory, wishing there was something more she could do to help him get through all of this. Her heart ached to see him struggling so hard to pull his life back together. She needed him to succeed not just for his sake, but for her own as well. Because if Spence could make sense of his new reality and get on with his life, well, maybe then she could do the same.

Chapter 17

❧ ❧

Two hours after arriving at the Reddings' house on Saturday night, Spence was on his second beer and his third helping of Mama R.'s rhubarb coffee cake. She'd really pulled out all the stops tonight and prepared way more dishes than four people could eat. All of his favorites were there, and she'd promised to send him home with a load of the leftovers. He'd barely made a dent in the last batch of food she'd brought him, but he wasn't about to complain.

While he'd figured Mama R. would make every effort to ensure that he and Melanie felt welcome, he hadn't been as sure about her husband. As it turned out, he hadn't needed to worry about it. Mr. Redding had kept up a low-key discussion about sports and the chances of his favorite teams to have a good season.

No, Spence's sudden tension had nothing at all to do with their host and hostess, but with his growing conviction that someone was watching his every move. He'd experienced the same burning itch on the back of his neck whenever the enemy had been lying in wait for them back in Afghanistan. He set his plate down and stepped away from the picnic table.

"Spence?"

He ignored Melanie's worried question and kept his eyes trained on the tree line, straining hard to see if he could pinpoint the enemy's location. There—just to the right of the path that led to his family home. Adrenaline pumped hard and fast through his veins, sending his senses into hyperdrive. When Melanie moved to stand beside him, he shoved her behind him. "Stay there. I promise I'll keep you safe. Whoever is out there will have to go through me to get to you."

Mr. Redding tried to intervene, his voice level and soft. "Easy, soldier. No one is out there, and no one is after Melanie. Just look around. You're not down-country anymore. You're right here in Snowberry Creek at our house."

When the older man put a restraining hand on Spence's shoulder, he shook it off. "I know where I am, sir, but there is someone out there. Watching and waiting."

And the closest thing he had to a weapon was a three-inch Swiss Army knife in his front pocket. One of the steak knives would've been better, but Melanie and Mama R. had already cleared the table of everything but the dessert dishes.

Mr. Redding stood his ground at Spence's side, but he clearly wasn't happy. "Melanie, why don't you go inside the house with my wife? I'll stay out here with Spence."

Neither woman moved an inch. Melanie spoke from behind him. "Spence, do you think it could be Leif or Nick out there? I know they weren't supposed to come over tonight, but I'm betting one of them couldn't resist the chance to check on you."

Even if her suggestion made sense, he was too caught up in the moment to back down. One way or another, he was going to confront the intruder. He started forward, heading right for the path with his hands clenched in fists. Mooch fell into step beside him, but the Reddings' dog and the three humans stayed right where they were. Good. No matter what happened, he didn't want them to get caught in the middle.

He knew long before he reached the edge of the yard Melanie had been right about who was lurking there in the shadows. Stopping just short of the trees, he called out one word. "Leif!"

As soon as the other man took a step toward him, Spence lunged forward to shove Leif up against a tree. "You son of a bitch! Are you trying to get yourself killed? What if I'd been carrying?"

At least the other man had the good sense not to come boiling right back at him. He held his hands up in surrender. "Sorry, Wheels. I was just out walking and spotted Mooch moving through the woods. I was worried he'd decided to come back here without you knowing he'd taken off."

Spence knew Leif well enough to know when he was telling the truth. "Once you knew he was with me, why didn't you retreat?"

"Because I wanted to know what was going on. Callie's parents said they were having friends over tonight, but they never said it was you and Melanie. What's up with that?"

If he'd come across as mad instead of hurt, Spence might not have had the strength to tamp his temper back under control. He shoved his fists into his pockets before answering. "Mama R. came to see me last week. She wanted me to come see the two of them and told me to bring Melanie if I needed reinforcements."

Leif stared past him to where she stood with Callie's parents. "If you needed a wingman, you could have called me. We've always had each other's back, or have you forgotten that?"

"No, I haven't forgotten a fucking thing."

Which was true, but things had changed and the fit felt all wrong somehow. Spence rocked back on his heels. "Look, like I promised Callie, I met with Troy Nash, my attorney. We've started wading through everything, and he'll let me know when he's heard back on a few things what my options are and what needs to be done. The bottom line is that I don't have any answers yet, but I am working on it. Can you let Nick and Callie know that progress is being made for me?"

Leif crossed his arms over his chest and gave Spence a hard look. "It would be better if you told them yourself, but I'll play messenger for you."

The big lump in Spence's throat made it hard to talk, but he forced the words out. "I owe you one."

Now Leif looked totally disgusted. "You don't owe me a damn thing. This is what friends do for friends."

What could he say to that? When he couldn't think of anything, Spence started to walk away but turned back after only a few steps. "How are you doing? Melanie tells me you've been seeing someone."

Even in the deep shadows it was impossible to miss Leif's smile, which eased the lines that pain had carved deep into his face. "Yeah, I am. Zoe is a former army nurse who served in Iraq. We met when she oversaw my therapy when I first got here. We've both been through some pretty rough stuff, but we're dealing with it."

So maybe there was hope for Spence, too. "I'm glad for you."

Something ran through the bushes behind them, causing both men to jump. Leif cut loose with a long string of curse words. He'd always had a real talent for that to the point where more than one time it had given rise to applause from his fellow soldiers. For some reason, that small memory eased the knot of tension that had Spence all tangled up inside. It was a little taste of normal and how things used to be between them—and it suddenly struck him that he had been looking for a sense of normalcy ever since he returned to Snowberry Creek.

"We'd better get out of these woods before something jumps out and gets us."

Leif laughed. "Yeah, some of the squirrels around here can be pretty vicious. Just ask Mooch."

Evidently, Leif's leg injury didn't prevent him for moving fast if he wanted to badly enough. Before Spence realized what Leif was up to, the man had him wrapped in a hard hug. It lasted less than a second, maybe two, in real time. But in Spence's head, it dragged on for an eternity. His lungs refused to work again until after he'd put several feet between them.

Leif held up his hands to show he was done with the sneak attacks. "Sorry, Wheels, but it had to be done. Maybe next time it won't be so hard for you. Try to fix whatever's out of sync in your head. I miss you."

He disappeared into the trees while Spence stood there, trying to draw a full breath. Melanie joined him in the shadows, her scent and touch giving him something solid to hold on to. She simply stood with him, letting him have all the time he needed to paste the broken pieces inside him back together.

When he no longer felt as if he'd shatter, Spence wrapped his arm around her shoulders. "Think we should be heading home?"

She nodded. "Mrs. R. has your goodies all bundled up and ready to go. All we need to do is say good-bye."

With Melanie as his anchor, they bid their farewells to their hosts. Mama R. hugged each of them. "Don't be strangers, either of you."

While she held Spence close, she whispered, "I'd love to have another barbecue where I could ask Callie, Nick, Leif, and Zoe to join us. No rush, Spence. Just let me know when you're ready."

God knows when that would be, so all he could do was nod to show that the message was received and understood. "Thanks for always being there for me."

Her eyes sparkled a little too brightly in the dim light. Aw, damn, he'd made her cry again, but she was still smiling. "You're family and we love you, Spence."

He hugged her again before getting into Melanie's car with Mooch. He hoped that the small gesture conveyed everything he had no words for.

Chapter 18

※ ※

Three days later, Spence sat flipping through the pages of an outdated sports magazine without really seeing any of the words. Was there some special service that provided doctors, dentists, and lawyers with old magazines? Because if they actually had subscriptions, wouldn't the newer editions be mixed in with the rest? Maybe there were more important things to worry about, but right now he appreciated the distraction.

He tossed the magazine aside when he heard the click of a door opening down the hall. Sure enough, footsteps were headed his way. When Troy appeared at the entrance to the waiting room, Spence stood up.

The attorney headed straight for him with a welcoming smile on his face. "Thanks for coming in on such short notice, but I knew you wanted to start getting this stuff resolved as soon as possible."

They shook hands. "Not a problem, Troy. It's not like I have a lot going on right now."

Okay, that must have come across more pathetic than

he'd meant for it to, because his friend's smile faltered. "Is everything okay, Spence? Anything I can do?"

"Just helping me wade through all this stuff is help enough. It's hard to make any kind of plans until I know how it will all play out."

That was close enough to the truth to satisfy the other man, at least for now. The real problem was that Spence had only one—maybe two—more nights of helping Will with the machinery at the millworks. After that, he had no further commitments, and therefore nothing to occupy his time. Without things to keep him busy, he'd be all alone with his memories. Already his nightmares were getting worse to the point that he was afraid to fall asleep when he was with Melanie for fear of what he might do.

It would be bad enough if he woke up screaming, but what if his screwed-up head told him she was the enemy?

Troy was no fool. If he picked up on how close to the edge Spence was running right now, he might just feel obligated to intervene somehow. The last thing Spence wanted to do was put his friend in that position. He braced himself to get through the next hour by doing his best to act normal. After that, maybe he'd take Mooch for a long run to burn off the tension.

Inside Troy's private office, he dropped into the chair that faced the two windows that formed the corner of the room. They faced the snowcapped Cascades to the east, which contrasted sharply with the barren mountains in Afghanistan where he'd spent much of the last two years. The panoramic view served as a reminder that he was home and safe, helping him to ignore stark memories of what life had been like over there.

Troy set a thick file on his desk. He pulled out two copies of a document and passed one across to Spence. "I've prepared a list for you of what needs to be done and in what order. Your decision on some items will obviously impact others, especially that top one. I'll give you a few minutes to look it over while I go get us each a cup of coffee."

Spence glanced up from the paper. "I'll take mine black."

The lawyer disappeared out the door. Good thing, too, because right now Spence couldn't make sense of anything that was written on the page. There was nothing wrong with his eyes; his mind just refused to process the information. He lifted his gaze to stare out the window again and reminded himself how much better he'd feel once he got through with all of this stuff. Once he did, he'd be free to live his life anywhere he chose.

He couldn't wait.

This time when he looked at the paper, the words shifted into stark clarity. The first line was brutal in its simplicity. *Do you want your house back?*

His whole world narrowed down to that one sentence. How the hell was he supposed to figure out the answer to that? Any memories he'd ever had of being happy there living with his folks had dimmed over the years. Far stronger were the hellish ones of existing within those same walls with his uncle and cousin. After he'd kicked their asses to the curb, rattling around in the place by himself hadn't been any fun, either. It wasn't until he enlisted in the army that his life had gained any real sense of meaning. Now even that was gone.

Without realizing what he was doing, he'd shredded the paper into pieces. Son of a bitch! He couldn't do this.

Not now. He wadded the pieces into a ball and tossed it in the trash on his way out the door. Troy was just coming down the hall.

"Spence? What's wrong? Did something happen?"

"No."

Okay, that was a lie. He tried again. "I can't answer any of the questions until I figure out the first one. I'm sorry for wasting your time, Troy. I'll call you as soon as I can come to some sort of decision."

He kept walking as he spoke, hoping to reach the door before Troy could stop him. No such luck. The other man did an end run to plant himself right in front of Spence. "Okay, I get why that one is a problem for you, Spence, but it's not going to go away on its own. I would also point out that your friends can't move forward until you do."

Spence snapped, "Screw that, Troy. Don't play the guilt card with me."

To give Troy credit, he didn't retreat an inch. "Okay, but I'll tell you this much. I cannot imagine the hell you've been through, but I do realize it's why you're having a hard time right now. I'm not pressing for immediate answers, and I'm here for you no matter what. Believe that even if you don't believe anything else. Having said that, you need to go out there and do a walk-through of the place. Figure out what it means to you, if anything. Even if you don't want the house itself, there might be a few things inside that you'll want to keep."

Troy stared at Spence until he gave in and made eye contact before speaking again. "If you want to do that, I can make sure no one is home when you go out there. Right now it's hanging over your head like a huge boulder ready to drop at any second. That won't change until you take control of the situation."

Okay, Spence got that Troy was trying his best to help. He might even be right. He slowly nodded. "I'll think about it and let you know."

The other man looked a bit happier. "Do that. I'll be waiting to hear from you."

Outside, Spence climbed on the Harley and started the engine. He wasn't sure where he was heading, but right now he needed the wind in his face and the sense of freedom the bike gave him. It took some effort, but he honored the speed limit as long as he was in town. But once he cleared the outskirts of Snowberry Creek, he ripped down the two-lane highway, hoping like heck that he wouldn't run into Gage Logan or any of his deputies.

After an hour of rolling down the highway, he reluctantly took a long, winding route back toward town. He'd enjoyed the ride, but it was impossible to outrun the demons that lived in his head. When he passed Liam's place, on impulse he hung a U-turn and drove back to the bar. Maybe beer could accomplish what the drive hadn't.

Inside, the bar was deserted. That was disappointing. He'd been hoping there would be enough people around to provide a welcome distraction.

Liam appeared just as Spence parked his ass on one of the stools at the bar. He immediately reached for a pair of beers and popped the tops. After sliding one across the bar to Spence, he took a long drink from his own.

"Thanks, man, but how did you know this is even what I wanted?"

A quick smile crossed Liam's face. "Didn't much care what you wanted. You looked like you needed it."

Spence laughed and raised the bottle in a mock toast. "Here's to perceptive bartenders everywhere."

Liam joined in and clinked his bottle against Spence's.

"Considering it's not even ten thirty, I'm guessing you've had a rough morning."

"It hasn't been my best—that's for sure." He frowned and shook his head. "A friend is trying to help me deal with some shit, and I acted like a jerk."

"If he's a friend, he'll get over it."

Spence hoped so. "Yeah, but I swear the list of people I should apologize to never gets any shorter."

"Common problem, my friend. If it wasn't, I wouldn't sell half the beer that I do." Liam picked up a rag and wiped down the already clean counter. "Are you any good at pool?"

Spence took another swig of his beer, trying to follow the sudden change in topics. "I've won my share of games. Why?"

"Because I'm in the mood to play a few rounds, but I don't have the patience to play with someone who doesn't know one end of a pool cue from the other." He tossed the rag back in the sink. "Are you good enough to make it worth my while?"

Spence reached for his wallet and pulled out a twenty and slid it across the counter. "That says I can beat you two out of three."

Liam picked up the bill and stuffed it in his shirt pocket. He added a second one from the cash drawer. "You're on."

As they made their way to the table, Liam's smile reminded Spence of a shark that had been hunting for some prey and just spotted a sure thing. Well, they'd see about that. Besides, if he did lose, twenty bucks wasn't much to pay for an attitude adjustment. Afterward, he'd call Troy and apologize for walking out on their appointment.

And if he won, he might just ask him to set up a day and time for him to visit the old homestead. Troy was right. Spence needed to figure out if there was anything left that could anchor him right here in Snowberry Creek. If not, he needed to clear the board, settle his debts, and hit the road.

He nodded at his opponent, who was busy chalking the tip of his cue stick. "It's your table. Why don't you break?"

Liam didn't say a word. He just leaned over the table and sent the balls flying with a sharp flick of his cue. That shark smile was firmly back in place as he lined up his next shot and went to work.

"Green in the corner pocket."

"I'm sorry, Ms. Wolfe. I wish I had a more encouraging answer for you. You have to believe that I argued long and hard that the bank should help you restructure the company's finances. I've also asked them to take another look at the new figures you sent and reminded them that the Wolfe Millworks was an important part of the economy here in Snowberry Creek."

Melanie struggled to keep a pleasant expression on her face, but she was losing the battle. She stood to lose more than that if she couldn't figure out how to convince the bank to reconsider its decision. "So, Mr. Lunt, tell me what I can do to help you convince them."

His gaze slid away from hers. Either he was lying about his efforts to change their minds or he knew an unpleasant truth behind their decision that he was reluctant to share with her. She had her suspicions what that might be. Mr. Lunt had been nice to her and helpful right up until this meeting, so she hated to put him on the spot.

However, unpleasant or not as they might be, she needed all the facts if she was going to make any headway toward saving the company.

It was time to show him she could play hardball. "I've provided you with every scrap of information you've asked for, good and bad, so I feel as if I've been completely honest with you. I would ask you to offer me the same courtesy, Mr. Lunt. What is the real reason the bank is hesitating to approve my application?"

He immediately reached for the glass of water and took a long swallow. After setting it back down, he picked up a pen and started doodling on the scratch pad beside his desk phone. "Okay, if you want complete honesty, here it is. If this were your father asking for the loan, he probably would have gotten it."

She sat up straighter in her chair and leaned forward. "So I'm being turned down because I'm a woman? I'd be very careful with how you answer that, Mr. Lunt."

To give the man credit, he looked genuinely horrified by her question. "No, not at all, Ms. Wolfe. Gender has nothing to do with it, but years of experience does. I am impressed by what you've accomplished so far, and your plan of action is solid. That's exactly what I told the committee. However, we owe it to our stockholders to be cautious with the bank's assets. It would make sense to work with your father to modernize the company because he had decades of experience in the industry. A year from now, when you've had a chance to prove yourself, I feel certain that we'd be leaping at the chance to work with you."

Yeah, but a year from now, there might not be a Wolfe Millworks. She kept that fact to herself. Rather than continue to pound her head against a closed door, Melanie rose to her feet and held her hand out to the banker. "Thank you for your time. Please let me know if you hear anything positive from the committee."

Feeling proud of her cool, professional demeanor, she smiled at him and walked away. It wasn't until she was inside her car and driving away that she gave in to the frustration that had been building from the minute she walked into the bank.

Pounding her fist on the steering wheel, she shouted, "Damn, damn, double damn!"

Glancing around, she was relieved to see that the street was deserted. The last thing she wanted was for rumors to start making the rounds that she was losing it. It was late enough that she could call it a day, but she wasn't ready to face going home yet. Maybe her attitude had more to do with the fact that Spence would be at the factory. She wouldn't interrupt his work with Mr. Cosgrove, but just knowing he was nearby might help her get through the next few hours.

Sure enough, his Harley was parked in its usual spot. Relieved, she retrieved her briefcase from the backseat and let herself in the back door of the factory. Several of the men were standing just inside, Spence among them. Their expressions were grim. That they fell silent when she walked in meant they were talking about her.

She smiled and nodded as she passed them and started upstairs. At the top, she hesitated before turning in the direction of her office and glanced back down to see what the group was doing now. In that short time, they'd scattered like cockroaches when a light came on. The only one left standing there was Spence. He offered her a sympathetic look and mouthed the word "later" before disappearing toward the front of the factory.

She let herself into her office and sat down in the oversized executive chair her father had preferred. For a moment, she flashed back to when she was a little girl and would play at his desk whenever she and her mom dropped by to visit her father at work. Back then, sitting there had been an adventure. Now it was a burden. And yet feeling sorry for herself wouldn't help anyone. Far better to prove Mr. Lunt's committee and everyone else who doubted her wrong. With that in mind, she started making a list of banks she could try next.

Spence forced his attention back to the pile of machine parts spread out on the counter. He'd been worried about Melanie ever since she accidentally walked in on her employees' bitch session a couple of hours ago. From the uneasy silence that had fallen over the group, she had to have realized she'd been the topic of conversation. Spence had gotten there right before she came in, but there was no way for her to know he hadn't really been part of the conversation. He'd only stopped in the hope he could figure out some way to convince them to give her a chance.

Mel wasn't stupid. She had to guess there was growing unrest among the workers. It made him angry on her behalf, but there wasn't anything he could do to fix the situation. For one thing, he was only a temporary employee, and everyone knew it. He didn't have the same stake in the game that they all did. Even so, they should give the woman a chance to prove herself. After all, no one had been let go other than the secretary, and technically she'd retired.

Melanie hadn't said a single negative word about the woman, which was probably a good idea. However, it pissed Spence off to know that Mrs. Cuthbert's mistake might have cost Melanie the one chance to save the company. Certainly, her actions had resulted in a lot more work for Mel. It was tempting to let the other workers know the truth of the situation, but Melanie had shared the information in private. He wouldn't betray her trust, especially since he seemed to be the only person she could vent her frustrations with.

Will slammed a big wrench down on the counter and laughed when Spence jumped about a foot. He turned to growl at his friend. "Damn it, Will, don't sneak up on a man like that, especially one who's just back from fighting in a war. I could have decked you or worse."

The old man didn't seem the least bit worried about the possible danger. He shouldered Spence out of the way to study the array of parts in front of him. After muttering something under his breath, he picked up two pieces and began fitting them together. "Boy, I don't know where your head is tonight, but it's definitely not on what you're doing. It shouldn't take more than half an hour to reassemble this mess."

Spence didn't much like hearing that, but the old man wasn't wrong. Rather than lash out, he picked up the next gear and handed it to Will. "Sorry. Guess it's a good thing this is our last night together."

Will paused to spit into his soup can. "Nothing good about it, Spence. Can't remember the last time I've actually looked forward to coming to work."

He took a long, slow look around their surroundings. "Near as I could tell, old man Wolfe didn't give a damn about the nuts and bolts of running this place. He and that wife of his spent all kinds of money on fancy clothes to wear to that country club while this place was slowly falling down around our ears."

Will pointed up toward the office that now belonged to Melanie. "Some folks aren't happy about his daughter taking over. They figure she'll be just like him and milk the company of every last penny and then close the doors."

This time it was Spence who picked up a hammer and took his frustration out on the defenseless table. "Melanie isn't like him at all, Will. She could have taken the easy way out and either sold the company or shut it down. Instead, she works here all day and then spends her evenings and weekends trying to make ends meet. She's damn near killing herself trying to save this place."

Will gave him a suspicious look. "And how would you know so much about how the boss lady spends her time, boy?"

Well, shit, he'd obviously revealed more than he meant to. Spence tried to forestall any more questions by saying, "I've got eyes, Will. She's here long after everyone else leaves, and she's one of the first ones through the door in the morning."

Will went back to work reassembling the pieces, but there was an odd glint in his eyes that said he wasn't totally buying Spence's explanation. At least he didn't call him on it.

When they had the motor put back together, Spence carried it back over to the lathe to reinstall it. Between the two of them, they got it bolted back in place in just a few minutes. After plugging the machine back in, Will flipped the switch and listened to it run. "Purring like a kitten. It's a damn shame that people aren't as easy to fix."

Where was Will going with this? Had he somehow sensed how shattered Spence was on the inside? The worst of the physical scars he'd brought home from the war were covered by his clothes. Outside of the medics who'd treated his injuries, few people had even seen them. He had to work far harder to hide all the cracks and crevices inside his heart and his head. The only time he felt close to whole was when he was in Melanie's arms.

Meanwhile, Will had kept right on talking. "... especially when they're scared. Folks here at the factory are nervous about the change at the top and how it will affect those at the bottom. Anyone with half a brain can see that lady is working hard to learn the job in a matter of months, one her father had decades to learn, but that's why they are scared."

He spit in his can again. "Me, I've seen too much in my life to be afraid of a little change. Shaking things up now and again can be good for the soul."

He paused to look over at Spence. "I'm thinking you have the opposite problem. The stuff you've seen and done, not to mention what was done to you, has left you raw and hurting from the inside out. If you and the boss lady are finding some comfort in each other's company, I say good for you both."

Spence glanced upward to where he knew Melanie was still working. "She deserves better."

Will's kindly expression turned to anger. "Better than what, boy? Better than a man who believed his country was worth dying for? Who sacrificed everything he had for that belief? If that's the kind of woman she is, why would you want her anyway?"

"She's not, but I'm—"

"Stop right there. Nobody bad-mouths you to me, boy, not even you." To his surprise, his old friend shook his big-knuckled fist right at Spence's nose. "Especially not you."

An instant later, Will backed away. "Sorry. I didn't mean for the night to end with hard feelings. I've enjoyed working with you again, Spence. I think you should talk to Ms. Wolfe about taking over for me so I can finally retire."

Spence was well aware of the compliment Will had just paid him. "Maybe I will. After I get a few things figured out and decide if I'm going to stay in Snowberry Creek, I'll give some thought to that idea."

Will bristled again. "What the hell is there to figure out? Snowberry Creek is your home. You've got friends here. Family, too, for that matter. Where else would you go?"

Will walked away, shaking his head as if he thought he'd been talking to an idiot. Spence found himself grinning. All things considered, maybe he had been.

Chapter 19

❧ ❧

"Are you sure you want to go alone?"

While waiting for him to answer, Melanie topped off her coffee and then Spence's. He hadn't said more than a handful of words all morning. It didn't take a genius to figure out that he was having some issues with this planned trip to his family home. When he didn't answer, she tried again.

"Spence?"

He frowned and looked up from staring at the empty plate sitting in front of him. "Sorry. Did you say something?"

She bit back her exasperation. "I asked if you were sure that you wanted to go alone."

He didn't hesitate. "I'm sure. You've already got enough going on without having to deal with my problems, too. It's enough that you're going to let Mooch out if I'm not back by early afternoon."

Okay, maybe he did think he was doing her a favor by not asking her to go, but it felt more like he was shutting her out. Had he drawn some line in his head that marked off the boundaries of their relationship? If so, he hadn't shared it with her. She'd make one more try and then give up.

"You've been there for me, Spence. How many times have you let me rant and rave over what's going on in my life? Seems only fair that I do the same for you."

He shoved back from the table and picked up his dishes. "Troy offered to go with me, too, but this is something I need to do by myself. Speaking of which, I'd better head out if I'm going to have time to get through the whole house."

Her heart hurt to hear the pain echoing in his words when she couldn't do anything to ease it. Who knows, maybe he was right that he had to face this particular hurdle on his own. After all, a lot of his past was tied up in that house. Now that she thought about it, she had the same kinds of issues with her family home. Wolfe House was her heritage as well as her burden. There were times she hated everything about it from the roof all the way down to the foundation.

She hurried to catch up with Spence before he reached the front door. "I'll be here when you get back, but I realize that you might need time alone to process everything. Just text me to let me know that you're all right."

"I will." He stopped long enough to give her a quick kiss. "And I'm probably blowing this all out of proportion."

But he wasn't, and they both knew it. His decision to visit his family house, to actually go through it for the first time since he came back, was a huge step. She could only pray it was a move in the right direction for him, something that would help him heal the wounds that were gradually tearing him apart inside. Instead of settling into his new life, he was growing more restless by the day. She wasn't sure when he actually slept or if he did at all. He spent way too many hours prowling outside in the yard between her house and the cottage with Mooch tagging along at his heels. And often in the middle of the night he'd leave her bed without a word. A few minutes later she'd hear the distant rumble of his Harley, and she'd lie awake listening for his return, needing to know he was safe. She hated all of it for his sake. Hers, too.

"What is it you said your counselor told you? One small step at a time? That's all this is, Spence. If it gets to be too much, leave and try again on another day. Eventually, it has to get easier."

Spence tightened his arms around her and rested his chin on top of her head. "That might be true, but I can't keep asking Callie and the others to disappear for hours at a time."

Why not? The bottom line was that she wanted Spence to be happy, no matter what it took or who it inconvenienced, because maybe that meant there was hope for her, too.

She broke off the hug and took a step back. "I'm going to the store this morning. Want to grill some steaks tonight?"

He turned so that he was no longer looking directly at her. "Better not count on me for dinner, Mel. I'm not sure where I'll be this evening."

With that chilling statement, he walked away.

Spence made it all the way to the curb without turning around. At the last minute, he gave in and braced himself to apologize to Melanie for shutting her out, but the porch was empty and the front door firmly closed. Rather than hike his ass all the way back into the house, he pulled out his cell phone and sent her a quick text. It wasn't a full-out apology, but it was a start.

He got in the car and turned the key. Melanie had insisted on him taking the station wagon rather than his motorcycle, the thought being he might want to bring a few things back to the cottage from the house. He figured the chances of that happening to be somewhere in the vicinity of a cold day in hell, but he could be wrong. Besides, it seemed to have been important to Melanie that she do something to help him out.

Before the car had rolled forward more than a few feet, he cursed and slammed on the brakes. How the hell had Mooch gotten out? The stubborn mutt planted his furry butt right in front of the car as if daring Spence to leave without him. Rather than waste time, Spence twisted around to open the rear passenger door. Mooch trotted around to hop in and then jumped over the back of the seat to land beside Spence, giving him a reproachful look as he settled in for the ride.

"Damn it, dog, this isn't some fun-filled outing we're going on."

That was true, but it didn't keep Spence from reaching over to scratch his buddy's back. "You can come, but don't complain if you get bored."

He put the car back into park and pulled out his cell phone to text Melanie a second time. Not sure how he managed it, but Mooch escaped and is insisting on going with me. No use in arguing with him when he gets like this. :-)

She answered immediately. Glad you'll have him with you. Let me know how it goes.

Will do. I promise.

After the brief exchange, the drive to his house was blessedly short. It was a relief to find the driveway empty and the place looking deserted. Troy had asked everyone living there to be gone for the day. That didn't mean that one of the current residents might not have taken exception to the temporary eviction notice and stuck around anyway. Hell, it had taken calling the cops the last time he'd wanted squatters thrown out of his house. Granted, Nick, Callie, and Leif weren't anything like his uncle Vince. He wasn't so sure about his cousin, Austin.

Either way, Spence planned to be in and out by mid-afternoon to further ensure that their paths didn't cross, which gave him about five hours to accomplish his mission and then retreat to safe ground. Funny to think about visiting his own home in military terms, but damned if they didn't fit. The gut-churning and hyperawareness of his surroundings as he got out of the car were all too familiar. He'd experienced the same exact feelings every time he prepared to go out on patrol, including the dry mouth that tasted of fear, the slight tremor in hands he hoped none of his buddies would notice, and the quiet prayers he murmured under this breath. Not knowing what the next few hours would hold for him made it all come rushing back. How many times had he, Nick, and Leif driven out of camp not knowing if any of them would be returning? Hell, look how that last mission had turned out, leaving all of their lives in shreds.

This couldn't be that bad. No one would die. No one would almost lose a limb. It wasn't that kind of mission. He was there to reconnoiter, study the lay of the land,

and then assess what his next objective should be. Piece of cake. No problemo.

Yeah, right.

There was no getting around the fact that this visit was going to be a flat-out bitch. He hated that his hands were shaky and his palms sweaty.

Shit, get it under control. You've been through worse.

Telling himself that Mooch needed a few minutes to make his rounds, Spence leaned against the front fender of the car and studied the changes in the exterior of the house. Nick and Callie had definitely left their mark on the place, including a few splashes of different colors of paint on the side of the house. Maybe Callie was trying to decide what color she wanted to paint the place. He'd vote for the blue. For sure, the new door he'd delivered looked good. Welcoming, even.

His pulse pounded in his head until he couldn't hear anything else. Maybe he'd start with a quick walk around the property. After all, there was nothing threatening about bushes that had been trimmed and grass that had been mowed. He noticed his mother's roses were staging a comeback. Good.

Having made note of the highlights of the front yard, he wandered around to the back of the house and saw more of the same. Another new door. Neat flower beds. A couple of lawn chairs he didn't recognize.

But what the hell was that thing sitting in the far back corner of the yard? His gut reaction was that the lacy white structure was something Nick had done for Callie. Chances were he'd even built the damn thing. If so, he hoped Leif had given Sarge some serious shit about it. He studied the octagonal structure. The right word didn't come to him immediately, but a few others came to mind: god-awful, sissified, silly, and completely unnecessary.

Mooch finally caught up with him. "Dog, why did you let them park that monstrosity there?"

The dog woofed softly, his tongue hanging out in a doggy smirk. He headed straight for the . . . gazebo. Yeah, that's what it was called. If Mooch could stand it, he could manage a quick peek inside. After that, he'd head on into the house and get started. Mooch's inspection of the gazebo lasted less than ten seconds, and then he was off to chase the squirrels back up the tree, leaving Spence to check it out for himself.

Okay, he could see why Callie would like it. The benches looked comfortable, making it the kind of place where she could curl up with a book. Definitely not his kind of place, though. He was about to walk away when he spotted something written on the back wall. It was too neatly done to be graffiti, but it seemed odd to think Nick would actually sign his work.

Spence took another step toward the small sign and then another one. Even from that distance he recognized Nick's scrawl of a signature. Leif's, too. What the hell? As soon as he got close enough to read the entire thing, he wished he hadn't. The words punched him right in the gut, knocking the breath out of him in a painful rush. He staggered backward to collapse on the bench behind him. They'd dedicated this . . . this damn frilly thing to him? What in the world had they been thinking? He'd rather have had them designate one of the barstools at Liam's place as the official Spencer Lang Memorial.

He stared at the words, still trying to make sense of the reasoning behind them. Nick and Leif had been his best friends. Brothers, really, a family forged in the fucked-up hell America's warriors faced day after day. But brothers or not, the bastards had come home without him. Started new lives without him. He'd been so sure they'd forgotten him, taking all their memories of him and burying them under that glossy granite stone in the cemetery.

Yet here he sat with those words staring down at him: *In celebration and remembrance of the life of Corporal Spencer Lang. Wheelman, we miss you. Sergeant Nick Jenkins, Corporal Leif Brevik, Callie Redding.*

Okay, so maybe moving on without him hadn't been easy for them. And what kind of selfish bastard was he to like the idea that they were torn up over the thought of him dying? He might not be happy with Nick and Leif, but right now he wasn't liking himself much, either. His eyes burned as he pounded his fists on the bench as hard as he could, the thick padding the only reason he wasn't doing serious damage to his hands.

He bit back the urge to howl as the shattered pieces of his life shifted yet again. The broken bits were mere fragments of memories: riding in the M-ATV with Nick and Leif; the vehicle flying through the air; waking up in pain and in chains; the long days spent in fear and darkness, knowing he'd driven over the bomb that had gotten his friends killed. How many times had he prayed for their forgiveness and then prayed for death?

Other images had been tossed into the mix now. Callie marrying Nick. Leif walking with a cane. Mooch chasing squirrels instead of dodging bullets. And Melanie with her gentle touch, bright red hair, and clear gray eyes that saw too much.

How the hell was he ever going to fit the pieces back together again? And what did he want the final picture to look like?

Finally, exhausted by the emotional turmoil, he leaned back against the wall behind him and closed his eyes. This was getting him nowhere. It was past time to get off his ass and move on, just as his friends had done, which meant going through the house. He forced himself to read the words one more time in the hope their meaning would give him the strength to walk out of the gazebo and head right into the house. Like the man said, one step at a time. Opening the front door, crossing that threshold, and finally realizing this would never be home again was one hell of a step.

Leif eased his truck into a spot at the far end of the parking lot, trying not to kick up any rocks that could chip the paint on his truck. Nick was busying looking around, probably trying to spot Spence's motorcycle. No dice.

"His bike's not here."

Yeah, as if Leif couldn't see that for himself. "He said he'd be here."

Nick laid his head back against the headrest and closed his eyes. "I don't get it. The attorney went to great lengths to make it clear that Spence didn't want us anywhere around him today while he went through the house. That we weren't welcome."

He held up his wrist so that Leif could see the time. "We were supposed to stay gone for another two hours, but then out of nowhere a text message asking us to meet him here. No explanations, not to mention that it had to be just us, not Callie. If she'd heard from Spence again, she would've said something.

"He'd better not be screwing with us." Nick slashed his hand across his throat. "I've had it up to here with this shit."

Leif wasn't much happier about the situation, but he wasn't ready to write Wheelman off completely. Maybe it was easier for him to be patient because for Callie and Nick, the old Victorian she'd inherited from Spence had been the foundation for all of their future plans. Now they were floundering.

"Let's go check in the bar for him. If he hasn't arrived yet, we'll knock back a couple of beers and maybe shoot some pool. Even if he doesn't show, the day won't have been a total loss."

Without waiting to see if Nick would follow, Leif got out of the truck and headed into the bar. Stepping inside, he waited by the door long enough for his eyes to adjust to the dim interior. At first he thought Nick was right about Spence blowing them off, but then he spotted Wheels sitting at a booth in the far back corner with three beers in front of him. Not only that, but Liam, the owner, was carrying three burger baskets in that direction.

Leif was about to head back out to the parking lot to haul Nick's slow ass into the bar when the door opened, saving him the trouble. Pitching his voice low, he said, "He's back there. Looks like he's either ordered us beers and burgers, or he's especially hungry."

Nick didn't look any happier than he did when he thought Spence had blown them off. "This just gets weirder and weirder."

"Yeah, well, we've been through weird stuff before and survived. Let's give the man a chance."

When Nick started to question him, Leif cut him off. "Let's not forget that Wheels has been through some seriously bad shit, Nick. There's no telling what happened to him over there. He might look okay, but we both know that he's got to be seriously screwed up inside. Hell, look how long it took the two of us to get back to anything even remotely close to normal, and we weren't guests of the insurgents for months on end."

Nick finally relaxed his shoulders. "It doesn't help that Wheels was wired wrong to begin with."

Leif laughed and for the first time thought maybe there was a chance that the three of them would get through this without bloodshed. On the other hand, maybe a barroom brawl would finally clear the air. Anything was better than the constant strain of living in the middle of no-man's-land.

He took that first step toward where Spence sat waiting for them. "I don't know about you, but I'd rather eat my burger while it's still hot."

Nick caught up with him. "Hope he remembered that I like mine with mayo and mustard."

"Yeah, I know, and don't forget the extra pickles. I'm betting he remembered."

Leif hoped so, because that would mean the Spence they'd both known and loved like a brother was still inside the grimly silent man waiting for them in the back of the bar.

Chapter 20

🌿🌿

Spence wanted to say he'd known that Nick and Leif would actually show up, but he tried not to lie to himself. And, boy, wouldn't he have felt foolish sitting there with three beers and three burgers with all the fixings and no one to share them with? The only question was why they were hovering over near the doorway.

Leif met his gaze from across the room and slowly nodded. Message received and understood. Evidently, Nick was having a hard time with this. No surprise there. Spence would give him a few more seconds and then go haul his ass over to the booth by whatever means necessary. He was already bracing himself for a fight when Nick abruptly led the charge across the bar.

He stopped short of the booth and stared at the burgers and fries. "I assume you ordered mine with mayo, mustard, and extra pickles."

Spence gave him one of his patented smirks, one guaranteed to set Nick's teeth on edge, or at least it always had. "Assume whatever you want to, Sarge."

He tugged the basket that held Nick's burger closer to himself. "If you're not hungry, I am."

Nick muttered a curse and slid into the opposite side of the booth and yanked the basket out of Spence's grip. Leif took a seat on Nick's side of the booth. No surprise there.

All three men concentrated on devouring their burgers and Liam's generous servings of sweet potato fries. The meal wouldn't last long as a diversion. Maybe all three of them were hungry, but Spence figured none of them was in a big hurry to get the real party started. He reluctantly dipped his last fry in the ketchup and popped it into his mouth. Leif cleaned out his basket a few seconds later with Nick finishing up right behind him.

Leif stacked the empty plastic baskets and tossed them on the table behind them, clearing the space between them of everything except their beers. Those wouldn't last long, either, so Spence caught Liam's eye and held up three fingers.

Nick launched the opening salvo. "You texted. We came. What's up?"

Spence's former sergeant usually yelled; he didn't growl. Maybe he was having to force the words out around a fist-sized lump in his throat, too. Rather than get straight to the heart of the matter, Spence lobbed his next comment directly at Nick, knowing he'd get a rise out of him.

"So, was it your idea to park that . . . that thing in the backyard?"

Then without giving him a chance to respond, Spence gave Leif a hard look. "And please tell me you tried to stop him. At least say you let the rest of the unit know he left the army to take up gazebo building for a hobby, and they gave him serious grief and misery over it."

He shuddered and rubbed his eyes as if trying to clear the image from his brain. "Because I'm telling you right now, I'm still feeling a little bit queasy. All those curlicues and white paint."

Leif laughed; Nick didn't. No surprise there.

"Rest assured, Wheels, I did indeed let everyone know. They were suitably horrified by the situation. I sent out pictures and everything. I've been told the video of him painting it went viral in certain circles."

Nick bristled nicely. "That's enough, you two."

Except it really wasn't. Spence smiled across at Nick. "I'm thinking a few cans of tan and army drab green spray paint would camouflage it. I'm certain the neighbors would be grateful."

His former sergeant flipped him off. "Fuck off, Wheels."

There was no real heat in the words, reminding Spence of so many similar conversations in the past. The context might have been different, but the trappings were familiar. God, how he'd been missing this. It was time to throw his friends a bone.

"Despite it making me break out in a rash, I couldn't help noticing you did a nice job on the actual construction, Sarge. I knew you grew up swinging a hammer for your old man. Didn't know you had a real talent for it."

Leif rejoined the conversation. "He didn't do it all by himself. I helped."

He looked right proud of himself, but Nick snorted and shook his head. "Yeah, right. Mostly you got in my way. And as I recall, most of the time you parked your worthless ass in a lawn chair and drank beer."

Spence could just picture it. "Sitting on his ass was always Leif's specialty."

The third member of their party looked offended. "I'll

have you know, Wheels, I was designated the official supervisor during the construction phase of the gazebo. I wouldn't have been doing my job if I hadn't watched him work."

Now that Spence had given his friends some grief, it was time to get to the hard parts of the conversation. "I saw the writing on the back wall."

The other two men sat up straighter and their faces became blank slates. The silence was so thick, Spence wasn't sure he could break through it. Luckily, Liam made a timely appearance at the side of the table with twice the number of beers Spence had ordered. He carefully set two in front of each man. "The extra round is on me. Make them last awhile. If necessary, there's more where these came from."

In other words, he'd picked up on the tension between the three men and was hoping the beer would defuse the situation. If they nursed their drinks, they'd benefit from the relaxing effect of alcohol. It was smart thinking and might even work. Spence set his beer back down on the table and waited.

It was no surprise that it was Nick who took the lead. "Don't hold back. Just spit it out, because I've got to be honest with you. It's been damn hard to figure out what's been going on in that thick skull of yours since you got back."

What did he want to say about that? In fact, what could he say? As he tried to come up with the right words, he ran his finger up and down the drops of condensation on his beer bottle. Maybe the simple truth was best. "It wasn't as bad as seeing my own tombstone."

Nick's face flushed red. "It's probably not much comfort, but we were both pissed as hell about that happening. You've got to believe your uncle Vince never told anyone you'd been found. If I knew where the bastard was right now, there'd be nothing left of him except for a grease spot on the road."

Leif reached for his second beer. "We made sure the marker was removed as soon as we knew. I had the caretaker at the cemetery put it someplace safe. Thought you might like to take a sledgehammer to it yourself. If not, I sure as hell would."

It was a relief to know Spence wouldn't have to look at that particular piece of polished rock again the next time he visited his folks' graves. "I'll get back to you on that."

He noticed neither of them asked him why he hadn't called them with the news himself. Maybe they'd already figured it out or maybe they just didn't want to set off another firestorm. Either way, he was relieved not to have to explain something he wasn't exactly proud of now.

Of course none of them had ever been great at talking about anything that smacked of emotions or touchy-feely stuff. It came as no surprise when they lapsed into silence and concentrated on drinking their beer. After a few minutes, Nick finally spoke up again. "So, Wheels, you called this meeting. What else is on the agenda besides giving me gazebo grief?"

Time for the hard stuff. "I went through the house. You've made some changes."

"Yeah, we have, but nothing that can't be undone if that's what you want."

No, that wasn't what Spence wanted. In fact, seeing so much that was different had actually made the visit less painful than he'd expected.

He leaned back in his seat, grateful for even that little

extra distance between him and Nick. "Describe to me what you had in mind for the rest of the place."

Leif broke in to ask, "Why, Spence? Somehow I can't see you running a bed-and-breakfast."

"Maybe I'm just curious." Spence pinched the bridge of his nose and prayed for patience. "But mainly because Sarge here always told us to always gather as much information as possible before formulating a plan of action."

"Nice to know that at least some of what I tried to teach you got through."

Nick pulled a pen out of his shirt pocket and grabbed a napkin from the dispenser on the table. Spreading it out, he made a rough sketch of what had to be the three floors of the house and the attic. It didn't take him long to have it all laid out for the three of them to study.

He marked a couple of small crosses on the rectangle he'd labeled with a 3. "We knocked out this wall and this one with the intent of making the third floor into a small apartment for me and Callie. We plan to make this side a combination kitchen and family room. The other half would be our bedroom and a small sitting room."

He sketched in a few more details on the attic level. "Eventually, we thought this would make a nice master suite and bath. Then we'd turn these two rooms on the third floor into bedrooms for any kids we might have."

Okay, now they were venturing into TMI territory for sure. Spence was still struggling with the whole idea of Nick and Callie being a couple. The thought that they were already thinking about a future with kids in it was too much to absorb. Rather than say so, he tapped his finger on the second-floor diagram. "So this is where you'd park any guests staying at the place?"

Nick nodded as he studied the rough sketch with the same intensity he used to bring to planning their next combat patrol. "We plan to modernize the plumbing in the existing bathroom and add at least one more. The kitchen will need upgrading with some commercial-grade appliances. We want to replace some of the existing furniture to make the living room and parlor more suitable for guests to hang out in. Callie has been restoring your mom's rose garden out front, so we were going to call the bed-and-breakfast Rose Blossom Place."

That was a nice touch, and it all made perfect sense. Spence wasn't surprised. Neither Nick nor Callie was given to doing anything halfway. Once they made a decision, it was all or nothing. Maybe he should do the same. He stared at the napkin spread out on the table as pictures from his past superimposed themselves over the rough sketch.

He thought of his parents and wished they were there to offer their advice. Or maybe he wanted their blessing for what he was about to do. That wasn't going to happen, but there was one thing he knew with great certainty. When they chose him to be their son, they wanted to give him the best life they could. They would want him to be happy, even if it meant walking away from the house they'd once filled with love and laughter.

And it wasn't as if he was throwing it away or letting strangers have it. No, this was Nick and Callie. They'd already put more effort into restoring the house to its former glory than Spence had in all the years since his parents' death. The bottom line was it could continue to remain an anchor around his neck or it could be a gift to the two people who would give it loving care every day of their lives.

In the end, the decision of what to do with the house was a no-brainer.

"I'll tell Troy to draw up the legal mumbo jumbo papers needed to make the transfer of title to you and Callie permanent. Not sure how long it will take or what it will involve, but he'll walk us all through the process."

This time it was Nick falling back to hit the back of his seat with a thump. Even Leif was looking a bit pale. Spence couldn't help himself. The look of utter confusion on their faces cracked him up big-time. In fact, he needed to preserve the moment for posterity. He snapped a picture of them looking totally dumbfounded with his cell phone.

The flicker of light from the flash broke Nick out of his stupor. "But we haven't talked price or anything, Spence. And then there's the money we've already spent on the place. Callie and I have enough savings to cover that, but it might make coming up with the down payment hard."

Leif leaned forward to rest his elbows on the table, clearly injecting himself into the conversation. "Don't forget my offer, Sarge. We're partners, remember?"

Nick was already shaking his head. "Yeah, but—"

Spence didn't want to listen to any of it and set his beer back down on the table with a little more force than was necessary. "Nick, I didn't say I'd sell the place to you. I said I'd sign it over to you. Consider it a belated wedding present or even an apology for being such an asshole when I got back. Not sure where all the anger came from, but it wasn't fair of me to take it out on Leif, you, and Callie."

He finished his second beer and eyed the third. No, he didn't need it. "I'll call Troy Monday morning and tell him to get things rolling."

Nick continued to argue. "Don't be stupid, Spence. That house is worth a lot of money. You can't just give it to us."

"Why the hell not? It's mine to do with as I see fit. That's the deal. Take it or leave it. It's your call. I'll give you twenty-four hours to decide. Come Monday I'll tell Troy either to transfer ownership of the house to you or to donate the damn thing and everything in it to charity."

He stood up and threw money on the table to cover the bill. "Oh, and one more thing. I want some time alone with Callie without you hovering in the background."

In an alternative universe, Nick's eyes would've been glowing in a jealous shade of green with just a hint of suspicion thrown in for good measure. "Why?"

Spence placed his hands back on the table and leaned past Leif to get in Nick's face. "Because she was my friend before you ever met her. Don't worry. I just want to talk to her. I'm not going to put a move on somebody else's wife."

He straightened up and shot a nasty look at the man. "It's a matter of personal honor."

Nick exploded. "You son of a bitch! I didn't put a move on your woman."

Leif groaned and braced himself to keep Nick from crawling over him to get at Spence. "Damn it, Wheels. You just had to go there, didn't you?"

Okay, so that had been a cheap shot. "Yeah, maybe I did, but I shouldn't have. Sometimes my mouth has an agenda of its own. Sorry, Sarge. You're entitled to one free punch if that will make you feel better."

He watched as Nick fought himself back under control. "Let me out, Leif."

The other man stayed put. "Not sure that's a good idea."

"Let me out, Leif. I won't ask again, not nicely, anyway."

Spence intervened. "Go ahead, Leif. You don't need to play referee."

He wasn't sure which one of them Leif looked more disgusted with. Most likely it was a tie. "Fine, but I'm not part of this. You two can bash each other's brains out as far as I'm concerned. Just know, Nick, if you end up bleeding, you're riding home in the back of the truck."

After Leif left the booth and limped his way across the bar to disappear into the parking lot outside, Nick got up in Spence's face. "I'll take a rain check on that punch, Spence, but you fucking well better never say anything like that again. For the record, if I hadn't thought you were dead and buried, I wouldn't have gone near Callie. As it was, all I meant to do was find a permanent home for your dog and then move on. I never expected to fall in love with her."

He retreated a step. "I was pretty much a basket case when I got here, thinking I'd gotten you killed, not to mention what happened to Leif. I don't know what would've happened to me if it hadn't been for her."

Spence knew a lot about living with guilt. He'd lived every minute he was in captivity thinking both his friends were dead. He might have been in hell, but he'd still been breathing. "Sarge, I'd be one sorry excuse for a human being if I can't eventually figure out how to be happy for my two best friends. I might still struggle with it a bit, but I'm trying."

He stuck his hand out and hoped Nick would accept the peace offering. When he did, Spence felt as though one small piece of his life was settling back into place.

"Now, we'd better head outside and let Leif know we're not going to kill each other, at least not over this. I'm sure some other reason will come up eventually, though."

Nick laughed. "Something always does."

On their way past the bar, Spence called out to Liam, "Good news. We're making it out of here without spilling any blood or beer on your nice clean floor. It was close, though."

Liam was busy stacking glasses on the back counter. "Glad to hear it. Leif's already been arrested in here once. I'm thinking Gage Logan wouldn't take kindly to a repeat performance."

Spence waved and followed Nick toward the door. "Seriously? Leif got arrested? Where were you in all of this?"

"I was finishing up my time with the army."

When they reached the parking lot, Nick looked around for Leif. Once he spotted him sitting in his truck, he turned back around. "The damn fool hooked up with your buddy Mitch Calder, and the two of them decided to take on some of the local talent. From what I heard, with Mooch's help, they made a fair showing for themselves. Luckily, Liam didn't press charges, but Gage made Leif attend the veterans' support group meeting."

Nick closed his eyes and took a slow breath. "That was before his last round of surgery, and he was still hoping for a full recovery. Obviously that didn't happen, but Zoe has helped him find some peace with that. The meetings help, too. We both go sometimes."

"That's good, Sarge." Spence gave Nick a light punch on the arm. "I'll call Callie to set up a time to talk to her."

Nick still didn't look happy about that, but he simply nodded. "I'll tell her. I'll also tell her about the house.

She won't think you're being fair to yourself, Wheels. I feel the same way, so don't be surprised if we come up with a counteroffer that we'll all be able to live with."

"You can try, but no promises."

Now that they were talking again, it was hard to walk away. Spence made himself take that first step to prove to himself he could do it. "I've got to get back to Mooch. He wasn't happy when I dropped him off at the cottage before coming here to meet you."

"Tell the mutt hi for me."

Nick started toward Leif's truck but turned back. "About Callie. You might want to meet her at the park along the river and bring Mooch. She misses him."

Not to mention it was a public place, meaning Spence wouldn't be alone with her behind closed doors. He didn't call Nick on it. "Sounds good, Sarge. Let me know about the house."

He headed for the station wagon. It had been a long day, and he ached as if he'd been on a forced march in the desert with a full pack and new boots. Once he got back to the cottage, he'd let Mooch out, let Melanie know he'd survived, and then hit the rack.

Chapter 21

※ ※

Melanie sipped her tea and stared at the succinct message on her phone. "Well, at least he kept his promise to let me know he was okay."

That didn't mean she was satisfied. She wanted details, or at least more than Spence's text that simply said I survived. Darn the man, didn't he know she'd been worried about him? Maybe he didn't care. After all, from the start they'd both said no promises and no demands. Those words, spoken with such sincerity at the time, now stabbed her in the chest. After all they'd shared, would he eventually ride out of town with no more than a friendly wave as he disappeared into the distance? Or more likely, another text message, something along the lines of I'm out of here. See you around?

No, she wouldn't jump to conclusions.

They both had things on their minds, a lot of stuff to deal with and get through somehow. This wasn't the time to let emotional entanglements take over. Neither of them knew how their lives were going to play out, especially over the next few months. Who knew where she'd be living a year from now? If she couldn't get the bank loan, she'd have to close down the company, and it would be time to move on from Snowberry Creek.

Another flash of pain ripped through her. When she'd first taken on managing the millworks, she resented having to uproot her own life for the sake of those who depended on it for their living. Now she didn't want to fail either herself or her employees. That didn't mean she was happy living here. Not Snowberry Creek, but specifically here in Wolfe House. She'd long grown tired of living out of a suitcase. Yeah, she'd unpacked, but she hadn't really moved in, either. She missed having her own place and living surrounded by her own possessions.

She strolled down the hallway and into the living room, pausing to pick up a knickknack here and then a framed family portrait there. The artfully arranged clutter left her cold. It was like living in a museum or maybe a hotel, a place people passed through but never left their mark on.

It was time to confront her mother on that particular subject. If she wasn't interested in coming back to live in Snowberry Creek, maybe it was time to put the house on the market. If they could get out from underneath the weight of the place, financially as well as emotionally, they could move on with their lives.

Rather than stay a minute longer when the walls were closing in on her, Melanie picked up her keys and purse off the counter. Maybe a quick trip to Something's Brewing would improve her mood. A tall coffee with a dash of cinnamon and one of Bridey's wickedly good brownies sounded pretty good about now. She closed the door behind her, putting its solid weight between her and the oppressive gloom that was her family home.

*   *   *

As she drove down Main Street, she wondered if Bridey would have time to sit down with her even for a few minutes. Probably not. Sunday was a busy day for her friend. If the shop was crowded, maybe the two of them could at least make plans to meet later in the week for dinner. They hadn't gotten together for a girls' night out in ages, especially since Bridey had Seth in her life. It was the same with Callie, although right now Melanie wasn't so sure Callie would be interested in hanging out with her.

On the other hand, it was time for Melanie to make the first move toward repairing their relationship. They'd been friends too long to let anything come between them. Besides, in a town the size of Snowberry Creek, it wasn't as if they could avoid each other forever. No sooner did that thought cross her mind when she caught a glimpse of the woman in question standing in the park as she drove by. It was as if Melanie had conjured Callie just by thinking about her.

She circled the block to head back to the park. Feeling better than she had all morning, Melanie parked her car and took off across the small rise that led to the creek, hoping to catch up with her friend.

But as she reached the top of the slope, Melanie came to a screeching halt. She'd found Callie all right. It was the person next to her who had Melanie gritting her teeth: Spence. She watched as the couple spoke briefly and then embraced. Not exactly one of those quick, haven't-seen-an-old-friend-in-a-long-time hugs, either. Afterward, the two of them walked over to sit down at a picnic table with Spence talking a mile a minute the entire time. Why hadn't he told Melanie that he had plans to see Callie? And where was Nick? She wanted to walk right up to the pair and ask, but she had enough of her mother's fear of making a scene in her to ensure that she wouldn't confront them. Not now.

But later, when she had a chance to corner Spence alone, she would get to the bottom of things. She backed down the rise, intending to return to her car. Unfortunately, she didn't make her escape fast enough. Mooch came flying straight at her, barking as if he hadn't seen her in weeks. Now what should she do? If she continued her headlong retreat toward the busy parking lot, that would only lead her furry friend right into danger. She might be mad at his owner, but she wouldn't risk Mooch getting hurt.

"Come here, boy."

The dog clearly thought it was a game and danced in and out of her reach. She finally succeeded in grabbing him by his collar. Kneeling beside Mooch, she debated what to do next. That decision was made for her when she heard Spence yelling the dog's name. Great. There was no way to avoid him now. Despite her current mood, she wouldn't let him worry about the dog.

"Come on, Mooch."

She kept a firm hand on the dog's collar as they walked back toward where she'd last seen Callie and Spence. Sure enough, there they were, both spinning in circles looking for the dog and calling his name.

She waited until Spence turned in her direction and called out, "I've got him."

His relief was obvious as he immediately headed straight for the two of them. There wasn't a touch of guilt in his expression, and Callie's entire focus was on the dog when she caught up with them. "Thank goodness you happened by, Mel."

Then she shook her finger at the dog. "Darn you, Mooch. Don't you dare scare us like that again."

Yeah, like that impressed the dog if his tail wagging like crazy was any indication. Right now he looked all too happy to have three of his favorite people surrounding him. Melanie relinquished control of the dog once Spence slipped the end of Mooch's leash through his collar and tied a solid knot to keep it there. When he straightened up, he gave the dog a disgusted look. "We were standing there talking when he took a big lunge forward and snapped the damn clip right off his leash."

"Well, now that you've got him under control, I'm out of here."

She had made it about five steps when Callie said something to Spence, but she spoke too softly for Melanie to make out what it was. She kept right on walking, not happy to be the topic of further conversation between them. Unfortunately, the sound of running footsteps warned her that she wasn't going to make a clean escape. A few seconds later, Mooch cut her off at the pass, with his master following right on his heels.

Spence stopped right in front of her, leaving her only two choices: stand her ground or try to outrun a man who was nearly a foot taller than she was. Opting for what dignity she could muster, she said, "Was there something you wanted, Spence?"

"Callie thought you looked upset, Mel. Is something wrong?"

She forced herself to meet his gaze head-on. "I saw Callie in the park and thought I'd ask her if she wanted to get together for a girls' night out. I hadn't realized that the two of you were . . . well, that she was here to see you.

I didn't want to intrude and was trying to leave when Mooch spotted me. Now I'll just be going."

He caught her arm before she could make good on that decision. "You don't have to leave."

Seriously, she had to spell it out for him? She glanced back toward Callie. "Yes, I do. The two of you obviously have a lot to talk about."

Then, before Spence could stop her again, she marched past him, determined that this time he wouldn't prevent her from reaching the sanctuary of her car. When he fell into step beside her, she wanted to scream. "Look, don't you have something better to do than bother me?"

"Nope. In fact, I was hoping you'd give me and Mooch a ride back to the cottage. We walked here."

By this point, she was nearly running. "Then you can walk back. That's what you would have done if I hadn't happened along."

"Actually, I would've gotten a lift from Callie."

She glanced back toward the park to where Callie stood watching the two of them with a funny look on her face. What was that all about? "It's not too late. She's still back there. I'm sure she'd be only too glad to take you home."

They'd reached her car. She pressed the button to unlock the driver's door. There was no way she was going to double-click it and let him in the passenger side. She tried to yank the door open. Before she could, Spence shoved his way between her and the door, successfully blocking her one escape route.

"Move, Spence."

No dice. She counted to ten, keeping her eyes focused on the logo on his faded T-shirt, and tried again. "Move, Spence. Please."

Still he stood there, a solid mass of sculpted muscle

and sheer stubbornness. What kind of game was he playing now? Frustrated beyond all measure, she snapped her gaze up to his, only to realize she'd badly miscalculated. He wasn't playing any game. Instead, he was clearly furious. What did *he* have to be mad about? She crossed her arms over her chest and waited for him to explain.

God save him from stubborn women. He'd just had words with Callie when she'd totally refused to accept the house as an outright gift. She and Nick would only consider his offer as long as he let them make him their partner in the bed-and-breakfast. She'd opened the negotiations insisting he retain seventy-five percent ownership in the house until they could afford to buy him out. He'd bargained her down to twenty-five percent, with them taking the seventy-five percent majority for doing all the remodeling and then managing the place.

Her look of triumph when she accepted made it clear that he'd been had. He should've known she was up to something when she'd conceded so quickly. At least he wouldn't have to be involved in the day-to-day details of running the place, but it would give him a permanent tie to Nick and Callie. His heart said that was a good thing.

Now he was standing there facing off with Melanie. Until Callie had pointed out that she'd acted upset, he'd had no idea anything was wrong. It would've helped if Callie had been a little more specific about her suspicions before sending him after Melanie. He was in no mood to play guessing games.

For the third time, the woman in question glared up at him and said, "Move."

No way in hell was he going to let her drive away and leave him standing there wondering when and how they'd gone off the rails. "I will after you tell me exactly what it is that I've done wrong."

"Oh, brother. You can't possibly be that dense." She rolled her eyes, her mouth set in that tight-lipped way that was guaranteed to make any male see red.

If it had been anyone else, he would have said "fuck it" and walked away, but this was Melanie. He'd developed a real talent for ignoring emotions, so he counted to ten and tossed his anger aside. Brushing a strand of her softer-than-silk hair back from her face, he aimed for calm and said, "Come on, Mel. I get that you're upset. Since we haven't even spoken since yesterday morning, I'm finding it hard to figure out exactly what I've done wrong."

She angled her head to look past him to where he'd been standing with Callie, but she still didn't explain. Suddenly, it clicked. "Son of a bitch, you think I'm meeting Callie on the sly? That the two of us are sneaking around together on Nick?"

She wouldn't look at him, but the bright flush on her cheeks was answer enough. "Seriously, Mel?" He laughed but there wasn't much humor in it. "I'm not sure which one of us you're insulting more by thinking Callie would cheat on Nick or that I would cheat on you like that."

Melanie jerked as if she'd been hit. What was going on in that pretty head of hers? "I admit I was jealous, but that's not what I was thinking. Not exactly, anyway."

Damn, he would've thought she knew him better than that, but then maybe not. It wasn't as if the two of them had been all that close back in high school, and if circumstances hadn't thrown them together now, chances were their paths might never have crossed. But even if he cut her some slack, she still should know Callie would never jeopardize what she had with Nick. Just like Mama R.

had said, if Spence and Callie had really wanted to hook up, they could've done it years ago.

"I need to go home."

Melanie's words were accompanied by a sniffle, meaning tears were imminent. They needed to take this conversation someplace more private. "Give me the keys, Mel. I'll drive you there."

"I can drive."

He wasn't going to budge and held out his hand. "Yeah, I know, but right now you're upset. I'll take you home where we can talk in private."

She pushed the button that unlocked the passenger door and dropped the keys into his hand just as his cell phone rang. Melanie pushed past him to walk around to the other side of the car while he checked to see the name on the screen. He groaned as soon as he saw who it was, but he couldn't ignore the call, not when the person calling was no doubt standing right where she could see him.

He kept his eyes aimed toward Main Street. "This isn't a good time."

"I was right, wasn't I?"

"Yeah."

"She didn't like seeing you hug me."

He sighed. "I've figured out that much. I am still working on the why."

Callie's laughter rang in his ear. "Here's a hint: Say you had happened upon the same scene, only with Melanie and Nick instead of us in the lead roles. How would you have reacted, especially if she'd never made it clear how much you matter to her or that she planned on sticking around for any length of time? I'm guessing here about how things stand between the two of you, so forgive me if I'm wrong. Either way, here's the bottom line:

Would you have assumed it was all innocent or would you have come out swinging?"

The phone went dead as he closed his eyes and considered what had happened a few minutes ago from Melanie's perspective. Callie was right. He would've kicked ass and asked questions afterward. He rested his arms on the roof of the car and stared down the street trying to come up with a plan before getting into the car with Melanie.

It didn't help that from his first night back in town Melanie had known he wasn't happy seeing Nick and Callie together. Hell, he'd hated their relationship with every breath he took. It had taken him all this time to come around to the realization that he wasn't jealous of Nick and Callie as much as he was jealous of what they had together. He could hardly blame Melanie for thinking ... well, exactly what she'd been thinking. Add in the fact that the two of them had been operating under the no-demands, no-promises principle, and she probably thought she had no claim on his loyalty at all.

God, he sure had a talent for leaving a trail of disasters in his wake. He'd barely made peace with his oldest friend and the two men who were as close as brothers to him. Now he'd inadvertently hurt the one person who had been there for him every minute since his surprise return to Snowberry Creek. He had to make this right somehow.

He opened the back car door. "Come on, Mooch. Let's go."

The two of them rode in silence until they reached the last turn before her house. "If we have to talk, can we do it at your place? I really can't face going home right now."

He waited until another car passed and turned down the street that led to the cottage. "Sure, as long as you give me a two-minute start going in so I can do a quick sweep through the place for anything disgusting or embarrassing."

She gave him a puzzled look. "O-kay, maybe we should go to my place."

Obviously his attempt at a joke had fallen flat. "I was talking moldy pizza and dirty underwear, Melanie, nothing more."

She sighed and stared out the passenger window. "I'm sorry, Spence. I don't mean to be such a downer. Maybe you should drop me off at home."

"Not happening, Mel. We need to talk. We can do that at Wolfe House or my place, your choice."

When she didn't answer, he continued straight for the cottage. No way he was going to leave her rattling around in that monstrosity of a house by herself. He'd never seen anyone who needed to be held more than she did right at that moment.

As soon as they were parked in his driveway, he got out and walked around to open her door for her. Taking Melanie's hand, he led the way toward the porch with Mooch trailing along behind them.

He unlocked the door and stood back to let her go in first. She had just a hint of a twinkle in her eyes when she walked by him. "I thought you wanted a head start."

Spence followed her into the small living room. "Maybe I decided you're tough enough to handle anything you might stumble across in here."

In truth, after all his years in the army, he normally kept the clutter to a minimum. Other than the paperback book he was reading, which was sitting by an empty glass on the coffee table, the room was pretty much just like it had been the day she'd given him the keys. If he'd been going to stay long-term, he might have made changes. But since living in the cottage was temporary at best, he couldn't be bothered.

Spence headed into the kitchen and opened the fridge. "Want something to drink? I've got beer, pop, and water."

He'd already snagged a beer for himself and was reaching for a bottle of water for her when she finally answered, "A beer sounds good."

She mumbled something afterward that sounded suspiciously like "a six-pack would be even better."

Pretending he hadn't heard the addendum, he popped the caps on the two beers and poured them into glasses. He never bothered with such niceties when he was alone, but Mel had been raised with a higher standard of manners than he had.

He wasn't surprised to find her curled up on the end of the couch with Mooch back in her lap. She sat with her face buried in the dog's fur as she scratched his back and murmured sweet nothings about how handsome the mutt was and how much she appreciated him keeping her company. Lucky dog.

Spence got one of the weird, lacy coasters the prior tenant had left behind and set Mel's beer on it. Rather than do the polite thing and sit in the paisley-print-upholstered chair, he dropped down on the other end of the couch.

Spence reached over to give his buddy a quick pat on the back. "Dog, I wish I had your knack for charming the ladies."

Melanie gave him a disbelieving look as she picked up her drink. "A handsome guy like you? I'm sure you've charmed more than your fair share of the female population over the years."

She thought he was handsome? That shouldn't please him quite as much as it did. It brought him back to the reason they were there.

"About what happened at the park."

Even if he hadn't seen Melanie wince, the death grip she had on her glass would've given her sudden rise in tension away. "Do we really have to do this?"

He ignored her question and picked up right where he'd left off. "I thought some context might help. As you know, I finally went through the house yesterday."

Her expression immediately turned sympathetic. "Was it really awful?"

Leave it to Melanie to be more concerned about him than herself. "Not as bad as I thought it would be. Seeing the changes Nick and Callie have started making helped a lot. That gave me something else to concentrate on other than all of the old memories."

"That's good, Spence. I was worried about you."

And he had known she would be, which oddly had also helped him get through it. "Afterward, I texted Nick and Leif to meet me at Liam's bar, which is why I didn't come right back here."

Her eyes flared wide. "And how did that go?"

He couldn't help grinning a little. "It helped clear the air between the three of us, although I won't claim everything is back to normal. I don't want to punch Nick anymore, so we definitely made progress."

"Sounds like it." Melanie studied him for a few seconds. "You're letting them keep the house."

"Yeah, I am."

He took a long drink of his beer, hoping it would ease the sudden constriction in his throat. "The minute I walked into the house, I realized that it had stopped being home to me when my parents died. Since then, it's just been a reminder of everything I've lost. While we were sitting in the bar, I asked Nick to tell me about what they had planned for the old place. He grabbed a napkin and started sketching it all out for me. You should have seen him. I've known Sarge for a long time, but I've never seen him look so excited about anything."

Spence had slipped that napkin into his pocket when he stopped to drop money on the table. After he'd gotten back to the cottage last night, he tucked it away in a zipper compartment in his duffel. Why, he didn't know, but it had seemed important at the time.

"So, I told Nick I'd have Troy transfer the title to them."

"You're just giving it to them?" Melanie didn't sound all that surprised; more like that it was something she'd been expecting all along.

"Well, I would if they'd let me. That's part of why Callie and I met up today. Nick had warned me they'd probably be making a counteroffer."

So now they were to the hard part. "I told Nick that I wanted to talk to Callie without him around. I know the way I handled, or actually mishandled, everything when I came home hurt her. It was important to me to make amends if I could. Try to talk things out, this time in person, so maybe we could get back to the way it used to be between the two of us. Having Nick underfoot would only have complicated things."

"How did the talk go?"

"Pretty well, all things considered. They won't take the house unless I remain part owner of the bed-and-breakfast they're going to open. They offered a seventy-five/twenty-five split in my favor. I got them to flip the percentages around, though. I wouldn't even have taken that much if they weren't so damn stubborn."

"You're a nice man, Spencer Lang."

Melanie shoved Mooch off onto the floor and scooted closer to Spence's end of the couch. "As long as we're all making apologies, I should do that, too. When I saw the two of you together, I overreacted. I admit I'm jealous of how things are between you two, but then I guess I've always felt that way. It's obvious that you had planned to build a life with Callie yourself and that you still have some pretty strong feelings for her. In fact, I'm pretty sure you even called me by her name when we kissed on my back steps the first time."

Oh God, had he really done that? Evidently so, considering how hurt Melanie looked right now. "If I did something that unbelievably stupid, Melanie, I am so sorry. Yeah, maybe I did have some vague idea of a future with Callie in it, but that's all it was. She and I are friends, but I swear that's all we ever were or ever will be."

He met Melanie in the middle of the couch, moving close enough that he could brush his fingers across her cheek. "To be honest, I don't have all that much knowledge about how relationships are supposed to work. I've moved around a lot since enlisting in the army, not to mention being deployed three times. There was never a chance for anything long-term. Hell, there weren't even all that many short-term things, either."

To lighten the moment, he added, "Which I will deny with my last breath if you repeat any of this to Nick or Leif. They must continue to believe all of the lies I've told them on the subject."

Melanie held up her fist with only her little finger poking up, her expression solemn. "I hereby pinkie-swear that all of this will remain confidential."

He reciprocated, tangling his pinky with hers even though it was hard not to laugh. "I seem to remember my folks laughing about an old sitcom that had something called the 'cone of silence.' We'll consider the cottage to be ours."

"Fair enough." Melanie held out her glass to clink against his. "Here's to shared secrets and good friends."

Relieved to see her looking happier, he took a deep breath and continued. "Anyway, what I've taken a long time to get around to say is that whenever I was with a woman, I was *with* only her. I might not be able to promise forever, but I could promise to be faithful for the duration."

He leaned in close enough to brush his lips across Melanie's. Hoping he wasn't about to screw up the one good thing he'd found in a long time, he forced himself to be completely honest with her. "I told you up front that I don't know how long I can stand to stay in Snowberry Creek, and that hasn't changed. But as long as you and I are sleeping together, there won't be anyone else for me. You have my word on that."

She stared up at him with those pretty gray eyes, which always seemed to see right to the center of his soul. "I believe you even if I wish things could be different for us."

Melanie reached up to trace the line of his jaw. "If circumstances were different, if neither of us had all this stuff hanging over our heads, do you think there might have been a chance for us? You know, long-term? Because I've got to tell you, Spence, that I've never had a relationship that feels quite so . . . right somehow."

What could he say to that? That sometimes those same vague ideas of how his future might look someday now featured a beautiful redhead and a spotted dog? He also didn't know what to make of the huge wave of relief that washed through him that she had reaffirmed her trust in him. "I would like to think so, Mel. For sure I've never felt so comfortable in so many ways with anybody else, not even Callie. The two of us have shared so much over the past few weeks."

Melanie's smile brightened a little. "Like ice cream in bed naked?"

Okay, that made him laugh. "Yeah, like that."

He leaned in closer to brush a kiss across her lips again. "So we're good? Even if long-term isn't in the picture right now?"

Melanie carefully set her beer back down on the table, moving slowly as if she were struggling to find the words for what it was she wanted to say. He'd almost decided that she was about to tell him she wasn't interested in continuing their relationship when she finally turned back to face him. The heat in her smile had a certain part of him on full alert, ready to leap into action. Then, wicked woman that she was, Melanie abandoned her end of the couch to straddle his lap. His brain quit working the second she rocked against his erection and wrapped her arms around his neck.

Then quiet, shy Melanie whispered right next to his ear, her warm breath sending a shiver straight through him, "So, what do you say to proving we can be so much better than just good?"

Chapter 22

✻ ✻

After two long hours in his attorney's office signing papers, Spence was ready for a break. He stopped to stare up at the clear blue sky above and breathed deeply of the cool morning air. The slight chill was one sign that summer was winding down. Another was the number of spiderwebs starting to pop up all over the place. Was it only the Pacific Northwest that marked the transition from summer to fall by the amount of arachnid artwork decorating fence railings and bushes? Heck, he'd even had a web spanning the rearview mirror on his Harley that morning.

Did the upcoming change in seasons also signal that it was time for him to be moving on? Would he already be packing if he had some plan in mind other than simply leaving Snowberry Creek?

His gut said it wasn't that simple. Shoving his hands in his pockets, he strolled down the block to hang a right onto Main Street. As he looked around, it all seemed so normal, so familiar. Yeah, he had some bad memories connected with the place, but who didn't have a few dark thoughts about their hometown? A few memories they'd just as soon forget? Look at Nick and Leif. There were reasons both of them had decided to settle in Snowberry Creek instead of going back to where they came from.

Frannie from the Creek Café spotted him and waved as he walked by. He waved back and wondered what kind of toxic chemicals it took to turn someone's hair that violent shade of red. Even his sunglasses did little to tone it down, but that was Frannie at her best. He couldn't even imagine the woman with her hair in any shade that approached a natural color.

The scent of roasting coffee drew him farther down the street. There was no way he could make it past Something's Brewing without stopping in for a tall latte and some of those brownies Melanie loved so much. No doubt she'd complain about the effect they might have on her hips or some other bullshit reason why she shouldn't eat them. He wouldn't listen, because he liked her hips just fine. Especially when he was kneeling behind her as they . . .

"Hey, Spence, are you okay?"

He blinked and spotted Bridey looking at him with a slightly worried look on her face. There was no way he could explain that he'd drifted to a stop in the middle of the doorway because he got so caught up in the erotic memory of what he'd been doing with one of her best friends just last night. Twice.

When the truth wouldn't work, go for the believable lie. "I just came from the lawyer's office and thought of something I should've asked him."

Her expression shifted to a bright smile. "That's a good thing you're doing for Nick and Callie, Spence. For that, whatever you want is on the house today."

Greed went to war with good manners. Unfortunately, the wrong one won. "My first impulse is to ask for a tall, double-shot latte and one of every pastry you have in the case. Since that would be over-the-top greedy, I'll settle for half a dozen of those brownies. I'll let you spot me the coffee, but I'm paying for the chocolate, no arguments."

She nodded and started transferring the pastries to a box while her assistant fixed his drink. He watched as Bridey piled the brownies on one side and then added a pair of cupcakes. As he reached for his wallet, he felt obligated to point out the obvious. "Bridey, I didn't order those."

She shot him a smug smile. "Never said you did. I tried a new recipe and thought maybe you'd be willing to give me some feedback."

He already knew there was no use in arguing with her. "If you're sure."

Her boyfriend, Seth, strolled out of the kitchen. "She's sure. She used to let me test all the new stuff, but she's decided I'm prejudiced and no longer trusts my opinion."

He grabbed Bridey for a quick hug and kiss. "Can I help that I like everything she does?"

Somehow Spence suspected Seth was no longer talking about cupcakes. That was okay. The man clearly adored Bridey. Over the years, Callie had kept him informed about their friends from high school, and he knew Bridey's first marriage hadn't turned out well. There was no mistaking that part of the heat in the pastry shop right now had nothing to do with the big ovens in the back.

It reminded him of the hunger that seemed to flare up every time he saw Melanie. Or hell, even thought of her.

He picked up his coffee and the boxed goodies. Maybe he'd drop by her office and tempt her into leaving early with the promise of some hot sex and brownies.

Bridey gave him another considering look. "Spence, you had that exact same expression on your face when you walked in. I don't know what you're thinking right now, but I'm betting it has nothing to do with your lawyer. In fact, I'm pretty sure if I could read your mind, it would leave me blushing."

Spence didn't bother to deny Bridey's conclusion. He just grinned and winked at her. "I'll let you know about the cupcakes next time I come in."

"Do that, and tell Melanie hi for me."

"Will do."

Melanie stared at the letter from the bank. A second reading hadn't changed a darn thing in the brief message. "Rejected" was the only word in the whole thing that really mattered. Oh, they tried to pretty it up with a bunch of other words like "regret" and "unfortunately" and "sincerely." She wanted to scream. Now what was she going to do?

A knock on her office door brought her impending temper tantrum to a screeching halt. Maybe she should be grateful; all she felt was thwarted.

"Come in."

The temp she'd hired through the local employment agency poked her head through the door. The young woman looked a bit confused at the moment. "There's a Mr. Lang here to see you, Ms. Wolfe. He says he doesn't have an appointment but that he does have brownies."

Bless the man!

"That's fine, Haley. Send him in."

Spence came in carrying one of the distinctive blue boxes from Bridey's shop. How many brownies had he bought her this time? No matter how often she told him that she shouldn't, he just smiled and waved all that temptation right under her nose.

She casually dropped the letter from the bank on top of the tray full of papers on the corner of her desk, hoping he wouldn't notice what it was. No such luck. The man had the instincts of a bloodhound. He dropped the box on her desk and stared right at the letter.

"You got the final answer from the bank."

He wasn't asking. He knew she'd been expecting to hear from the bank anytime now. She retrieved the piece of paper that might well herald the end for Wolfe Millworks and held it out to Spence's outstretched hand. "It comes as no surprise that they said no."

As Spence scanned the letter, his expression turned hard. "Assholes."

She laughed. "Actually, they would say they were prudent businessmen."

"Same thing if you ask me." He tossed the paper back down on her desk. "So what's your next step?"

At least she didn't have to put up a brave front with him. "I'm not sure. I suspect that any other bank I'd talk to would come to the same conclusion, especially if they ask if I've been turned down for a loan lately."

"It's crazy they'd use one bank's poor judgment as an excuse for their own."

There was no use in pretending the chance of successfully obtaining a loan elsewhere was very high. "I can't say for sure, but they all seem to follow the same criteria when it comes to handing out money. It's like Mr. Lunt said, they don't want to see the millworks close, but my lack of experience in running a company gives them pause."

"Well, that sucks." Spence dropped into one of the chairs facing her desk and propped his feet on the edge of her desk. Her father would've fainted at the sight, but it didn't bother her. On the other hand, anyone else would think Spence was relaxed, but she knew him better than that. Despite the calm facade, his mind was working a hundred miles an hour.

While she waited for him to tell her what had him thinking so hard, she reached for the box he'd set in front of her. Flipping the lid open, she breathed in the rich, chocolaty smell of temptation. As if it had a mind of its own, her hand delved right in to pick up one of the brownies. What could she say? Obviously she was a person of weak character and no willpower. Besides, the letter from the bank definitely topped out on her chocolate emergency scale. She was entitled to splurge. But to be safe, she closed the box and pushed it back closer to Spence.

The movement must have caught his attention, because he nodded toward the box. "By the way, Bridey wants our feedback on the cupcakes. Seth said she no longer thinks he can be impartial when it comes to her baking. I bet the lucky bastard still gets to try everything before she puts it out for the general public. I think I'm jealous."

Spence was kidding, but she had other reasons to be jealous of what Bridey and Seth had going for them. Yeah, their relationship had gone through a slight rough patch, but now the two were engaged and planning a wedding in the near future.

Did it make Melanie a bad person to be envious of

her friends who had found the love of their lives in the past year?

Probably.

Maybe she wouldn't feel that way if she hadn't had her own taste of what it was like to be half of a whole, because that's what she shared with Spence. They spent some nights in her bed, and some in his. He'd even taken to packing her a lunch before she left for work in the morning. Tonight was his turn to cook dinner, but she'd be right there pitching in to help.

In truth, they were really only playing at being a couple even if her heart didn't seem to know that. They both knew he wasn't likely to remain in Snowberry Creek for much longer. If the factory closed, she wouldn't have anything left to tether her here in town, either. She had to wonder where the two of them would be in a year. Would they still be in touch? Rather than ask, she changed the topic.

"How did it go with Troy today? Did you run into some kind of snag?" Spence had been staring off into space, his eyebrows drawn down low and his green eyes looking a bit grim.

He didn't answer immediately. When he finally did, the serious expression had vanished. "No, Troy had everything ready for me to sign, so it all went pretty much as expected. We took care of transferring the title of the house, set up the agreement on the bed-and-breakfast, and a bunch of other stuff."

"That's good."

Although she didn't really mean that. She secretly hated each step forward he took toward hopping on that Harley and riding out of town for good. At the same time, she could tell that things were getting better for

Spence. It had been several days since he left her bed to go prowling the grounds in the darkness with Mooch tagging along for moral support. He had to know that his friends didn't want to see him leave, especially her. Maybe now was a good time to test the waters and see how he reacted.

"Now that you've worked things out with Callie and Nick, have you given any more thought to staying here in Snowberry Creek? You know they don't want you to leave, and they aren't the only ones who feel that way." She hesitated before adding, "I don't want to see you go, either."

He was already shaking his head. "That's nice of you to say, Melanie, but I'm not sure what I'm going to do. I've been thinking for a while now that the best thing for me would be to hit the road on the Harley and see where the highway takes me. I've been moving around so much over the past ten years that I'm not sure I can stay in one place for any length of time. I still have a few things to iron out with my attorney, but after that . . . well, we'll see."

He lapsed into silence again. This was the first time he'd mentioned having made any plans for leaving, and it hurt that he hadn't mentioned them to her. Rather than bugging him for any further explanations she really didn't want to hear, she polished off her brownie, gave herself a stern lecture on why she didn't need another one, and went back to reviewing the work orders they had scheduled over the next few days. She was pleased to see that the numbers were up again.

Another ten minutes passed in silence. Suddenly, Spence's boots hit the floor with a loud thump. When she looked up, he was already heading for the door. "Spence?"

He didn't even slow down. "I've got to go. I'll see you at dinner tonight. My place, right?"

"Yes, although I can cook if you'd rather."

"Nope, I've got it covered. See you at sixish."

Then he was gone. She hurried over to stand at the window to watch as he left the building with deliberate purpose, evidently a man on a mission. What was he up to now? Spence buckled on his helmet and straddled his motorcycle. As he circled the parking lot aiming for the exit, he looked straight up at her and waved. Busted—but what was going on with him? If necessary, she'd ply him with wine and hot sex to see if she could get him to open up to her.

For now, she needed to get back to work. Before sitting down, she carried the box with the rest of the brownies and the cupcakes over to the filing cabinet and locked it inside. Out of sight, out of mind. Right. It might only be her imagination, but she was pretty sure she could still smell the chocolate calling to her from across the room. Doing her best to ignore it, she began reviewing the short list of applicants to replace Mrs. Cuthbert.

Spence drove in circles for two hours, still trying to decide the best way to proceed. It would be complicated, far more so than convincing Callie to accept the house. Earlier, when he'd walked into Melanie's office, he'd known immediately that the bank had turned her down. She'd done her best to put up a brave front, but he was learning to read her moods. The rejection had hurt her deeply. It had made him furious, to the point he'd had a hard time not heading straight for the bank to pound on somebody. That wouldn't fix a damn thing, but he was a soldier and trained to protect what was important, what mattered, what was his.

And the bottom line was that Melanie Wolfe mattered.

So if he couldn't fix her problem with his fists, maybe he could find another way. It would be tricky, for sure. He'd need Troy's help again, because he was going to need a smoke screen if he was going to make this work.

His decision made, he turned back toward town in the hopes the attorney could see him again on short notice. This would be his one last mission before he left Snowberry Creek behind. He might not have a home here anymore. But before he left, at least he could make sure another one of his friends got what she needed.

Chapter 23

Melanie stared at the phone in the kitchen. It had been a bitch of a day, and she'd rather be sharing a bottle of wine with Spence than making another phone call, especially this one. But she knew procrastinating wouldn't make it any easier, so she reached for the receiver and dialed the number. When the answering machine picked up, she breathed a sigh of relief. Yeah, it meant everything was still up in the air, but she gave herself points for trying.

"Hi, Aunt Marcia. Sorry I didn't catch you, and I know Mom has been calling. I've been really busy lately, but having said that, I do need to talk to her about a few things. The kind of stuff that would be better done in person. Would it be all right if I drove down for an overnight visit? I won't be home this evening, so just leave a message on this number to let me know what day works for you, and I'll be there."

After hanging up, she grabbed her keys and the bottle of wine and bolted out the back door. It was a good thing that she and Spence had made plans to spend the evening at the cottage. At least she wouldn't be sitting around the house alone and dreading her aunt's call. Or worse yet, her mother's. She'd left a couple of messages, but Melanie hadn't responded, figuring it was her usual demand for more money. That was part of what Melanie needed to talk to her about. And wouldn't that discussion be fun?

When she reached the cottage, she was surprised to discover the front door was locked and Spence's motorcycle missing. Had she gotten the time wrong? No, she was sure he'd said six o'clock. She had a key to the cottage on her key ring, but she didn't feel comfortable letting herself in with no one home. Before she could decide what to do, a muted bark reminded her that one of her tenants was inside. The least she could do was let Mooch out for a run.

She unlocked the door and blocked Mooch's escape while she reached inside for the leash and the Frisbee Spence always kept on the table by the door. Once she clipped the leash to Mooch's collar, she stepped back and let him out. He hit the porch at a dead run that had her stumbling down the steps in his wake.

"Slow down, dog. Spence won't be happy when he gets home if you've managed to break my neck."

Evidently, Mooch didn't care what his master thought. He charged around the small yard, nose to the ground, until he completed one full circuit before finally stopping to take care of business. When he was finished, she led him around the side of the house and turned him loose in the backyard of her family home.

"Come on, Mooch, I'll let you have a quick romp, and then we'll come back and wait on the porch."

Once he was off the leash, Mooch ran circles around her until she sent the Frisbee flying through the air. The dog tore off across the yard and made a high leap to grab it out of the air. He came trotting back and dropped it at her feet, his tail wagging like crazy. With a flick of her wrist, the disk went sailing with Mooch hot on its trail. She wasn't sure which of them enjoyed the game more. For sure, it felt darn good to be doing something besides worrying about things she couldn't change.

The next time she tossed the toy, Mooch caught it. This time, instead of bringing it to her, he froze in position with his ears up. "What is it, boy?"

The dog yipped in response and trotted a few steps toward the cottage before looking back at her as if to ask, *Are you coming or what?*

Then she heard the familiar rumble of a motorcycle. "Go ahead, boy, I'll catch up."

When she reached the driveway, Spence had parked the bike and was pulling a couple of sacks out of his saddlebags. "Damn it, dog, settle down."

She smiled because even as Spence crabbed at the dog, he was setting the bags back down so he could give Mooch a thorough scratch. Yeah, he was such a big softie. Then he tossed the Frisbee for him before picking up what had to be their dinner.

When he spotted her, he smiled and held up the plastic bags. "Thanks for letting the idiot out, and I hope you don't mind Thai food. I know I promised to cook, but things took a little longer than I expected."

"Thai sounds great, and it was a long day at the office for me, too. It felt good to work out a few of the kinks playing with him."

Mooch returned with his prize but headed straight for

the porch with it. Melanie picked up the bottle of wine she'd left there and took one of the bags from Spence so he could unlock the door. The three of them trooped through the living room straight into the kitchen. While Spence got out plates and glasses, she gave Mooch fresh water and filled his food bowl.

Despite the three of them moving around one another in the small kitchen, it was cozy, not crowded. Something else she shouldn't get too used to, knowing it would make it that much harder to watch Spence ride away for the last time. Even so, she wouldn't let that stop her from enjoying every minute they had together.

"Rats, I knew there was something I forgot," he said.

She put the lid back on the bin of Mooch's kibble. "What's that?"

Spence's hands settled on her shoulders and turned her to face him. His smile was sly, his green eyes darkening as he leaned in close to capture her mouth with his. Her heart fluttered in her chest as he tasted and teased until she parted her lips in invitation. His tongue swept in, taking charge, taking her from zero to sixty in five seconds flat. She dug her nails into his shoulders and held on for dear life.

When he backed off on the kiss, she was glad she wasn't the only one whose breath was coming in ragged gasps. She traced the curve of his smile with a fingertip. "I'm glad you remembered. I would have hated to miss out on that."

"It was my pleasure. Now we'd better eat or dinner will get cold." He kissed her on the tip of her nose. "Besides, I'm really hoping I'm going to need all the strength I can muster tonight."

"Well, then by all means, let's get you fed."

*   *   *

She was into her second glass of wine and thinking about making a move on the man sitting next to her, when her cell phone buzzed. It went silent after a few seconds but then immediately started ringing again.

"Are you going to answer that?"

She didn't even look at the screen to see who it was. "I asked my aunt to leave me a message tonight. It's probably her." Even though she'd asked Aunt Marcia to use the landline, not her cell.

Spence tightened his arm around her shoulder and took her wineglass from her hand and set it safely out of reach. "Good. We have better things to do than talk on the phone."

"I like the way you think. Now kiss me."

Before he could carry out her order, the phone started up again. Clearly someone was determined to talk to her. She picked up the phone and immediately wished she hadn't. It was her mother calling, not her aunt. As much as she wanted to ignore the interruption, her dutiful daughter syndrome kicked in.

"Yes, Mom, what is it?"

Spence watched all the life drain out of Melanie's face as she listened to whatever her mother was telling her. If he was reading her expression correctly, it wasn't anything life-threatening. Probably more of her mother's constant demands for more money.

Or maybe it was something else, considering Melanie had just shifted to sit on the far end of the couch. Clearly she didn't feel comfortable with whatever her mother was ragging on her about with him sitting beside her. It was tempting to pry the phone out of the death grip Melanie had on it and simply disconnect the call. Or better yet, he could tell Mrs. Wolfe to get off Melanie's back for once. Didn't the damn woman realize how hard her daughter was working to salvage something from the mess her husband had left behind?

None of those were good choices, so he settled for giving Melanie some space. "Come on, Mooch, it's time for you to patrol the yard."

He squeezed Melanie's free hand and headed for the door with the dog at his heels. He'd give her about ten minutes to wrap up the call and then he'd do it for her.

His countdown had almost reached zero when Melanie finally stepped out on the porch. He whistled Mooch back and joined her on the front step. "So I'm guessing she found out about us."

"She said if I was going to indulge in a fling, the least I could do was be discreet. Seems the neighbors are talking."

Melanie threaded her fingers through his and laid her head against his shoulder. "I don't know which makes me madder: that some busybody felt obligated to tell tales or that my mother managed to make something that's so special sound cheap and tawdry."

What could he say to that? What they had was special, but a couple of weeks ago her mother wouldn't have been entirely wrong. From the outset, they'd both said their relationship had no real future. He was only planning to be in town temporarily, and she didn't know what was going to happen to her family company. It had become all too easy to forget the rules they'd established when hanging out together felt so right.

"I'm sorry she said such hurtful things."

"Well, she's not going to be happy with me anytime soon. I've already told my aunt that I need to make a trip to Portland. It's time to quit coddling my mother and lay the facts out for her to see for herself. With the bank turning the company down for a loan, I have fewer options when it comes to keeping all of us afloat financially. Putting the house on the market is the next logical step."

If Spence had harbored any doubts about the plan he'd put into motion that afternoon, they were gone now. "I hope it doesn't come to that, Mel. It would be too bad to see Wolfe House pass out of your family's control."

She shrugged. "I'm not so sure about that. Maybe I'd feel differently if the place wasn't more of a museum than a home. Besides, if Mom's going to stay in Portland, I sure don't need to keep rattling around in a house that size."

"Maybe."

"I will admit that I've found there are some things about being a Wolfe that matter to me. I want to remain a part of the community and support some of the charities my parents did. That feels right to me." Melanie glanced at him out of the corner of her eye. "Tell me you don't feel better ... freer somehow ... you know, now that you've signed the house over to Callie and Nick. That's got to be a huge relief."

Yes, it was, but then he'd made the choice because he'd wanted to, not because of money problems. He wanted Melanie to be free to make that same kind of choice. "When you go visit your mother, let me know if you want me to come with you."

"That's sweet of you to offer, but I can't ask you to do that."

"You're not asking, Mel. I'm offering."

She released his hand to slide her palm down to his leg and give it a quick squeeze. "And is that all you're offering? Because I seem to remember you saying you needed all your strength for something."

That warm pressure from her hand wandered on, stroking the inside of his leg up to the top of his thigh and back again. As a tactic designed to change the subject, it was a dandy. The second stroke was a little slower and a lot more adventurous. The next one had his eyes about to roll back in his head. He caught her hand in his and used it to tug her up to her feet after he managed to stand up himself.

Spence whistled to get Mooch's attention. "Hey, buddy, it's time to come inside."

The dog looked up from the bush he'd been sniffing. Maybe he picked up on something in Spence's voice, because he immediately headed right for them. Good, because thanks to the effect of Melanie's touch, Spence could barely walk, much less run.

As soon as they were all inside, he swept her up in his arms and carried her straight into the bedroom. He wanted her, needed her, and that made him even more determined to make the most of every minute they had together. In a perfect world, he would have been able to offer her a future together. But he couldn't, not when he was still so broken inside. He didn't know if they'd make it out of this relationship without regrets, but damned if she'd ever doubt that he wanted her, that he cared.

Chapter 24

❧❧

Nick had asked Leif to tag along with him and Callie to their appointment with Troy. They were signing off on their portion of the paperwork about the house, which didn't really involve him. Sarge's excuse was that they needed Leif's moral support, saying the three of them were jumping off a cliff together by opening two businesses at the same time with no idea of whether their parachutes would open.

Not a bad analogy. A high percentage of new businesses failed. That was a fact, but Leif had a good feeling about all of this. Maybe it was because there was so much right in their lives now. As long as Nick and Callie were together, they'd be happy. Him and Zoe, too. If they fell flat on their collective asses with the bed-and-breakfast and the remodeling business, they'd pick themselves up and press on.

Troy appeared at the door of the small waiting room. "Hi, everybody. Sorry to keep you waiting."

Nick stood up and held out his hand. "No problem. Troy, you remember our friend Leif Brevik."

The attorney shook Callie's hand, then Nick's and Leif's. "Of course. Why don't we head into the conference room? There's more room in there than in my office."

Signing the papers hadn't taken all that long, but the attorney didn't seem to be in any great hurry to show them to the door. Clearly something was bothering the man. Right now Nick and Callie were busy studying the last paper they'd signed, the one that gave them legal title to the house. Maybe they hadn't noticed the worried look on Troy's face.

Leif nudged Nick and then gave the attorney a hard look. "You're concerned about something. What's wrong?"

Troy actually jumped as if Leif's blunt statement had startled him. His face flushed red and the worry was replaced by what looked like guilt. "I'm sorry. It's something I can't discuss with the three of you."

Leif sat up taller. The man hadn't actually said that the matter didn't concern the three of them, only that he couldn't discuss it with them. That left only one logical explanation: Spence. "What's he done this time?"

"What has who done?" Callie asked as she glanced around the table at each man in turn.

When the attorney didn't respond, Leif answered her. "Spence has done something that has Troy here worried, but he can't tell us what it is because of attorney/client privilege or some such shit. Not to mention, I'm betting Wheels is still planning on leaving town."

Troy remained grimly silent but gave the briefest of nods—twice. Meaning Leif was right on both counts. Son of a bitch, what was Wheels up to now? Well, there was no way Leif would get the answer to that question sitting here. He exchanged looks with Nick. Yeah, they'd have to track Spence down and find out for themselves. The tricky part would be not outing Troy in the process.

Leif reached for his cane. "Well, we should be going. Places to go. Certain people to see."

Nick and Callie stood up with him. Troy shook everyone's hand again and led the small parade back down the hall to the door. "Thanks for stopping by. If there's ever anything I can do for you, don't hesitate to call me."

As they filed past, he stepped in front of Leif. "Tell Spence hi for me when you see him."

"I will."

When they reached the parking lot, Nick held out his keys to Callie. "I'm going to catch a ride with Leif."

She ignored the keys. As she glared at her husband, she said, "Tell me what you two have planned."

Leif stepped back. No way he was going to get caught in the middle between the pair. "Nothing, Callie."

She shot him a disgusted look. "Right. So Nick is blowing off our lunch date for nothing?"

Well, shit, this wasn't going well. "Nick, you want to take the lead on this?"

Nick pocketed his keys. "We're just going to go talk to Spence. Shoot the shit. See what's going on with him."

Callie crossed her arms over her chest. "And if he doesn't want to spill his guts? What then? I know how these discussions usually end. I'm telling you right now, I don't want you coming home with bloody noses and bruised knuckles."

Her husband clearly wanted to argue the point, but there was no denying that she was right on target. "Callie, Nick and I have years of experience in dealing with Spence. Sometimes a good right cross is the only way to get through to him."

"Not happening, gentlemen."

He couldn't believe what he was hearing. "So you want to let Spence go ahead with whatever screwball thing he's doing that has Troy that worried?"

That didn't go over well. Callie turned her anger in his direction. "He was my friend long before he was yours, Leif. No one cares more about what happens to Spence than I do, with the possible exception of Melanie Wolfe. So I'm thinking we need to have a barbecue at the house and invite both of them. That way, after a few beers, we can gang up on him and see where it gets us."

Nick finally smiled and flexed his right hand. "And if that fails, promise me we can still try our way of convincing him to talk."

Callie's smile matched her husband's. "It's a deal."

Good. That much was settled. "So what excuse can we come up with that won't make him suspect this is an intervention?"

"We should keep it simple, like a potluck. Tell him it's a chance for old friends to get together. We'll limit it to three couples besides Spence and Melanie: Nick and me, you and Zoe, Bridey and Seth. Eight people is plenty. We don't want a huge crowd of witnesses."

"Good thinking. Figure out the day and time, and I'll let Zoe know to save the date."

He had started for his own truck when Callie called his name. "Leif, maybe we can add one more thing to the agenda. I would really love it if we could convince Spence to stay here in Snowberry Creek."

"Me, too, Callie. Me, too."

Chapter 25

❦❦

Melanie braced herself for the worst and knocked on her aunt's front door. Marcia had agreed to be gone when Melanie arrived, but she had made it clear that she'd only stay gone an hour at the most. After that, she'd be back to pick up the pieces. Not exactly encouraging as to how much success she thought Melanie would have in explaining a few harsh realities to her mother.

The door finally opened.

"Why are you here?"

Melanie forced a smile. "It's been a long time since we saw each other. I thought I'd surprise you with a visit."

True enough, but not the real answer to the question. Her mother knew it, too. "If you were missing me all that much, you wouldn't have been avoiding my phone calls."

And Melanie had answered one that she should have ignored, but she wasn't there to talk about Spence.

Her mother finally unlatched the screen door and held it open. "I'm also guessing that Marcia being conveniently absent right now isn't just a coincidence."

Melanie followed her mother into the living room. She was struck again by the sharp difference between her aunt and her mother. The living room in the Wolfe House was filled with museum-quality antiques, the kind that people were afraid to touch for fear of breaking something. Aunt Marcia's home was meant to be lived in, the furniture solid and comfortable.

Melanie waited until her mother perched on the edge of the sofa before sitting down beside her. She booted up her laptop and set a stack of bank statements and other papers beside it. Her mom looked at it all as if it were a rattlesnake poised to attack her. "What's all this?"

"I brought the most current statements on everything because I'm here to update you on the status of your finances. Our finances, really, since I'm running the company."

"And if I had other plans for this morning?"

Before Melanie could formulate a response, the door opened again, and Marcia appeared in the doorway. "Sorry, Mel. I know I promised to stay gone, but I decided you'd both do better with me here to referee. If I'm wrong about that, I'll apologize later."

"It won't be a problem, Marcia, because I'm not interested in anything Melanie has to show me. It's all lies anyway. Edmond was a fine businessman. He wouldn't have left things in such disarray."

Melanie picked up the first bank statement. "We're going to go through all of this page by page. Ask questions as you have them. I'll explain everything as clearly and concisely as possible. When I'm done, you can decide what you want to do with the house and the company."

Her mother jerked as if Melanie had hit her. "What

are you talking about? There are no decisions to be made. The house stays in the family, and the company goes on as it always has."

Once again Marcia joined the conversation. "Sandra, Melanie has been trying to make you see the truth for months, and you've refused to listen. It's one thing to keep up appearances for the sake of Edmond's memory, but not at the sacrifice of your daughter. Look at her. She's driven all the way down here to talk to you in person rather than ask you to come to her at a time I'm guessing she could ill afford away from the office. She's also put her own career on hold to step in when you needed her most."

Sandra frowned and focused her eyes on Melanie as if really seeing her for the first time. But rather than crumple as she always had done in the past, she braced herself and sat up straighter. "Fine. I'll listen."

Melanie glanced at Marcia, who just shrugged. "Okay, here's where we are."

Two hours and a headache later, Melanie escaped to the backyard, leaving the two sisters alone to talk. She could count on Marcia to give her sister good practical advice, and she would have better luck making Sandra face up to the hard truths that Melanie had laid out for them.

Her mom hadn't liked a single thing she'd said, but at least she no longer doubted what Melanie was telling her was anything but the truth. It helped that Melanie had brought along all the paperwork concerning the loans her father had taken out so that her mom could see the hard evidence for herself.

As Marcia had pointed out, accepting that Edmond Wolfe hadn't been perfect didn't change the fact that he'd loved Sandra and she'd loved him. The important thing now was for them to band together to do everything possible to protect the legacy of the Wolfe family. If it became necessary to sell the house to save the company, so be it.

Her mother was still mulling that part over. To give them both a break, Melanie had grabbed a cold drink from the refrigerator and headed outside. She settled into one of the chairs on the deck and drew the first easy breath she'd had all day.

She really hoped her mother would come down on the side of saving the company. Despite the headaches that came with running the place, Melanie would miss it. Besides, the idea of telling all the employees that she was going to have to put the company up for sale made her sick. Even if it did sell, that was no guarantee that would save their jobs. Someone might buy the place with the intention of stripping it of every asset before closing it down.

She sipped her diet cola and tried to shut off the constant stream of worry that kept her head pounding. No dice. There was too much she should be doing back at the office. She'd originally planned to stay overnight, but now she thought she'd head back home after she and her mother finished up their discussion.

Given a choice between sleeping at her aunt's house and snuggling up with a handsome guy, well, there was no contest. Once she was on the way back to Snowberry Creek, she'd give Spence a call to let him know a few ideas about how they might celebrate her return.

The door behind her opened, and Marcia stepped out onto the deck with Melanie's cell phone in her hand. "You had a call from a Mr. Lunt. I didn't want to answer for you, and he hung up before I could get out here. I thought it might be important."

Melanie glanced at the screen on the phone. Evidently, he'd left her a voice mail. What could he want now? Wasn't turning her down in writing enough?

Her aunt dropped down on the next chair. "I'm guessing this isn't good news."

"I'm not sure. He's the banker I was working with, trying to restructure the company's debt load."

She had to listen to the message, not that she wanted to, especially right now when her head was already pounding. Bracing herself for whatever bad news he had to deliver, she punched in her password and put the call on speakerphone so Marcia could hear it, too. The woman already knew everything there was to know about the Wolfe family finances. One more bit of information couldn't make things any worse.

"Hello, Ms. Wolfe. I would appreciate greatly if you could give me a call at your earliest convenience. There has been a new development with regards to your file, one that is most promising. I'd rather not discuss the details in this message, so I'll be waiting to hear from you."

Melanie replayed the message twice more before setting the phone aside. Marcia stared at it with her. "What do you think it means?"

"Honestly, I have no idea. His letter made it perfectly clear that they wouldn't be able to help us."

"Are you going to call him?"

Melanie bought herself a few seconds by finishing her drink. "I don't have any choice if there's a chance he really does have good news for me. If they've changed their mind, it will buy us some more time to decide what to do about the house."

Just the possibility that the bank was going to toss her a lifeline left her hands shaking. On the plus side, her headache was gone.

Her aunt rose from her seat to give Melanie a quick shoulder rub. "You can do this, champ. Get in there and fight!"

Melanie laughed and patted her aunt's hand. "Thanks, coach. It means a lot to me that you've been in my corner through all of this. No matter how it turns out, I'm grateful."

She pushed the button to return the banker's call. Mr. Lunt answered on the second ring and quickly gave her a brief overview of what had changed since they last spoke. When he was finished, she set up an appointment for the next afternoon to come in to discuss everything in more detail. After exchanging a few more pleasantries, he ended the call. Melanie sat frozen, unable to think, much less speak. Not coherently, anyway.

Her aunt stared at her, her expression slowly changing from hopeful to worried. "Melanie, what did he say?"

Lurching up from the deck chair, she knocked her pop can onto the deck. With a swift kick, she sent it flying through the air to bounce off the wall behind her. "I'm going to kill that sneaky son of a bitch!"

Her aunt looked horrified. "The banker?"

If it were only that easy. "No, not him. Spencer Lang. That man is dead meat."

With exaggerated care, she picked up the can and crushed it with her bare hands as she pretended it was Spence's neck. "I'll be leaving now, Aunt Marcia. I'll let you know where things stand after I talk to the banker tomorrow."

"Are you okay to be driving, Mel? You're awfully upset right now."

Faking a calm she certainly didn't feel, she hugged her aunt. "I'm fine, and I really need to get back to town."

Marcia held her out to arm's length. "I'm guessing this Spencer Lang means a great deal to you."

Yeah, he did even if she hadn't actually admitted how much, not even to herself. Maybe it was time to put a label on the powerful jumble of feelings he'd managed to stir up deep inside her. "I love him, Aunt Marcia."

"And that's a bad thing?"

"It is when we promised to make no claims on each other. I've known all along that he planned to leave Snowberry Creek. And now the big jerk has gone behind my back to the bank and offered to cosign on the loan. It's his way of telling me good-bye."

The door behind them opened, and her mother stepped out onto the deck. "Well, are you going to let him get away with this? We don't need money from the likes of him."

Marcia gasped. "Sandra, your daughter is hurting, and she certainly doesn't need your snobbery right now! If Melanie loves him, I'm sure he's a fine young man."

Her mother glared right back at her sister. "If he doesn't think my daughter is worth sticking around for, he doesn't deserve her, Marcia. I'd live in a hovel before I'd take a dime from an idiot."

She joined the group hug, surrounding Melanie with the familiar scent of Chanel No 5. "Sell the house. Heck, sell my jewelry if that's what it takes to keep the company afloat."

Then, just as her sister had done, she took half a step back to give Melanie a hard look. "But only if that's what will make you happy, Melanie. Otherwise, we'll put the company on the market so you can be free to choose your own life. Before you meet with the banker tomorrow, decide what you want and then we'll figure out the best way to proceed."

"And if what I want is Spence Lang?"

Her mother blinked back some tears. "My advice? Go after him with everything you have. That's what I did when I met your father. He was dating someone else at the time, someone his family thought was more suitable." Her smile turned wicked. "I wasn't Edmond's first choice, but I made darn sure he figured out I was the right choice."

So why hadn't Melanie heard about that before now? As much as she'd love to hear more details, now wasn't the time to ask. She had miles to drive and plans to make. "I'll call you both tomorrow when I know more."

Her mother patted her on the cheek. "Do that. And, Melanie, I know I've been useless to you all this time. As corny as it sounds, your father was my soul mate, and I've been lost without him. However, that's no excuse for having failed you, and I promise to do better from now on. If you need me to come home, I'll start packing right now."

Amazing. Melanie had no doubt her mom meant every word. Better yet, it was the first spark of life she'd seen in her mother since the funeral. "I'll keep you posted, Mom."

She hugged her mother and her aunt one last time. "Wish me luck, ladies. When I get done with Spence, he won't know what hit him."

Marcia followed her through the house to the front door. "One more thing, Melanie. Before you beat him up too badly, remember that his heart was in the right place."

"I know." And she really did understand. "The thing

is that he's never felt as if he belonged anywhere, especially after his adoptive parents died. After he enlisted, he bounced all over the world, which hasn't helped. I'm not sure he knows how to put down roots anywhere."

"So if he can't stay, what are you going to do? Does keeping the family company going mean more to you than he does? Because we both know it could come down to that choice."

The familiar burden of all those people who depended on Wolfe Millworks for their income settled right back on Melanie's shoulders. The image of all their faces flowed through her mind, each a reminder of how much there was at stake. "I guess I need to figure that out."

Marcia hugged her one last time before letting Melanie walk out the door. "Like Sandra said, if you need us, we'll be there."

Three hours later, Melanie turned off the interstate onto the two-lane highway that would take her straight into Snowberry Creek. She'd been driving alone with her thoughts for over three hours and still hadn't come to any conclusions. Maybe divine inspiration would strike the second she saw Spence, but she wasn't counting on it. Just before she hit the city limits, her cell phone rang. In no hurry to get home, she pulled off the road to take the call.

"Hey, Callie, what's up?"

She found herself nodding long before Callie had finished filling her in on the plan Spence's friends had concocted. As much as she wanted Spence to stick around just for her, it wouldn't hurt to have more people make it clear that he belonged right there in Snowberry Creek with them.

"My only input would be that the more the merrier. I

know Will Cosgrove has been trying to get Spence to hire on in his place at the millworks. That old man has never shown any interest in retiring, so I'm thinking that it's his way of trying to get Spence to stay. Your folks mean a lot to Spence, too. I'd even ask Gage Logan to put in an appearance."

She hesitated and then added, "I think my mother would like to be there. My aunt, too."

Callie actually gasped. "Really? Your mom? What's changed?"

"Three hours ago she told me that she hadn't been my father's first choice, but that she made darn sure he figured out she was the right choice for him. That's when she told me that if I felt that way about Spence, I should go for it."

Her friend's laughter rang out in the car. "Seriously? She actually said that? It's hard to bring that picture into focus, but I'll take your word for it. We'll add them to the list."

Melanie was feeling better by the second. "Thanks for doing this, Callie. It means a lot. And if . . ."

The next words were proving difficult to say. She closed her eyes and tried again. "And if he decides to go, at least he'll never doubt that he'll be missed."

There was a brief silence on the other end of the line before Callie spoke again. "I know it's hard to do right now, but we've got to have a little faith in the guy. There was a time I thought Nick was going to walk away, too, but look where we are now. Don't give up on Spence."

"I won't."

"Good. And if all else fails, Nick and Leif plan to knock some sense into him. Gage may end up arresting them, but that's a risk we'll have to take. Desperate times and desperate measures and all that. Now I'd better go tell Nick there's been a change in plans. We'll need to double the food order."

"Let me know what I can do to help."

"Just show up. We're kind of considering you to be the big gun in this battle. The man would have to be an idiot to walk away from you. Talk to you soon."

Feeling better than she had in hours, Melanie put the car back in gear and drove toward home—and Spence.

Chapter 26

Spence stood at the front window, his forehead pressed against the cool glass. Lately, his nightmares had made themselves blessedly scarce, maybe because of how Melanie had helped keep him anchored here in Snowberry Creek. But without her presence somehow the cottage had turned into a cage, one with walls that were slowly closing in on him. Even with all the windows open, the air was too thin to breathe. His head might know he wasn't back in that damn hellhole in Afghanistan, but that didn't seem to count for much right now. For what seemed like the hundredth time, he turned away from the window to pace the length of the living room and back again, the smooth wood cool against his bare feet. The short distance didn't help.

Where the hell was she?

On his next lap, he extended his route to include circling through the kitchen; the few extra feet didn't help. Neither did nearly tripping over Mooch.

"Damn it, dog, go lie down and stay out from underfoot."

The dog backed away to slink across the room to take refuge on the back of the couch. Son of a bitch, he was acting as if Spence had really kicked him. "Cut me some slack here, Mooch."

When the dog didn't look any happier, Spence gave up on trying to outdistance his demons. After grabbing some doggy treats, he flopped on the couch where he could pet his buddy and try to make amends. "Sorry, dog. I shouldn't take my bad mood out on you."

A pair of sympathetic brown eyes said he understood and forgave him. They both took comfort from the close contact. "I wish I knew what was going on with Melanie, boy. Women are a mystery that this poor soldier will never solve."

Especially while he was hopelessly mired in his very own pity party. He thought for sure Melanie would call him after she spoke to Mr. Lunt at the bank. Instead, there had been nothing but silence. He'd tried to call her several times, but each time it had gone straight to voice mail. Her phone must be dead; she wouldn't screen his phone calls. At least he hoped not, because that would mean that she was avoiding him.

Hell, he didn't even know if she was still in Portland visiting with her mother and aunt. He'd also avoided checking her house to see if there were any signs of life. If she was back from her road trip, why hadn't she come to see him?

Had he really and truly fucked up this time?

"What do you think, Mooch? Did I screw up big-time by trying to fix things for Melanie?"

The dog sighed and laid his head on Spence's leg. "Yeah, I don't know, either. Maybe I should have talked to her first, but you know how stubborn she is. It would be just like her to refuse help because she wants to do it all herself. She might have issues with her parents, but the truth is that she inherited a full dose of the Wolfe family pride."

He leaned his head against the back of the couch to stare up at the ceiling. No answers there, either. Had Nick and Leif had to maneuver through a minefield like this with Callie and Zoe? He'd like to think so, although that didn't mean he'd call them for advice. He could just hear the huge pile of grief they'd give him for screwing up again, not to mention that they'd never let him live it down.

Of course, if he followed through on his plan to leave on his road trip as soon as next week, he wouldn't be around for them to hear it. He'd run out of excuses to hang around much longer. That thought should make him feel a whole lot better than it did.

"So, Mooch, we do have one problem I haven't quite figured out." He dug in his pocket for another dog biscuit. "Here's the thing. I don't know where I'm headed once I leave here."

He let the dog munch on that problem along with the biscuit. "Then there's the fact that I don't own a car or a truck, which makes taking you with me a bit tricky."

Mooch stopped chewing to shoot Spence a suspicious look. He was probably only picking up on something in Spence's voice or maybe in his body language, but he clearly knew something was up. Either way, he sat motionless and as if waiting for the other shoe to drop.

"I guess I could always leave you with Nick and Callie until I get settled somewhere and can send for you."

He rubbed Mooch's silky ears. "But I'm thinking maybe you'd be better off with them on a permanent basis. You love people, and there will be plenty of those around when the bed-and-breakfast takes off."

And he knew it would. Hell, the only reason he could stand to leave was believing his friends would live the life they wanted here in Snowberry Creek. Sarge and Callie would have their bed-and-breakfast. He especially loved the name they'd given it: Rose Blossom Place in honor of his mother's love of roses. Leif had Zoe and his partnership with Nick. All of that was good.

And Melanie? He'd made sure she'd have Wolfe Mill-works if that's what she wanted, which he was convinced she did. She might grumble about a few things, but there was no missing the pride she took in seeing the numbers improve. Once she had it all under control, maybe she'd even have time for a personal life. No doubt she'd eventually hook up with some guy who would fit in with the country club crowd and make her mother proud. She might not think that last part mattered, but it did.

Yeah, he wanted all of that for her.

Even if he wanted to punch something at the very thought of someone else sharing Mel's life, holding her in his arms, and sharing her bed. Memories filled his mind with what it had been like to rise above her and see her peaches-and-cream skin flushed with passion. He loved the way she called his name as she urged him to take her harder, faster, further. God, he'd never forget the perfect fit of their bodies as they surged together. How the hell was he supposed to find the strength to walk away from all of that?

He had about the same chance of coming up with a reasonable answer to that question as did Mooch. Maybe a long walk would help. They'd head toward Main Street and maybe grab a burger somewhere. The one place he wouldn't go was anywhere near the Wolfe House. He couldn't stand the thought that Melanie had come back from Portland and had no interest in seeing him again.

If that was true, it would only play into his plan of leaving town with no strings attached. He should be happy about that, but he wasn't. He was pissed.

"Come on, dog. Let me grab my shoes and socks, and then we're out of here."

Sitting on the edge of the bed, he'd only put on one sock when a heavy fist pounded on the front door. He picked up his boots and the other sock and headed out into the living room. There was a brief silence before the banging started again. By this time, Mooch was pitching a fit, barking and dancing around in front of the door. He wasn't growling, though, which meant the idiot raising all the ruckus was someone the dog knew and liked.

Great. There was a pretty short list of possibilities, and none of them were people Spence wanted to deal with right now.

"Spence, I know you're in there, so answer the damn door."

The heavy door muffled the voice, but he would have recognized that irritated baritone anywhere. What the hell did Leif want now? Only one way to find out. He yanked the door open and walked away, leaving it up to Mooch to make their guest feel welcome.

By the time Leif got past the ecstatic dog, Spence was lacing up his second boot. "So, what brings you here?"

Leif planted his size thirteens right in front of where Spence sat on the couch, his arms crossed over his chest. "I'm here to fetch you."

Spence studied the man, trying to see through that carefully blank expression to determine what the hell was going on. "Fetch me where?"

"Does it matter?" Leif looked around the small house. "It doesn't look like you have much on your agenda for the evening."

Pitiful, but that didn't mean he had to admit it.

"I was just getting ready to leave." That much was true. "Melanie and I have plans."

"Don't try to bullshit me, Wheels. It won't work."

Okay, so that had been a lie. But how did Leif know to call him on it? He studied Leif's whole demeanor. He wasn't exactly smirking, but he was coming damn close. The bastard was up to something; that was for damn sure.

"I repeat, I was sent to fetch you. Now that you've figured out how to tie your shoes, get your lazy ass up off the couch. We have places to go. People to see."

Spence's pulse kicked up a notch. He unfolded off the couch to his full height, which gave him several inches over Leif. "And if I don't want to see people?"

Leif flashed his cell phone. "I have reinforcements on speed dial."

"Seriously?"

"Yep. The only reason Nick didn't come with me in the first place is that I reminded him how you were always so reasonable to deal with."

Okay, neither one of them could keep a straight face after that bald-faced lie. "What did you really say?"

"That you wouldn't be able to resist my charm?"

Snicker. "Try again."

Leif lost most of his bluster. "Okay, fine. I told everybody if we ganged up on you, you'd refuse just out of pure cussedness, and that's the honest truth."

"And who exactly is this 'everybody' you mentioned?"

"You'll find out when we get there. I've also got orders to bring Mooch with us." He reached down to pet the dog, who had parked himself right at their feet. "How you doing, buddy? Is Wheels treating you okay?"

The four-footed traitor actually whined and tried to look pathetic. "Don't buy what he's selling, Leif. See that fat belly? He's eating me out of house and home, not to mention he just devoured a handful of dog biscuits."

Leif straightened up. "So, are you coming along peacefully or do I need to call Sarge?"

Anything was better than staying trapped here at the cottage. "Grab Mooch's leash while I lock up."

Fifteen minutes later, what had started off sounding like a bad idea suddenly got a whole lot worse. Leif turned into the driveway at Mama R.'s house and said, "We're parking over here because the driveway next door is full."

"Straight up, what's really going on?" Spence glared over Mooch's head at the other man. "The whole truth, Leif, or I'm not getting out of this truck anytime soon."

His friend twisted around to face Spence more directly. "Nothing bad, Wheelman. That much I can promise. I'm sure you'd rather get the explanation directly from Melanie and Callie. This was their idea." He swallowed hard and looked away. "Mostly, anyway."

Anger started burning along Spence's nerves. "And what is their objective? Tell me now."

"We started off calling it an intervention. But I promise, it's really a bunch of people who care about you getting together hoping to convince you to stay here in Snowberry Creek."

What the hell were they thinking? Were they all crazy to think this was a good idea? Because it sure as hell wasn't. If he'd had trouble breathing in the cottage, it was nothing compared to how choked up he was right now.

"I can't do this, Leif. Take me back."

At least his friend realized he was as serious as death about that. "We'll just take it slow here, Wheels. Why don't you get out and walk around the Reddings' backyard? Give yourself a couple of minutes to think things through. If you still want to leave, I'll take you anywhere you want to go."

Spence nodded and fumbled for the door handle. He and Mooch spilled out of the truck and took off toward the koi pond in the back. Leif got out, too, but he kept his distance. Spence might thank him later, but right now all he could do was focus on the soothing murmur of the water. Mooch lay down to watch the fish dart through the pond, his tail moving in a slow sweep across the grass.

Spence's pulse gradually dropped back down below the imminent heart attack range. That didn't mean he was ready to venture next door. Instead, he sat down on the swing and set it to swaying gently. He wasn't sure how long he'd been sitting there before he realized he was no longer alone. The breeze rippling across the water carried with it the slightest hint of Melanie's perfume. Maybe she wasn't avoiding him after all.

"Come sit down. I promise I won't bite."

"That could prove to be disappointing." She set a large flat package on the picnic table and joined him on the swing, taking his hand in hers. "Are you okay?"

If it had been anyone else, he might have lied, but this was Melanie. She'd seen him at his worst and never flinched. She could handle this. "I'm just coming down off a major panic attack."

"Anything I can do to help?"

He tugged his hand free to wrap his arm around her shoulders and pull her close. "Just your being here is enough."

Mooch joined them, his feet skidding on the vinyl seat when the swing moved again. He finally flopped down with his head in Melanie's lap.

Melanie glanced up at Spence. "We meant for this to be a good thing, you know."

"I know. And somewhere on the outer edges of my panic, I do appreciate everyone's good intentions."

He sniffed the air. "I'm guessing Nick's barbecuing some big hunks of meat."

She giggled. "Mostly steaks, although after a heated discussion, he conceded to throw some chicken on the grill, too. Something about it being for those who aren't manly enough to eat their meat rare enough to still be mooing. That's pretty much a direct quote, by the way."

Spence chuckled. "Yeah, that sounds like Sarge."

They lapsed into silence for a few minutes. Finally, Melanie asked, "Think you can handle facing the folks next door anytime soon?"

He didn't want to, but it wasn't in him to tell her no, not when she was speaking to him again. He'd feel better if they cleared the air between them first. "I've got to ask you something first."

Without waiting for her to respond, he blurted it out and then waited for the fireworks. "How pissed are you over my offer to help with the financing at the bank?"

The explosion wasn't long in coming. Between one second and the next, Melanie went from sympathetic to furious. She jumped up from the swing so abruptly poor Mooch tumbled off the seat with her, hitting the ground hard in a scrambling mass of black and white fur. She immediately knelt down to check him over for damage, apologizing profusely as she did. That didn't mean her eyes weren't ice-cold and glaring at Spence the entire time.

After verifying Mooch was all right, Melanie straightened up and pointed a finger right at Spence's face. "If you want to do this now, fine by me. You had no right to go behind my back like that. I won't be one of your special projects, Spencer Lang!"

The last vestige of his smile vanished in an instant. "What the hell are you talking about, Mel? I don't have projects, special or otherwise."

"The heck you don't!"

Holding up one finger, she started counting off all the examples she could think of. "Mooch was a project. Bringing him home was your idea even if it was Nick and Leif who made it happen. You couldn't stand the thought of that dog going back to starving in the streets."

He started to protest, but she held up her other hand. "No, don't interrupt. I didn't say that what you did was anything but good, but this is my tirade. You can have your own when I get done."

When his mouth snapped shut, she held up a second finger. "You volunteered to help Will get all of the machines tuned up and running right again. Yeah, that helped me and the people that use them every day, but the fact is that you did it for Will. It doesn't take a genius to know he's having trouble keeping up, so you helped out your old friend."

The rest of the fingers on that hand popped up while she pointed toward the woods that separated the Reddings' yard from the one next door. "I don't doubt that you really have issues with your family home, but the truth is you gave up the house next door to make sure Callie got her chance at that bed-and-breakfast she's been telling everyone about. Not to mention that signing the house over to her and Nick served more than one purpose. Once Leif and Nick finish doing all the work on that old beauty, their fledgling remodeling business will have some serious street creds that will attract more work for them in the area."

She paused to take a quick breath and then launched back into her lecture. "So that left me, the last person in this town that you give a damn about. You couldn't let yourself get on that Harley and ride out of Snowberry Creek until you knew you'd made sure I'd never forget you or what you did for Wolfe Millworks. Well, I won't have it, Spence. It's not up to you whether my family's company succeeds or fails."

He looked totally bewildered. "But I've got the money, Mel, and you need it."

"Yes, I do need money, but I don't need yours!"

Okay, that probably wasn't the best way to put that, because suddenly she had a totally irate man lunging up out of the swing to stare down at her with eyes the color of jade. "So that's the bottom line, isn't it? If some stuffy banker offers you a handout, you'll take it. God forbid that money come from a friend!"

He leaned in close, crowding her, until she retreated a step. "Or is it because the Wolfe family is too good to take money from a Lang?"

She so wanted to smack him, but her mother had raised her better than that. "Don't you dare accuse me of being a snob!"

He crossed his arms over his chest, clearly not ready to listen to her. Well, she was made of sterner stuff than he suspected. "Yes, my folks had issues with image. I'll grant you that much. But just so you know, earlier this week my mother advised me to decide whether or not you were worth fighting for. If so, she told me to go after you, no holds barred."

That got his attention. "She really said that?"

Melanie took back that step she'd given up and then another until she was standing so close that she had to tip her head back to look up at him. "Yes, she did. And if you don't believe me, you can ask her yourself. She's next door at the barbecue. She and my aunt drove up this afternoon to help out. She even brought a casserole, so cut the woman some slack."

After giving him a few seconds to come to terms with that little bombshell, she continued. "So I've spent the past two days thinking about everything in my life. I learned a lot, some of which I'm not all that proud of, but some that I am. I've spent years resisting being a real part of my family. I now know that it was the pressure from all sides to fit the Wolfe family image that I hated, but my heritage is still important to me. I also know my family has done a lot of good things for this town, and I'd love to continue that tradition. The bottom line is that I figured out what matters to me and what doesn't."

He was starting to look a bit panicky again, but she wasn't about to stop now. There was no telling how long he'd stick around after tonight.

"My family home isn't important to me, but it is to my mother. If I can save it for her, I will. On the other hand, she told me to sell it if that's what it took to save the company, if that's what will make me happy in the long run."

This next part was not her proudest moment. "I also

finally figured out that on some level I'm still trying to prove to my father that I was a worthy heir even if I'm a woman. The stupid thing is that I'm not sure I could have convinced him of that even if he'd lived to see me take over the helm. He was what he was, but I loved him. I still do."

She blinked back the burn of tears. "But regardless of the reason, I'm not ready to let Wolfe Millworks go out of business or even pass into other hands. It's my family heritage, and I'll fight tooth and nail to keep those doors open. However, I can't do it alone, and I need to be honest with the people who work for me. I plan to call a meeting with everyone to let them know where we are on things. It's their livelihood, and they deserve the truth. I also want them to know that if we do go down in flames, it won't be for lack of trying on my part. Having said that, Spence, there's one thing I need to have in my life or none of the rest means anything."

It was time to move in for the kill. She placed her palms on his chest. Good, his heart was pounding as hard as hers was. That gave her the courage she needed to lay the rest of her cards on the table. "That one thing is you, Spence. If you leave, I leave. If you can't find peace here in Snowberry Creek, then we'll keep moving until we find the right place."

His mouth dropped open in obvious shock. "But why, Melanie? You can't walk away from everything you've fought for, especially not for me." His voice was rough and deep with pain.

"I can and I will. If necessary, I can hire a manager to take over. Like my mother said, some things are worth fighting for, and for me, you're at the top of the list. I love you, Spence, and I think you have strong feelings for me, too. I'm not asking you to commit to anything other than to give us a chance."

He seemed to be at a total loss about how to respond, his expression confused and worried. "Melanie, I . . ."

When he hesitated, she forced herself to step back and give him some space. She'd needed a couple of days away from him to get her own head straight. He deserved some time to filter through everything she'd just dumped in his lap.

"I'm going to the party next door. If you don't show up in half an hour, I'll bring you something to eat." She hesitated and then added, "Or if you'd rather, I'll have Nick or Leif deliver it. Your choice."

When he didn't immediately respond, she had her answer. "Okay, then. I'll get going."

Before walking away, she picked up the package she'd brought with her. "This was supposed to be part of the celebration at the barbecue, but I think you need it now."

Then she kissed his cheek and walked away.

Chapter 27

❦ ❦

Spence started to follow her but stopped himself before he could go more than two steps. He'd already hurt her enough for one evening. The flash of pain in her pretty eyes when he didn't ask her to be the one to bring him dinner had made him physically ill.

He stood frozen in midstep, moving neither forward nor backward. And if that wasn't a perfect metaphor for his life right now. Mooch brushed against him, whining as he went past. When the dog circled back a second time, the nudge was harder, enough so that Spence snapped out of the freeze-frame moment to sit back down on the swing. Happier, the dog jumped up on the swing and curled up beside him.

Stroking his buddy's head, Spence stared at the package Melanie had left with him. The wrapping paper, which was printed in the same camouflage as his ACUs, made him smile. Whatever was inside measured about fifteen inches square and maybe an inch high, although one edge was slightly thicker. He reached over to pick it up.

"Well, dog, staring at it won't tell me what's inside."

He'd always been a ripper when it came to opening presents. Not this time, though. He went slowly as if it mattered whether or not the paper got torn. Yeah, it was a delay tactic, but he didn't care. When he finally peeled away the last bit of tape and saw what was inside, his pulse kicked up into high gear again. It was a scrapbook. He knew that much because it said so right on the front.

No way he wanted to see what was inside. Running his fingers in circles over the pebbly surface of the faux-leather cover, he finally gathered up the courage to open it and look at the first page. Inside the cover was a note in a familiar handwriting.

> *Spence: I started putting this together for you the day you left on your last deployment. I think it's only right that Melanie finished it for you since you came back to us. I hope our combined efforts serve as a reminder of how many people love you and that you're an important part of our lives.*
>   *Callie and Melanie*

One by one, he turned the pages, studying the pictures and savoring the memories they stirred up. Even the few that hurt so much he could hardly breathe. Not all of the men he'd served with had returned home, and some that did come back faced a life that wouldn't ever be the same. And selfish bastard that he was, he hadn't even thought about reaching out to them since he'd been home.

The next page had him smiling. He remembered that basketball game. The winning shot had been his, costing that squad of marines a pretty penny. That had been shortly before Mooch came into their lives. He tilted the book so that Mooch could see it.

"Hey, buddy, here's the first picture of you we ever took."

The dog lifted his head long enough to check it out, and his tail thumped on the seat. Maybe he understood what he was looking at; maybe not. It didn't matter. Spence turned the next page.

Shit! Callie had included pictures from her wedding. Sarge looked so damn happy looking down at his beautiful bride. Spence's conscience stirred to life. "I made an ass of myself that night."

They might have forgiven him, but that didn't mean he wouldn't apologize again. There were pictures of Leif with a pretty brunette. Considering the besotted look on his face, she had to be Zoe. He seemed to remember her from high school. Maybe a couple of years ahead of him, not that it mattered. She and Leif looked good together.

The list went on. There were pictures of Mama R. and her husband sitting on this same swing. Melanie had taken pictures of several people at the millworks, most prominently Will standing in front of the last machine he and Spence had serviced. Bridey and Seth smiled up from the next page. The photo had been taken in her shop with both of them holding up a cup of coffee as if toasting him.

Right now his eyes were too blurry to make out the captions under each picture, but he'd read them later. Besides, none of them really needed explanations. He smiled at the picture of the cottage and winced at the close-up of the pink poodle shower curtain. Yeah, there was a memory that did not deserve to be preserved.

And finally, there were pictures of Melanie and him. They'd been taken at a distance, most likely by Callie. She was sneaky that way. There was one taken from closer up, and that was the one that nearly stopped his heart. Melanie was smiling up at him, but it was the expression on his own face that left him stunned. It was the exact same one Nick wore in the picture from the wedding and Leif had shared with his Zoe.

Everything inside his head shifted and spun. All those broken pieces he'd been living with for months on end suddenly snapped back together in one cohesive whole. He loved Melanie, he loved his friends, and he loved Snowberry Creek. It was just that simple.

He closed the book and carefully tucked it under his arm. "Come on, Mooch. We have someplace to be."

Melanie had loaded up a plate for Spence, but no one would take it to him. Unless either Nick or Leif manned up in the next ten seconds, they were both going to be wearing it.

"Come on, guys. You know he's hungry. You don't have to stay. Just set it down and walk away."

She hated the sympathy in Callie's eyes, who shook her head and held up her hands as she backed away when Melanie tried to hold the plate out to her. "Maybe he is, Mel, but it's not us he wants to see even if he's too stubborn to admit it. You hit him with a lot all at once, but he's a big boy. He can take it."

"But he—"

Leif's deep voice cut her off. "Sorry to interrupt, but you might want to see who's headed this way."

The crowd parted to let her see. "Spence."

He'd just cleared the woods. His steps stuttered briefly when he saw everyone staring at him. But then his shoulders snapped back and he continued his determined march straight toward them. Toward her. Mooch paced at his side, his head raised high, his ears pricked forward, as if this moment in time carried enormous significance for them both.

Spence didn't slow until he reached the edge of the crowd. His eyes sought out Callie. When he spotted her standing next to Nick, he held up the scrapbook. "Thank you for this. Can you hang on to it for me for a few minutes?"

It was Nick who took the book. "Sure thing."

Melanie ached for Spence. Others might not see how close to the red zone he was running right now, but she did. But until he gave her some kind of signal, she had to stay right where she was.

He cleared his throat twice before he spoke again. "I want to thank all of you for coming tonight, and I apologize for being so late to the party."

There were several murmurs of "No problem" and "That's all right."

He ignored the comments as he ran his hands over his buzz-cut hair, maybe trying to gather his thoughts. His jade green eyes scanned the crowd, stopping to study each person in turn. "I'm not one for long speeches, but I'm going to try. Mama R., you and Mr. R. gave me a sanctuary when I needed it most. Will, you taught me so much, and not all of it had to do with grease and gears."

The old man laughed. "You were a quick learner, boy. Best I ever trained."

Spence flushed, but it was clear the compliment was appreciated. He continued on around the circle. "Gage, thanks for not giving me a ticket on my first day back. Bridey, I love your shop, and how you make everyone feel welcome. Seth, I hope you deserve her."

The artist hugged Bridey close. "M-me, too."

Spence made his way to Callie. After shaking hands

with Nick, he took her in his arms. "Callie, I can't imagine what would have become of me without you in my life. You're the sister I never had."

That last remark eased the tension pumping in Melanie's veins, but only a little. He'd yet to even look at her.

When he stepped back from Callie, he turned to Nick and Leif. "And you two are my brothers. I lived for months believing you were both dead. No, I barely existed for those months because I couldn't imagine a world without you in it. The idea almost killed me. I may not have handled my return to town very well, but I hope you know nothing has ever made me happier than finding out that you were both alive and well. The truth is we've walked through hell and lived to tell about it."

Melanie wasn't the only one who had tears streaming down her face when the three soldiers exchanged a three-way hug, their big shoulders shaking with emotion. When they finally broke apart, none of them had dry eyes.

Spence was running out of people. When he moved to stand in front of her mother, Melanie held her breath. "Ma'am, I earned the reputation I had in high school, but I'm not that guy anymore. I hope the two of us can start over and get to know each other as the people we are now."

Sandra held out her hand and shook his. "I would like that, Spencer, but a lot depends on what you have to say to my daughter."

Spence nodded. "Fair enough. So, if you'll excuse us, everyone, I would like to borrow Melanie for a few minutes."

She'd never seen people scatter so quickly as Spence walked toward her. He took her hand in his and led her the short distance to the gazebo. Inside, he headed straight for the back wall where his friends had carved their tribute to him. He traced the words with his fingertip.

"My first reaction to this was anger mixed with relief that someone actually cared that I was gone," he said.

She spoke for the first time. "A lot of us cared, Spence."

"I know that now, even if I was too fucked up when I got home to realize that."

He sat down on the nearest bench and tugged her down beside him. "I would never have made it this far without you, Mel. From that first night you've been my anchor, the only thing that made sense to me. Thanks to you, even my nightmares are all but gone."

Leaning his head back, he stared up at the ceiling. "You were right. I wanted to fix things for other people because I couldn't figure out how to fix me."

"You're not broken, Spence. You've just needed some time to adjust to this new part of your life."

He raised her hand to his lips and kissed it. "That explosion in the street that day shattered me, Mel, and I wasn't exaggerating when I said thinking my friends had died almost killed me. I wanted to die with them."

God, she hurt so much for all three of them. "I know, but all three of you are so strong. You've each moved past the pain of that day. That's a good thing."

He studied their entwined hands. She didn't know what he was thinking, but she loved the simple connection between them. After a few seconds, he gave her hand a soft squeeze. "I've been putting the pieces back together for a while now. They don't all fit the way they used to, but that's not necessarily a bad thing. But I want you to know the things you said earlier and that scrapbook finished the process. I know what I want my life to look like now."

"Care to share that vision?"

His mouth curved up in a slow smile. "I see me here in Snowberry Creek, living in a small cottage with a beautiful woman and one scruffy dog. She and I both work at the same place, you know, as partners in the family business, using my money and her brains. She is up on the second level, taking care of the big picture while I work down on the floor, maintaining the equipment. That way, together we keep the whole company running smoothly."

"And does this woman have a name?"

For the first time, he looked straight at her. "Right now it's Melanie Marie Wolfe. I'm hoping she won't mind changing her last name to Lang one of these days."

Suddenly, the pieces of her own life were coming together in a beautiful landscape. "I would guess it would all depend on who had asked her to do such a thing. He'd have to be pretty special to her. In fact, she'd have to love him a lot."

A pair of strong arms lifted her onto his lap. Spence whispered near her ear, "You told me you loved me earlier, Melanie. Fool that I was, I let you walk away without answering you, and for that I apologize."

"And if you had it to do over, what would you have said?"

"That I love you and have loved you from the night you fainted in my arms at the cemetery." He brushed his lips across hers. "Marry me, Melanie, and I promise you'll never regret it."

"Will you still take me on night rides on the Harley?"

"Anytime."

"Then, yes, Spence, I'll marry you."

A huge whoop went up outside of the gazebo. So much for the privacy they'd asked for. Spence muttered a curse, but then he grinned and shook his head. "Life in a small town."

She laughed and kissed her warrior lover one more time. "And we wouldn't have it any other way."

And don't miss Leif's story in

More Than a Touch

also available in the Snowberry Creek series.
Available now from Signet Eclipse
wherever books are sold.

The crunch of tires on the gravel driveway out front announced the arrival of the first guests. Leif glanced out the front door to see if he recognized anybody before heading off to the kitchen to let Callie know it was showtime.

"Gage and his daughter just pulled in, and there's a pair of pickups right behind him."

He made the announcement from the safety of the dining room door. The kitchen had been declared off-limits to him, Nick, and even Mooch. Since right after breakfast, Callie and Bridey had been preparing for the potluck dinner they were hosting for the crew of volunteers Nick had recruited for the afternoon.

She had just taken a huge tray out of the oven. The scent of fresh brownies wafting through the air made Leif's mouth water, but Callie knew him well enough to keep the pan safely out of his reach. She smiled at him. "Can you let Nick know, too?"

"Will do."

The last time Leif had seen Nick, his former sergeant when they were deployed together, he'd been heading around to the backyard to set up the tables and chairs that Callie had borrowed from a local church. The shortest route was through the kitchen, but he knew better than to try to go that way. Instead, he did an about-face and went back through the dining room toward the front door. On the way, he whistled for Mooch. The dog came running but skidded to a stop when he spotted the leash Leif had snagged off the table.

When the dog tried to avoid capture, Leif lost patience. "Damn it, Mooch, hold still. There are too many cars pulling in right now for you to be outside without the leash. Otherwise I'll have to lock you in the den for the day."

Not that he would do any such thing, but it did the trick. Finally, Mooch slunk over to lie down at Leif's feet, looking pitiful. Yeah, right—he had it cushy here in Snowberry Creek, and they both knew it. After clipping the leash onto Mooch's collar, Leif patted his furry friend on the head. "Okay, boy, let's go greet our guests."

Outside, Sydney had her father by the hand and was towing him across the yard. "Come on, Dad. Mooch is waiting for me."

"Slow down, Syd. There's no reason to run."

Even so, Gage made no real effort to stop his daughter's headlong rush toward the porch. In his role as chief of police for the town of Snowberry Creek, the former Army Ranger was as tough as they came. But when it came to his daughter, he was pretty much a pushover. Leif liked that about him. He stepped out onto the porch with Mooch hot on his trail. As soon as the mutt spotted Syd, he yipped happily and wagged his tail like crazy.

"Hi, Gage. Hi, Sydney. Mooch has been watching for you."

That much was true. The dog had spent most of the morning lying on the back of the couch, which afforded him a clear view of the driveway out front. Leif eased his way down the steps to join Gage and his daughter in the front yard.

Before handing off the dog's leash, Leif set the ground rules. "Syd, I know you're really good with him, and I don't have to worry about Mooch when he's with you. But until everyone has arrived, I don't want him running loose. Too many moving cars. I've already told him that it's either the leash or he's locked in the den. So if he tries telling you otherwise, ignore him. Okay?"

The nine-year-old giggled at the notion but nodded vigorously as she took control of the leash. "Come on, Mooch. We can still have fun."

They took off running, carefree and happy in the way only children and their four-legged friends could be. Leif called after them, "Syd, can you tell Nick that people are arriving? He's out back."

She nodded as they dashed.around the far end of the house. Gage stood next to Leif and watched until the pair was out of sight. "Thanks for letting me bring Syd with me. My folks offered to watch her today since this is supposed to be a work party, but she was so excited about the chance to play with her buddy."

"Not a problem. Callie brought over a couple of her favorite Disney DVDs in case Sydney gets bored and wants to watch a movie. "

Gage looked pleased. "I'll let her know. Meanwhile, I'll grab my toolbox and head around to see what Nick has planned for us."

When Gage went off to get his gear, Leif crossed to where the other new arrivals were unloading stuff from their cars. Two of them were strangers, but he recognized Clarence Reed, the owner of the local hardware store. Normally the older man wore neatly pressed khakis with a plaid shirt and a sweater vest, all topped off with a flashy bow tie. Today he was dressed in a chambray shirt, jeans, and sturdy work boots. The change in style looked good on him.

"Mr. Reed, it's good to see you again!"

"Hi, Leif." After they shook hands, Mr. Reed introduced his companions. "These are my sons, Jacob and Joshua. And that plastic container there in the backseat has two of my wife's blueberry pies in it. Just a fair warning: Neither of my boys can be trusted within ten miles of anything she bakes, so I'll take them inside for safekeeping. While I do that, do me a favor and tell Nick to put my boys to work as soon as possible. It's the only way these two will stay out of trouble."

His sons, both of whom towered over their father, just laughed. Leif made a point of eyeing the pies when Clarence got them out of the car. "If I slip you a few bucks, would you hide one of those in the den? Even half of one would be good."

Jacob, who looked to be in his late teens, was already shaking his head. "We already tried bribery and got nowhere. I figure if Dad said no to his own flesh and blood, he's gotta say no to you, too. It's only fair."

Joshua joined in. "Dad said the only way we could earn a piece of Mom's pie was to work as hard as we could this afternoon."

If that was the going price for a piece of Mrs. Reed's pie, Leif could pretty much kiss any chance of tasting one good-bye. Considering the shape his leg was in these days, there was no way he could keep up with Mr. Reed, a man twice his age and half his size, much less his two able-bodied sons. On the other hand, Callie's friend Bridey had brought along two of her cheesecakes, and she was a soft touch.

"You guys should find Nick in the backyard somewhere. I'll be along as soon as everyone else arrives. Nick will assign jobs, but I think Callie has told him he has to make a speech first. That should be fun. There's nothing Sarge hates more than public speaking."

After another fifteen minutes of directing traffic and parking, Leif finally joined the rest of the small crowd gathered in the backyard. He caught Nick's eye to signal that the last of the scheduled crew had arrived. Nick immediately ducked inside the house, no doubt wanting Callie by his side when he kicked off the afternoon's festivities. While everyone waited, Leif pulled one of the lawn chairs closer to the porch where he'd have an unobstructed view of the proceedings. Trying not to wince, he lowered himself onto the seat and stretched his legs out.

He'd skipped his morning dose of painkillers because they made him too sluggish to work around power tools safely. Right now he regretted that decision. Damn, his leg hurt, but he was determined to ignore the throbbing pain that dogged his every step. There was no way he'd let it rule his life. Not now, not ever.

The sound of the back door opening snapped him back to the moment at hand. Bridey walked out ahead of Callie and Nick; she headed right for him with a can of pop. When she handed him the drink, she also slipped him a couple of pills. "Nick thought you might need these about now."

Was it that obvious? Leif glanced at the pills and was relieved to see they were just aspirin. They wouldn't knock out the pain completely, but maybe they'd at least blunt its sharp edges.

"Thanks, Bridey."

She patted him on the shoulder as they waited for Nick to get the show on the road. The sergeant looked a bit twitchy up there on the porch, but he finally cleared his throat and started speaking. "I want to thank everyone for coming today. I promise not to work you all too hard, and it means a lot that you all volunteered."

One of Clarence's boys called out, "Or in our case, got volunteered!"

Clarence shot his son a dirty look but then grinned. "His mother begged me to bring them with me. Something about wanting an afternoon off from having to worry about what the pair of them were up to."

Someone from the back shouted, "Can't say as I blame her."

Everyone laughed, including Jacob and Joshua. It had been a long time since Leif had been around the kind of humor that arose from everyone knowing everyone else's business in a close-knit community like Snowberry Creek. As a teenager he'd hated it and was only too glad to leave his hometown behind when he'd enlisted. Odd to realize now that he'd actually been missing this kind of camaraderie after all these years. Meanwhile, Nick picked up where he'd left off.

"Well, however you came to be here, Callie and I both appreciate it." He paused to take her hand, his smile fading a bit. "As you all know, Callie inherited this place from our good friend Corporal Spencer Lang."

At the mention of Wheelman's name, everyone in the

crowd grew silent. They'd all lost one of their own. Thank God Nick kept the pause too short for Leif to lose himself in the past for long. "In Spence's memory, we're not just going to restore the house and the grounds to their former glory. As of today, we're making it official that we'll be converting the place into a bed-and-breakfast and naming it Rose Blossom Place, after his mother's favorite kind of flower."

Everyone clapped as Nick and Callie hugged each other, looking so damned pleased to be sharing their future plans with so many friends. Leif might have been jealous under different circumstances, but Sarge deserved to be happy. Besides, maybe now the couple would stop feeling guilty about having inherited the place and just be glad for the gift Spence had given them.

As the applause died away, Callie left Nick's side long enough to pick up the surprise she'd had Leif stow in the back corner of the porch earlier in the day. She held up the brightly wrapped package. "There's one more thing. As most of you know, Nick's going to have to leave soon to finish out his tour in the army. Once he's back, he'll open his own remodeling business here in Snowberry Creek."

After another round of applause, she handed Nick the package. "Go ahead and open it."

He shot Leif a WTF look before tearing into the paper. When he had it unwrapped, he studied the certificate that Callie had had framed for him. His eyes were blinking like crazy as he turned it around and held it up to show everyone else.

"It's my business license. As of right now, I guess Jenkins Renovations is officially up and running." Nick swallowed hard and once again pegged Leif with a long look. "And just so you know, Leif, I left room for your name if you ever decide you want to throw in with me. We'll hold that spot open until you're ready, regardless of how long it takes."

When Nick jumped down off the porch, Leif pushed himself up to his feet. What could he say? They both knew his current goal was to resume his army career. But as he looked around at the people scattered across the backyard, it hit him that there were worse places to end up than here in Snowberry Creek.

He and Nick exchanged one of those awkward man hugs that never felt comfortable but still meant so much. "Thanks, Sarge. That means a lot. No promises, though."

His friend nodded. "I understand. I just wanted you to know that you've got options."

Leif's throat clogged up with the volatile mix of emotions that seemed to be his constant companion these days. The look in Nick's eyes made it clear he was having the same problem, but he once again spoke to the crowd. "It's time to kick off the work on Rose Blossom Place. The goal today is to move all the furniture from the third-floor bedrooms down to one of the spare rooms on the second floor. Once everything is out of the way, we'll start knocking down walls and ripping up carpet! First of all, though, Leif and I will take a couple of ceremonial swings with the sledgehammer to get things started off right!"

While everyone else gathered up their tools and got their assignments, Leif headed inside to start the trek upstairs. It was a long haul to the top, but damned if he'd miss seeing Nick take out that first chunk of plaster. Right now, the plan was to turn the third floor into a private apartment for Nick and Callie.

Nick had confided that he'd also drawn up plans to convert the large attic on the fourth level into a master bedroom-and-bath combination so that there would be more room if they expanded their family. It was hard for Leif to get his head around the idea of Nick already thinking about kids, but good for him.

He reached the third floor just as the rest of the crew came pounding up the steps. Earlier, he and Nick had shoved all of the furniture in the first bedroom to one side. Everyone crowded into the small room, lining the walls as they waited for Nick to take that first ceremonial swing. Using the camera on his cell phone, Leif prepared to preserve the moment. He loved that Sarge made a production of it, pretending to spit on his hands and taking two practice swings with the sledgehammer. Then he threw all his strength behind the first blow to connect with the old plaster-and-lathe construction. Dust and wood splinters flew.

"Damn, Sarge! Nice job."

Nick grinned and traded Leif the tool for the camera. "Your turn."

He hefted the sledgehammer, liking the heavy feel of it in his hands. Like Nick, he took a couple of trial runs before finally really cutting loose. The impact sent a jolt screaming up his arms, but it felt good. Kind of like hitting a home run back when he played baseball in high school.

All the other men hooted and hollered while Nick stood next to him and grinned. "I've always known you had a real talent for wrecking things, Corporal!"

Leif handed back the sledgehammer and clapped his friend on the shoulder. "I learned from the best, Sarge."

Nick looked around the room at the other men. "We probably shouldn't bash up any more walls until we get the rest of the furniture out of the way and the carpet ripped up."

He handed Leif a clipboard and a mechanical pencil along with a pair of screwdrivers. "Here's the list of jobs that I'm hoping we can get through today. I've already told everyone where they should start and to check in with you when they're finished."

Next, Nick pointed at a separate list on the second piece of paper. "I put you down for taking a bunch of stuff off the walls, including light switch covers and the like. There are boxes and packing tape in the closet over there to put it all in. That should keep your lazy ass busy when you're not playing supervisor. Any questions?"

"Yeah, one. As supervisor, does that mean I get to tell you what to do?"

His friend smiled and shook his head. "You can try, but you might want to remember which one of us has the sledgehammer."

Laughing, Leif hung the clipboard on a nail that was sticking out of the wall. "Good point, Sarge. Guess I'll get started on those light switches now."

"You do that, Corporal."

Zoe parked at Callie's parents' house and cut through the woods to deliver the pan of lasagna she'd promised to bring to the potluck dinner. From what she understood, the gathering was in honor of Callie and her fiancé kicking off two new business ventures. Interesting that Callie had decided to stop flitting about the country to stay in Snowberry Creek and turn the old Lang place into a bed-and-breakfast. That should make her parents happy. Nick was going to oversee the necessary renovations to bring the old house up to code and then open his own remodeling business.

Although Zoe was several years older than Callie,

they'd known each other back in high school and had become reacquainted since they'd both moved back to Snowberry Creek. When they'd run into each other at Something's Brewing earlier in the week, and Callie had mentioned the work party they had planned for today, Zoe had offered to donate a casserole to the cause.

She could hear the deep rumble of male voices before she had even cleared the woods. Pausing at the edge of the lawn, she studied the scene in front of her. Men were sprawled all over the porch and even on the grass. Evidently, the work party portion of the day's activities had come to a close. Before she could decide whether to wade through the scattering of bodies to reach the front door or head around to the back of the house, a dog spotted her and sounded the alarm.

Several of the men sat up long enough to see what had set the dog off, but they immediately resumed their relaxed positions. Only one stood up and made his way toward her, using a cane to support himself as he cut straight across the yard in her direction. She started forward to save him having to come the whole distance.

When they met in the middle of the yard, she smiled. "I'm sorry if I'm late. Callie told me dinner wouldn't be until after six."

"No problem. You're not late." He offered her a reassuring smile. "We got through Nick's checklist faster than expected and knocked off early. Callie and company are busy out back putting the finishing touches on dinner."

That was a relief. Zoe would've hated spending a good part of her afternoon putting together her mother's best recipe for lasagna to find out everyone had already eaten.

"It's nice to meet you. I'm Corporal Leif Brevik."

"Zoe Phillips." She held up her foil-covered casserole dish. "I'd shake hands, but mine are a bit full at the moment. However, it is nice to put a face to the name. Callie has mentioned you."

The man's grin kicked up a couple of notches. "Should I claim everything Callie said is a pack of outrageous lies or take credit for all the marvelous things she said about me?"

Zoe laughed. "Well, Corporal, I'd hedge your bets and do a little bit of both. She did say you were a good-looking charmer. She got that part right."

She suspected Leif normally had a fair dose of the swagger that was second nature to soldiers, but her compliment had him blushing. Cute. She hadn't been kidding, either. Leif would turn women's heads in any crowd. A shade under six feet tall, he had nice broad shoulders, although he could stand to put on a few more pounds. He wore his dark hair longer than regulation, so she had to guess he was on leave, maybe something to do with that Velcro-and-plastic boot on his left leg. His brown eyes were framed with ridiculously long lashes and laugh lines. Like she'd first thought, a good-looking charmer.

Leif was talking again. "I'll walk you around back. I was heading that way to grab a couple of beers for me and Nick when I spotted you."

She suspected he was making up that last part, but if he wanted to provide escort, she wasn't going to argue. "Lead on—and I wouldn't mind a cold drink myself."

"You got it."

When they reached the backyard, Leif veered off toward a row of coolers lined up along the side of the yard. As soon as Callie spotted Zoe, she set down a giant bowl of salad and headed straight for her. "I'm so glad you could make it! I also really appreciate your bringing something, too. We'll need it."

Zoe stared at the huge array of food arranged down the length of two long tables. "Wow, that's quite a spread."

"It is, but we've ended up with a good-sized crowd tonight." Callie held out her hands. "Why don't you let me take that for you? Grab a drink and relax. We'll be eating as soon as we finish reheating the last few casseroles."

Zoe surrendered the lasagna. "Careful. I took it out of the oven just before I left, so it's still hot."

While Callie found a spot for the pan on the table, Leif appeared at Zoe's side with her drink. "I hope you like amber ale; this is one of my favorites. Ever since we got here, Nick and I have been working our way through all of the local microbrews."

"This is fine. Thank you." She took a sip and looked around the yard. "That gazebo looks new. Was that part of the plan for the B and B?"

"Right on both counts."

A catch in his voice hinted that there was more to the story, but she didn't press for details. Still, it did make her curious. "Mind if I take a closer look?"

"No, go ahead."

He looked hesitant about following her, but then Callie called his name, which settled the matter. Zoe stopped a few feet away from the gazebo to admire the gentle curves of the roof and the lacy look of the latticework that formed the sides of the structure. The design was simple but elegant. She stepped inside and immediately wished it was hers. For sure, Callie's future guests would love it.

As she turned back to see if Callie could use a helping

hand, she noticed some writing on the back wall. Stepping closer, she read the words written there in black paint. As soon as she did, she almost wished she hadn't. Leif and Nick had built the place as a memorial for their friend and fellow soldier Spence Lang. It was a lovely gesture, one that also explained the odd note she'd heard in Leif's voice when she'd asked about it. It was tempting to find the man and give him a big hug.

Soldiers were a tough lot, but she knew firsthand how much they suffered when they lost a friend in battle. She immediately took a mental step back from the sign and the painful memories it triggered. Now wasn't the time for any dark thoughts. It was an evening for celebrations. She stepped out of the gazebo just as Callie picked up a pan and banged it with a wooden spoon to summon the hungry crowd.

They came pouring around from the front yard, pushing and jostling one another like a bunch of kids. The women immediately took refuge on the far side of the table. Zoe thought that showed good sense and joined them. Picking up a serving spoon, she began dishing out the food as the line filed by.

When it was Leif's turn, he smiled at her. "Can I save you a seat?"

"I'd appreciate it. I'll be along as soon as the line dies down."

"Want another ale?"

"That would be great."

A pair of teenagers right behind Leif grew restless. "Leif, get a move on. We're hungry. Besides, we want to get in the dessert line early to make sure we get some of Mom's pie."

Leif rolled his eyes. "I don't want to hear about it. You

two get to eat her pie all the time. Do the decent thing and let the rest of us have first dibs."

Bridey joined the conversation. "Leif, I'm disappointed. Here I made a point of bringing my strawberry cheesecake because you like it so much."

He gave her a guilty look. "Aw, come on, Bridey. We're talking blueberry pie here! Besides, I planned on having a piece of your cheesecake, too."

Looking disappointed, Bridey shook her head. "Sorry. Too late."

Although Zoe was sure Bridey was kidding, she intervened on Leif's behalf. "Can't he have both? I'm sure he's put in a long day doing all kinds of manly things."

Leif looked hopeful. "That's right. I have. I personally took down at least a dozen light switch covers and knocked a big hole in the wall. I also checked things off a list."

The other woman wasn't buying it. "Seriously? You think checking things off a list warrants a piece of my cheesecake AND a piece of pie?"

The Reed brothers complained again. "Quit holding up the line, Leif. Flirt on your own time."

Leif shot his younger companions a dirty look. "Hush, children. To answer your question, Bridey, maybe I don't deserve both, but I have been known to carry out a strategic raid when the objective is worth the risk. Stealing a piece of your cheesecake definitely falls into that category."

Then he winked at Zoe. "I'll save you that spot."

After he continued on down the line, Zoe realized Bridey was giving her an odd look. "What?"

Bridey whispered, "What do you think of Leif? He's cute, isn't he?"

Zoe's first instinct was to deny that there was any kind of attraction going on. "I just met the man a few minutes ago!"

Then it occurred to her that she might be treading on someone else's territory. "Sorry, Bridey. I didn't know you were—"

Realizing that their conversation wasn't exactly private, she lowered her voice, too. "Interested in him."

"I'm not, I'm sad to say. He's a great guy and a real cutie, but that's as far as it goes. For one thing, I don't know how long he'll be here. No use in getting involved with someone who's not going to stick around."

Bridey immediately turned her attention back to serving the next guy in line. As Zoe waited for him to reach her station, she followed Leif's slow progress across to where he'd staked out two lawn chairs. Bridey was right. He was a cutie, but Zoe wasn't one for short-term flings, either.

Surely one evening of good food and conversation wouldn't hurt anything, though. With that in mind, she served the last few people in line and then fixed her own plate. As she loaded it up with a variety of salads, Bridey stopped her. "Tell him I'll cut him pieces of both the cheesecake and the pie and hide the plate in the cabinet over the stove. Never could resist a pair of puppy dog eyes like his."

Zoe laughed. "I'll tell him—well, except for the puppy-dog-eyes part. No use in letting him know we're both suckers for that kind of thing."

She picked up her plate and headed over to deliver the good news.